Sting Magic

Other Series by Sarah K. L. Wilson

Dragon School

Dragon Chameleon

Dragon Tide

Bridge of Legends

Tangled Fae

Sting Magic

Empire of War & Wings
Book 1

Sarah K. L. Wilson

Published by Sarah K. L. Wilson, 2020

STING MAGIC
First Edition. June 15, 2020

ISBN : 978-1-7772645-0-5
Cover Art by Luciano Fleitas
Written by Sarah K. L. Wilson
www.sarahklwilson.com

For Cale, always.

BOOK ONE: HATCHING

Though wind should blow,

We fly, we fly,

Though death shall loom,

We fly, we fly,

Though hunger grip,

We fly, we fly,

Though fate shall snare,

We fly, we fly.

- Songs of the Winged Ones

Elsewhere in the Winged Empire

"Launch on my mark!" Azur bellowed, his throat raw from what felt like hours of calling the battle. In truth, it had only been minutes. They'd been taken by surprise, their merchant ship coming around the southern point of the island only to be set upon by Rajadeer triremes. His heart leapt the moment he saw them and it was still stuck in his throat. "Launch!"

The arrows flew, but there were few trained archers on a merchant ship – even when there was spare money to hire protection – and most of the flight fell short into the water. Azur clenched his jaw and tried not to think of how few were left.

On the other side, their foes readied grapples for boarding. They wore the scarlet hoods and face coverings of Rajadeer – as if there was any doubt.

Azur looked up to the skua bird decorating his sails and made the sign of the bird across his chest. One tap to each shoulder and one to the forehead. A bee buzzed irritatingly around his head.

This was it.

They had minutes left.

Rajadeer boarding parties left no survivors.

"Prepare for melee!" He bellowed down the line as coshes and knives were pulled from belts.

No hope, then. Just the chance to fight until death. He bit his tongue and tasted blood.

He felt his lips forming the world of the old Invocation, "Fly us to the great beyond on the wings of the dawn. Shelter us under your wings."

The enemy ship crashed into theirs, grappling hooks already in the air.

"Cut them loose," he cried.

He reached for his axe but a gust of wind lifted him from his feet and sent him flying into the mast. He wrenched himself up from the deck as it careened from side to side. What in all the Storms and Seas was this?

In the chaos of his crewmates finding their feet, it was hard to see anything, but he rushed to the ship rail, eager eyes searching for any answer.

He clung to the rail as beside them, the Rajadeer trireme rose into the air, inch by inch. On its deck, the captain of the ship – noticable by the gold band in the red cloth wrapped around the lower half of his face – met Azur's eyes in shock.

For a moment they were one, both terrified and confused.

Azur looked up, and up, past the ship and the mast to the great purplish-white spirit bird holding the ship – a bird both there and not there – mostly invisible in the bright of the noon sun but with flames of white picking it out against the azure sky.

The trireme was completely out of the water, the barnacle-encrusted hull held fast by translucent purple-white talons larger than Azur was. Water poured in streams from the hull, casting up a spray of brine.

Azur's mouth fell open as the great wings flapped – once – and his merchant ship spun in the grasping green waves, shoved into their embrace by the force of the wind.

By the time they'd righted themselves – their ship bobbing back to the surface – the purplish-white osprey had flown so far away that the little ship in its grip was the size of the one neatly constructed within a bottle back at the Winged Empire Shipping Administration.

They were going to live another day. Relief made him feel light on his feet as he spun to see a Winged Empire tern sailing across the waves to lend them aid. White sails billowed as they harnessed the wind and the masthead bore a majestically carved tern with a beak sharp enough to split the hull of an unlucky merchantman. It had been lacquered white and polished to gleaming so that the light reflecting off it hurt Azur's eyes.

And standing on the hull – arms outstretched, hair and clothing rippling in the wind – rode an Imperial Wing, his eyes far away as he directed his bright spirit bird.

Behind him, a smaller man stood majestically, the white swans of the Imperial House decorating his blue coat and a golden band around his brow. Le Majest. The crown prince of the Winged Empire was here at the edges of the Empire instead of dancing in the halls of Paradise City like he should be. It was like a strange dream.

Azur blinked twice and then tore his eyes away from one wonder to watch the other. He looked back at the osprey just in time to see it snap the Rajadeer ship in half, dropping the wreckage and the tumbling red-veiled raiders into the sea. The bee shot out from its orbit around Azur's head toward the wreckage.

No one challenged the Winged Empire. Not if they had any sense.

CHAPTER ONE

I slashed out with my sword, hacking at the tendril of Forbidding that whipped out at me from the tangled green tree. Yesterday, this oak had been healthy and thick with vibrant leaves the size of my palm. Today, it smelled of rot and something that looked like a snake slid under the bark and seemed to bulge out from its trunk as it clawed toward me.

One of the branches unfurled, waving in the air toward me. I severed the snatching branch with one blow, pivoting on my left foot and whirling into a crouch to hack a second branch right before it caught the back of Alect's cloak.

"You'll have to be faster than that," I warned my younger brother as I slid my foot back from where a root arched out of the ground, hungrily pawing at my foot.

We were getting close to the heart. One more good blow and we'd be able to plant a flame within the tree. Something buzzed in my ear and I swatted at a fluffy bee.

"I only have to be faster than you," Alect teased, striking with his axe and hacking an opening into the oak about the size of my palm. I shook my head in resignation. Whoever didn't open the heart had to set the fire. That was our rule for fighting Forbidding-taken trees.

"I've got your back," he said solidly, for all the world like a grown man instead of a gangly fourteen-year-old.

Fighting the Forbidding, like many things in life, had a lot to do with trust.

You had to trust your fighting partner. You had to trust your sword. And you had to trust your own good judgment and intuition. Mine was telling me that something was off today. Something was about to go wrong. I sure hoped it wasn't this Forbidding fight.

I clenched my jaw, sheathed my sword, and dove under the darting strands of Forbidding that sliced out from the tree. I shoved a tiny nest of dry grass into the heart of the tree and eased my flint out of my belt pouch. That was one thing I couldn't afford to drop at a time like this. I was striking it with my belt knife before most people could have arranged the grass. But we learned to light fires quickly on the frontier edge of the Winged Empire.

You learned or you died.

I struck again, shifting my angle.

Success.

A spark took in the clump of grass and I blew gently on it, refusing to look over my shoulder and let anxiety distract me. The spark flared into flame.

Behind me, I heard a grunt and barely turned in time to deflect the root rising up and shooting toward me.

I rolled across the grass and came up clutching the root as it snaked toward my throat. It was too slippery. It was too strong.

It slid around my neck and I gasped, dropping my knife in my desperate attempt to open a space to breathe.

This must be why I had such a bad feeling today.

I couldn't draw in a breath. I flailed, panicking now.

Come on, Aella. Think of something.

The edges of my vision began to sparkle and dance. I wasn't ready to die.

And then the root went slack and I fell to the rocky ground, gasping and heaving.

I scanned for Alect and saw him bent double, clutching his knees as he tried to catch his breath, too. In one hand, he held his sword. In the other, the end of the severed root.

Fighting the Forbidding was all about trust.

The fire took to the tree at that exact moment, and it went up like it had been dried and aged for two summers. Forbidding-taken things burned hot and fast. And it was the only way to drive back its eternal creep.

I scrambled to my feet, hurrying to pull the mustang from the tangle of roots that had locked it in place. They were slack now – the magic in them as dead as the tree the fire had killed.

"Sometimes I wonder," Alect said as he came to join me, axe hacking through the thicker roots holding the mustang. "What it's like in a place without the Forbidding."

"Like the Continent?" I asked. The main continent of the Winged Empire lay south of our shores. I'd never seen it. I was proud to say I'd been born here in Far Stones.

"Sure. Or anywhere really," he said, looking over to where the land curled up like a wave of the ocean. The trees and ferns on that patch of ground grew upside down. It would need to be burned too – eventually. The edges of it slithered like snakes beneath the lip of ground. Always snakes. It made my skin crawl.

"You'd hate it. Everyone there has enough to eat, pretty clothes, oil for their hair, and all the latest contraptions," I said dryly.

"Yeah, that sounds awful."

We shared a grin.

"And they live under the ever-watchful eye of Le Majest, the great Winged Emperor."

"He can't watch everywhere at once," Alect teased. He was lean for fourteen, but with his sleeves rolled up I could see our constant battles on the Empire's frontier were starting to bulk up his arms and shoulders. Just like my own arms had grown strong and taut.

Soon enough he'd be making his choices about the life he'd lead away from home. So would I.

I tried not to think about that. The only thing I'd ever wanted was my family. And they seemed to slip away a little more every year as my siblings grew and started lives of their own.

"They say he has a thousand eyes in every street and a thousand ears listening at every door," I said in my spookiest voice, trying to distract myself from the things that actually scared me. "And they drag you from your home in the night and bring you to his Vultures."

"Yeah, I'm sure frontier kids are their top priority," Alect said. "But maybe we won't be frontier kids for long. Maybe big bold Aella will test as a Wing tomorrow at the Hatching and go practice ancient magic on the mainland."

He waggled his eyebrows at me.

"Big bold Aella," I said, putting a palm on my chest to indicate myself, "is more than happy here in Far Reach. Besides, Alect. No one has Hatched here since Amalia and that was an aberration."

I gave the vines a final tug and the mustang whinnied, shook his mane, and tumbled out of the clutches of the dead Forbidding Oak, rolling his huge eye at me and plummeting into the forest.

I sighed. He'd been hard enough to catch last time. He'd be even harder now that he was spooked.

"Come on," I said wearily. "We'll have to catch him later. It's almost dark."

"The old man won't like that we lost the mustang. That's the fourth one this month," Alect said, his expression dark.

"He'll be more worried if we're out past nightfall," I said, retrieving my fallen knife and backing away from the burning tree.

I whistled for the dogs, hearing their yapping echoing out over the stony ridge. They ran toward us, tongues lolling from their mouths and I looked around at the landscape wreathed in Forbidding with a tired slump to my shoulders.

It was getting worse.

Every day, we fought back the Forbidding as it tried to reclaim the land we'd hacked out of it in the first place, and every day it seemed to fight harder and harder. That tangled dark mass – unnatural and twisted, part spirit and part real – wore on a person.

But if I could choose any other place in the world, I'd still stay here. It was home. It was where my family was. It was where you could live free and clear, as hard as it might be.

I was never going to leave.

"What will you do if you Hatch tomorrow, Aella?" Alect said and the way his voice trembled a little, I thought he was more worried for himself than for me.

"I won't Hatch, Alect. And neither will you. No one in Far Stones ever Hatches and that won't be changing now," I said.

But as we walked down from the rocky ridge toward the lights of our farmhouse, I thought I saw a flicker of something glowing – a faint purplish-white between the reaching tentacles of the dark Forbidding. It made a little stab of terror shoot down my spine. There was something different about this Hatching. And I wished I knew what it was.

Seven Years Before

I gasped as the spirit egg appeared in Amalia's hands – as translucent as the owl on the Imperial Wing's shoulder but slightly pink and glowing brighter and brighter.

Magic. I couldn't help but let that word echo in my head again and again as I watched her. Magic, magic, magic.

"Now, say the word," the Imperial Wing – a Winged Empire magic manifestor – breathed. She was entirely focused on Amalia as she guided her Hatching. There was a slight curve to the corners of the Wing's mouth as her lips parted and stayed that way. She seemed to be anticipating a particular pleasure. Everyone else in our town shifted uncomfortably, their expressions identical – worried, nervous, expectant.

"Hatch," Amalia whispered.

Her whisper echoed out over mothers clutching children close and men holding their pipes in mid-raise. Most touched a talisman or stroked some of the feathers sewn into their belts. Amalia's friends gripped their skirts or jackets with worry. Most of us had never seen anything happen when a Wing came to town. Certainly not this.

The seconds drew out, long and tense. I held my breath, waiting.

Something cracked.

The crowd gasped all at once.

I leaned forward, nearly toppling from my father's shoulders as he fought to keep me upright.

Peep.

The faint sound shattered the air around me as we all sighed.

A bit of spirit eggshell fell from the glowing egg, disappearing as a little beak popped out. I felt like I could hardly breathe. There was a sudden struggle in Amalia's hands and a whooshing sound as everyone leaned forward, breathing again.

The little chick emerged from the egg and shook itself.

Amalia gasped, her face full of sudden delight. She looked up at us all, beaming.

Behind her, her father's face twisted with grief.

Hatching changed everything. Magic left nothing the same.

Ragged cheers erupted from behind me as all of Far Reach burst with hesitant joy.

Our first Wing had Hatched.

CHAPTER TWO

We hurried into the homestead yard, still laughing together.

Whatever thing I thought I'd seen in the woods was long gone and I was getting excited about seeing our family and enjoying the dinner my sister Raquella had been roasting all day.

Our dogs ran ahead, announcing themselves with excited barks.

From the stables, I heard Retger cursing at their enthusiastic greeting and I couldn't help the grin spreading across my face.

Hatching was always my favorite celebration of the year because it meant the days would grow longer and summer would swell across the Far Stones and fill our bellies with good things.

Contentment settled over me like a warm blanket as I joined Alect at the well.

I washed my hands and face in the bucket sitting beside the well and took a look at the yard around our homestead. Keeping it tidy was my job and with the last horses being brought into the barn, it was up to me to catch any stray handkerchiefs tumbling across the mowed fields between the barn and the house, or to pick up any abandoned buckets beside the sheep and chicken pens, or tie up the dogs if they got too loud from all the excitement.

Their barks had quieted now that we were home. Likely, I'd find them curled up on the wide veranda the way they usually wiled away a feast night. A dog's life was a good one but they made my life better, too, just by being alive.

I looked toward the edge of the forest, cautious after that strange glowing spot I'd seen before, but the tree line looked the same as on a normal day. There were no signs of the Forbidding creeping down from the woods. No twisted, magic-ruined creatures slipping through the shadows or tangled trees lying in wait.

"Did you find the mustang?" Retger asked us as he came to the bucket to wash up.

"Already tangled in a Forbidding tree," I said, tapping the sword at my hip. "We lit the tree and cut him loose but by the time he was free he was too spooked, and we lost him."

Retger grunted unhappily and Alect gave me a wry look. I snickered silently. Our older brother got more and more like the old man every day.

"Worried about the Hatching tomorrow?" Retger asked, clapping us both on the shoulders. We celebrated Hatching ever year – but this was one of the years when an Imperial Wing would attend the ceremonies. New manifestors could only Hatch under their guidance.

I shook my head, trying to dispel the tension forming in my belly. There was no reason to be worried. I tapped my shrike talisman for luck and turned back to tidying myself.

"Not hardly," Alect said. "If they want to pay me a boatload of money and teach me magic, I'll stand where they want and do what they say."

But I knew he was joking. No one would give up their freedom for money and a touch of power.

"Let's get inside," I said, making the sign of the bird unconsciously. One tap to each shoulder and one to the forehead, a plea to the deity to preserve us.

Inside the homestead, the conversation would already be starting as our family settled along the long dining room table or around the wide fireplace in the great room. Long as the table was, there wasn't room at it for everyone – not with ten children and their children.

I was the second youngest, and seven of my older siblings were already married, with only Raquella – who was almost eighteen – and Alect still at home with the old man and me.

We glanced around the yard from long habit and checked over our swords. I felt the shrike etched into the pommel with my fingertip and my eyes trailed up to the shrike totem set outside the homestead. Our family sign.

It was fitting. Shrikes impaled their prey on long thorns, and so would we if we were attacked.

We'd shown that today when we freed the mustang and that wasn't even the first time this seven-day.

I nodded sharply. It will be okay, Aella. Weird feelings of dread happen sometimes. They don't mean anything.

So why were my teeth still on edge?

"Did you settle the horses?" Alect asked Retger as we started to walk to the homestead. I kept my gaze on the treeline, still worrying.

What had happened to those dogs? It wasn't like them not to be underfoot.

Hadn't they run right to the house? I had heard them in the barn with Retger, but now they were gone.

"Sure did. I thought that was your job," Retger grumped as we headed in.

"Yep. I would have done it if I was here," Alect said. "Did you see that black Oska had last summer? A chest like that? That's power. That mare can pull a cart full of timber or race down a trail – either one as easily as the other. I'm telling you, no one on the Far Stones raises horses as good as Oska's. No one."

I ignored the horse talk. I was scanning the trees for the dogs. No sign of them anywhere. But was that the purplish-white glow again? I shook my head. I must be seeing things. It was the excitement, that was all.

We opened the door to the house and tumbled inside, smiling together as the scent of honeyed carrots and roasted chicken wafted over us. My mouth was watering before I had my boots scraped.

I pushed through a knot of my laughing nieces and nephews as they plowed into Alect's legs.

"Give us a bear ride, Alect." one of them called before Anfrea – my oldest sister and the mother of four of the children – hurried over to herd them back to the long table. Weariness etched lines on her face, but her smile was warm as she nodded to me.

"You've grown, Aella. You're taller than I am."

The children were arranged around the dining room table as their mothers filled plates for them. It was late and they needed their beds. We'd eat when they were finished and tucked away.

As much as I loved the children, it was my older brothers and father in the Great Room who held my attention. I was dying to hear what news had come up the mountains from the coast.

"That's what they're saying," my oldest brother Abghar said, from his place leaning against the mantle. He tamped down his pipe but there was fire in his eyes that made him look younger than his thirty years. "The tax is up on minerals of any kind. Iron. Copper. The nails for the new barn were three times what I'd saved for. Three times. The Empire thinks they can just keep taxing us and there will just be more and more to take, but it's not true. We are not bottomless wells."

There was a murmur of support from the rest of us and I was nodding my head with them.

With all the success of my father's homestead, Alect and I had to go without new boots this year, despite the holes in the ones we had. There was no money for extras – not even boots – after the Frost Season tax. I'd watched my father frowning as he combed through the seed. Last year had been a hard harvest and we hadn't kept the seed we would have liked to, but with taxes so harsh, we couldn't afford to buy extra seed from anyone else. We'd have to make do with what we had and that meant tightening belts and going without.

My brother Oska wrapped an arm around me, squeezing me into a side hug.

"You've grown again, Shrikling," he said quietly, under the sober voice of my brother-in-law Royn. "Keeping those Forbidding manifestations at bay?"

"Of course," I whispered back with a grin.

"You'd best be quiet voicing that, Abghar," Royn said loudly. "The farm next to mine was run by a man named Heligar." Royn and my sister Anfrea live two days' ride east of us. "Heligar said the same at the last village meeting. It was deep into the Frost Season, but I saw no smoke from his farm all the next week, so I went over to see if he'd taken ill. He was gone. So were his animals. Someone fixed a seal of the Winged Empire to his door. No entry. No one in town will talk about it." He sighed. "We took in his cat. Poor thing was half-starved."

"Aye, and so it is in Karkatua," my brother Awet said grimly. He pulled his long brown hair back into a knot as he spoke. We all had the same tangle of brown curls and sharp features dotted with freckles. "I've seen both men and women disappear after a complaint like that. My sister-in-law took in a pair of children whose parents had disappeared in the night."

"If no one says anything," the old man – my father – said from the chair at the fire, "then they can do as they please. It will be them today and us tomorrow until the only ones left are those willing to kiss dust for the Imperials. I'll not live like that. And neither should my children."

There were pained murmurs among us, but I saw my siblings looking worriedly at the children gathered around the dining room table, already noisy as they dug into the tantalizing food.

"So we take a stand?" I asked, but Abghar was already shaking his head, worry creasing his face.

"It's no easy thing to pit yourself against the Empire when you have small mouths to feed. How can we put our prosperity before their lives?"

"What lives will they have if they keep taking everything from us?" Alect argued.

There was a sound – barely audible – that tickled my ears. It sounded out of place. I frowned, trying to think of what it could be. A tool sliding down from where it had been left? Had Retger failed to bar the barn door? I gripped the shrike talisman on the handle of my knife as I stood up on my toes, concentrating.

The dogs weren't barking. They would bark if someone was here. So I shouldn't be worried, right?

"We can't be silent. No matter the risk," the old man said, his silver-streaked curls tumbling out of his leather hair-strap as intensity seized him. "We must be strong. We must be relentless."

I opened my mouth, about to ask if anyone had heard the sound, when the door crashed inward with a bang. The force of the impact rocked the room leaving the door hanging from a single hinge like a drunk stumbling out of Cardinal Tavern.

My sister Raquella screamed.

CHAPTER THREE

I froze.

What in the ...

Still no barking from the dogs. Sweat broke out on my neck.

Before my father could even rise from his chair, fabled Imperial Claws rushed into the house, swords drawn. I'd only ever seen an Imperial Claw – the soldiers of the Winged Empire – twice before in my life. They looked larger now – more intense in color and fury.

I gasped, fumbling at my waist for my belt knife without thinking, but I was already too late.

"Don't move," they roared as they rushed into the entranceway, armor and weaponry jingling, their boots hard on our polished wood floors.

Abghar tried to push forward, but he was caught in the doorway to the entrance, a drawn sword at his throat preventing him from reaching my sisters and the children in the other room. Retger and Oska were right behind him, pressed against his back, eyes moving wildly as they looked for an opening.

“Step back,”a grizzled warrior with an unshaven chin and a thick scar on one cheek murmured as he stepped forward, blade still at Abghar’s throat.

The nearest Claws stood in a line across the door to the Great Room, swords drawn, faces stony, like pieces from a game of Wings and Claws rather than real people.

They wore the traditional blue short-coats of the Claws, a design of golden eagles stitched in gold threads across their coats and marching up the sleeves to collars so high and stiff they looked like they might cut their chins. Their knee-high boots and breeches were black. More gold thread climbed up the outer legs of their breeches, swirling to give the impression of greater majesty in a design of curved talons. They were a long way from their Imperial home across the sea, but they seemed determined to bring that world with them.

My eyes widened at the sight of them. So many. And here. In Far Reach. They were as foreign to us as the Rah-Mehn of Rajadeer.

“Please! Don’t hurt the children,” Anfrea pled, her voice strained with fear.

I craned to look around the Claws and saw my sisters, Raquella, Anfrea, and Adigale standing in a trembling line, arms crossed over their chests, protecting the dining room with their bodies. Little faces peered around the edges of their skirts and breeches.

I swallowed down a lump in my throat. Vulnerability and fear warred within me, choking my breath and making my hands shake.

Soldiers poured into our home as porcelain crashed in the kitchen. They must have come in the back door as well as the front, smashing the washbasin on the way in.

My breath turned ragged. What did they want? Why were they here? We were no threat to the Empire. And that was all that Claws were rumored to care about. They were the Imperial Army – the sword of the Emperor to defend his land and bring more and more people under the Winged banner.

I made the sign of the bird as Claws pushed past Abghar, their boots hard on the wood plank floor. They surrounded us, ringing the Great Room before we could do more than reach for our own weapons. I could barely hear over the sound of my heart pounding in my chest.

This was worse than facing the Forbidding. Worse than taxes that stole from our pockets.

Flight of wind protect us, mercy of the skies fly over us, give us peace and protection, let us soar from this terror on the wings of eagles.

My prayer felt too weak.

From behind the Imperial Claws, a dark shadow emerged.

Tall and slender, with a dark short-coat embroidered richly with the thick wings and curved neck of a crowned white crane, the man stepping from the shadows stood in stark contrast to the blue of the Imperial Claw's uniforms. Swan wings twisted around the arms of his coat and white feathers were sewn in overlapping layers over the crossed belts slung over his chest. The scarves wrapped round his neck under his high collar were stitched to look like feathers. There was something familiar about him.

The Claws stood at attention, making the sign of the bird in unison at the sight of him.

"Search the house, Sergeant," he said in a drawling, Imperial accent. His hair was oiled and the scent of roses rolled off of him as strongly as the stench of the pigpen in the heat of summer.

He turned his face and my eyes narrowed at his profile. I'd seen that somewhere...but where?

"Look. Everywhere." His bright eyes glittered.

I stiffened at the thought of these soldiers rummaging through our things – breaking even more irreplaceable items. The washbasin had been a wedding present for my mother and father. The old man liked to tell us about her pride in the basin when she'd been a blushing bride, long before bearing ten children and dying of the Frost Fever. I hadn't seen another one sold here in my whole life. These things might be common in the heart of the Empire, but here on the new continent across the sea, they were rare and precious.

We took good care of what we had. Nearly everything was irreplaceable.

"What's the meaning of this?" my father asked stiffly. "We've done nothing wrong. We're just eating dinner as a family before the Hatching."

The dark figure stepped into the light of our home so that I could finally see his face properly.

He was not much older than I was. Maybe not any older at all. Thin and pale with full red lips and blue too-large eyes, he was far too pretty to be an Imperial Claw. He was far, far prettier than I was. But the cruel slant of those full lips told a story of more than beauty.

I knew where I'd seen that face before. My eyes widened.

I'd seen its profile on the backs of copper coins.

"You'll bow when you address me and call me Le Majest or I will have your head," he said with a slight tremble to his low voice.

My father's lips formed a tight line and I saw them trembling, as if he was deciding what to do, but when his eyes fell on my sisters and the tiny faces peering around them, he frowned and bowed, awkwardly.

"Le Majest," he managed in a choked voice, his silver-streaked curls tumbling from their binding band to cover his face as his head bowed.

The soldiers standing in a ring around the Great Room stiffened as if expecting an attack, while a grey-haired Claw with a scar where one eye should be, strode up the staircase into the loft. These were no regular soldiers. These Claws guarded the Imperial family. That made them Swan Claws. I'd heard legends of the Swan Claws and their brave acts. I'd also heard of their atrocities.

In Haberno, they had fought their way through twenty times their number to rescue a single bottle of wine of the vintage the Emperor claimed was his favorite and then cut their way back through a hundred miles of enemy territory to bring it to him.

In Javens, they'd murdered an entire town because the village idiot wrote a poem about them.

What in the world were they doing here?

There had to be thirty of the Swan Claws spread around the room – more than the room could comfortably hold. They packed around us, smelling of sweat and nerves.

A second man entered the house from behind the crown prince. His blue eyes – so blue that they almost seemed purple – narrowed as he surveyed us. From his full lips, a small white stick jutted. He was dressed as an Imperial Wing in tight trousers, knee-high boots, and a sharply cut black short-coat. He made me think of a sapling held back, ready to burst forward the moment it was let loose. Though his expression was mild on his stony face, his sharply trimmed black hair and dark brown skin made his eyes seem even bluer – as if they held some bright patch of the sky inside them.

"Area is secure. No one else creeping around in the rocks or woods," he reported. He sounded so much like a veteran, and yet he had to be the same age as the prince – barely older than I was. Maybe the same age as Raquella.

Le Majest nodded imperiously – how else would he nod? As if he was play-acting at being himself.

"And the Forbidding?"

"Far enough back not to be a threat. For now." His eyes were on me, though he was giving a report to the prince.

What did he want with *me?* I didn't like that considering look in his eyes, as if he was weighing me and finding me wanting.

He chewed on the splinter and his lips twisted around it in a considering frown.

The crown prince nodded his head toward the dining room and the rest of the Claws pushed into it, shoving Anfrea and my other sisters out of the way.

Glittering swords flashed and children shrieked, leaving a tight feeling in my chest.

"Don't touch him!" My sister Helissa's voice was too high, her son Carsell's sobs almost choking it out.

"The rest of you," the crown prince barked. "Kneel."

My eyes bulged as my brothers and brothers-in-law looked warily at one another.

The prince shrugged one shoulder at the Imperial Wing.

"A display is in order. Show these creatures what it means to serve Le Majest of the Winged Empire."

The Wing pursed his lips and opened his hand.

A huge bird – translucent white with just a hint of purple glow – filled the room above us, pressing down, down, down. It was so large that I couldn't make out its features. But I could feel the pressure of it forcing me down like a powerful wind pushing on me.

My heart hammered even louder. This was the flicker I'd seen in the woods. It had been watching us. Waiting for us to come home. *He* had been watching us.

Reluctantly, my brothers fell to one knee, muttering, "Le Majest."

Those cool blue eyes fell on me as the crown prince waited for my obeisance.

Hatred – hot and sharp – twisted my guts.

Whatever he was doing here – whatever he wanted – he wasn't worth half of one of my brothers, and yet he forced us to bow and kiss dust for him. Fury warmed my chest in a way I'd never felt it before. I called to me, begging me to unleash it.

I fought the push of the bird, refusing to relent as its pinions pushed against my head and shoulders.

"And you, girl?" The prince gave me a tight smile, but his voice was full of threat. "I'm sure we'd all want to show proper honor here, wouldn't we?"

Behind him, the Imperial Wing took the pick from his mouth, studying me. He adjusted his stance like he was flexing a muscle – just waiting to use it.

I glared at him. He was pathetic – working as a bully for a prince who was ... what? Intimidating free men on the far frontier of the Empire? That made no sense. What was he doing here?

I refused to kneel to that.

A hand snaked out and pulled me down – Alect. He shot me a warning glance. Even my younger brother knew it was a bad idea to go against the Imperial Crown.

I swallowed. But I couldn't dislodge the fury welling up in me. It made my lower lip tremble like I might cry. They were treating us like criminals.

"Do the honors, Osprey," the prince said.

The Imperial Wing's mouth twisted, his Imperial drawl full of disdain. "You have the privilege of addressing his Imperial Majest, Juste Montpetit. Heir to the Imperial Throne, Lord of the Far Stones, Owner of this land and all who dwell within, on his formal Grand Tour of the Empire."

I glanced furtively to either side of me. My brothers and brothers-in-law all shared the same look. Barely concealed fury.

We weren't anyone's property.

We were free people who had chosen to come to the Far Stones. We had carved out lives in this unforgiving country, battling the Forbidding and its strange tangling, fighting their relentless shadows, taking on the swift and violent changes of the seasons, without flinching and without complaint. No one had the right to pretend our hard work was theirs. No one had the right to own us.

But none of us spoke. We didn't dare, with the children in the other room. I heard one of them begin to cry softly.

"You will lay down any weapons at my feet," Juste Montpetit said, striking a pose that was surely meant to be majestic as he pointed at the slightly curled toes of his boots.

Maybe I should be trembling at the honor of seeing the heir to the throne of the Empire face to face. But what was he going to do to us? Rulers didn't march into the homes of free people to do anything kind.

I wasn't impressed by him. All I could manage to think was that he was too pretty and too delicate for a land like ours. These stones would break his pretty fingers and smash that long straight nose. Even if he bent and broke us, this land would take our revenge.

"As part of my Grand Tour of the Empire, I have decided to display my ambitions for this great nation to the people on the outer edges of our reign. Starting with you. Weapons. Lay them down."

I felt like a Forbidding had stepped into my house. I froze, uncertain of what to do.

"Now," he barked and the soldier nearest my father put the tip of his sword to my father's neck. A line of blood ran down it as the old man's lips moved in what I was sure had to be a curse. But though the steel in his eyes was cold and harsh, he drew the sword from the scabbard at his side and laid it before him.

The shrike on the pommel glittered in the firelight and my heart sank. We'd etched those shrikes on our weapons with our own hands – shrikes for House Shrike. They were ours. They belonged to no one else.

And we needed them. I'd used mine today to bring down a Forbidding tree. I'd used it two days ago to slay a Forbidding bear, twisted and ravaged into a creature that fed on merciless slaughter, more snake than bear in the way it swayed side to side and struck with a neck too long to be real. Without a weapon, I might not last a week in Far Reach.

And my father had just given up his sword.

So much for making a stand no matter the cost. So much for being relentless.

Someone in the dining room whimpered and Alect drew his sword, tossing it to the ground without hesitating.

My sister Adigale was trying to calm the crying child, but at least two more were sobbing now, too. I saw their fathers twitching as they fought the urge to battle their way to them. Hands shook next to sword pommels and eyes grew wild.

"All of you will disarm," Juste Montpetit said, his expression twisting into something cruel. "Or we'll have to make an example of you for your neighbors. *Small* corpses are the best incentives. Or so my father has always said."

His father.

Le Majest of the Winged Empire.

Everyone I knew trembled at his name. And spoke of him with lips twisted with spite.

But that had been from afar. Now, what we hated was right here, just steps away. And I was powerless before it.

The rush to unsheathe their swords was so fast that my brothers were blurs of movement.

The soldiers around the crown prince tightened their guard.

Raquella screamed and my eyes shot to her as my hand gripped the pommel of my sword. The Imperial Claws nearest her put their blades to the throat of little Ambren in her arms. She tried to move to shield the toddler with her body, but the swords moved with her.

I caught a flicker of terror in her wide eyes and then the blue-coated bodies blocked her from view.

The prince's smile widened.

My brothers flung their swords to the ground with curses and wet eyes. They clattered when they hit the ground – too loud over the children's sobs and the little gasps of fear.

Tears of frustration pricked my eyes, too. They couldn't do this to us.

Without swords, we'd be defenseless on the trails and in our fields. Forbidding creatures could tear us – or our little ones – to pieces and we'd have no defense.

But they had to know that. They must not care.

My gaze went to the Wing. He snapped his fingers and the massive bird disappeared, but his gaze held mine – intense and searching. I tried to put all my hatred into my gaze. He should be ashamed of himself. He should die of that shame.

"These weapons were made for only one thing and they are very good at that one thing," Juste Montpetit said. There was so much satisfaction in his eyes that he couldn't mask it, even though he was trying to cover it with a show of fatherly lecturing. "They were made for killing. An axe may split wood and a knife may gut fish. But a sword or dagger is only for killing men. And no Imperial subject needs one."

"How do you expect us to defend our families?" Royn asked

quietly, his hands forming fists at his sides. "How will we fight back the Forbidding and the Forbidding Beasts?"

"I'm stationing Imperial Claws here. That is protection enough. If you need their help, fly a red flag high on a pole and they'll come to any settlers in need."

"They can't get here in time," Royn protested. "We'd die before they could make it, even if we sent out a pigeon immediately."

I held the gaze of the Imperial Wing. Something stirred within those blue depths. But if it was pity, he didn't act on it. I memorized his face. When I saw him next, I wanted to remember the face of my enemy.

"Our Imperial Claws are the best in the world. They are committed to the protection of our citizens," the crown prince said smoothly.

"They won't be able to see the flags from over the mountains."

"Our Claws will do whatever is necessary for the promulgation of our Empire." His cultured drawl never faltered.

"That's not an answer." Royn's face twisted with emotion he could no longer control.

Juste Montpetit nodded and the Swan Claw closest to Royn turned his sword and struck him across the temple with the hilt.

Royn groaned, spitting blood as he fell to the floor. Retger caught him before he could smash his face on the floorboards. He hugged his brother-in-law's unconscious body to his chest, tears of frustration leaking from the corners of his eyes and his fists balling with the need to act.

I felt it, too. I wanted to fight them all. I wanted to make them feel as helpless as I felt right now. I leaned forward, fighting against the desperate need to *act*.

"Please don't do this," my father said. I'd never heard him beg. I didn't know he knew how. His fingers were white where they dug into the wood floor for strength. His voice was raw. "Please don't leave us defenseless."

"Our Imperial Claws are dedicated to the protection of our citizens."

"Please, I beg you." He was groveling now, on all fours. My brothers were stiff and red-faced around him. I couldn't even look at him. Not like that. I kept my eyes away.

I felt, carefully, for the sword still at my side. They had no right to take our defense. To steal our only protection. To make my father grovel.

They had no right.

My breath was coming quickly now. I needed to act fast. If I could just think of some way to turn this all around ...

Heavy footfalls came down the stairs and the Sergeant returned, his arms full of weapons – swords, bows, halberds. Everything we had. Everything we'd saved up for or made. Everything we'd carefully sharpened and oiled and cared for every evening of my life.

"I found it all. Tucked here and there," he said. "Under beds, hanging on walls, hidden in closets."

They weren't hidden. They were just kept close. In Far Reach, you never knew where you might need a weapon.

I leaned forward, just enough to put my weight in my toes. If I moved fast, I could ... I could ...

Juste Montpetit stepped into the room and lunged toward me so suddenly that I didn't have time to flinch before his narrow sword blade was already through the back of my hand, pinning it to the leather wrappings around the handle of my sword.

I couldn't help the cry that escaped my lips.

"I said all the weapons, girl." His voice was ice and sharp as a whip crack.

I gasped at the pain, my hand trembling as blood spilled hot from the back of my hand, running down my leg and into my breeches. I blinked back tears, refusing to cry out or moan at the sharp pain shooting from the wound.

Alect's eyes were huge as he watched me, his hands trembling at his sides. He shook his head as if he could read my thoughts – as if he knew I was measuring the distance between me and the crown prince.

"Take that sword from her," the crown prince said, wrenching his sword from the back of my hand. I couldn't help gasping, but I refused to allow any other sound as I clutched my injured hand to my chest.

The Imperial Wing took a step forward and leaned in so close that I could make out the black freckles dotting the tops of his dark cheeks. He snatched my sword from the scabbard while the others searched my family roughly, looking for any weapons they'd missed. His eyes met mine for a brief instant – their bright blue still startling. He winked and then shook his head slightly as if he was trying to warn me against fighting back anymore.

My lips twisted. As if I wanted advice from *him*.

But there was no use in fighting. We were outnumbered and outmaneuvered. They even had magic on their side.

"We'll be taking these," Juste Montpetit said with a false warmth to his voice – as if he was doing us a favor. "We are so pleased that you can join us in making the Empire a truly safer place."

I shook from head to foot. Not with pain – though that was there. Not with shock – though that was probably there, too. With red, roiling rage.

I wanted to spit.

I wanted to bite him with my teeth just to show him that I wasn't defenseless.

He could take every weapon from us and still we weren't weak. Not us. We were the relentless and he would pay for this.

He started to stride away, but he turned in the doorway to face us as if he'd just remembered something. It was too rehearsed to be real.

"Oh," he said with half a smile. "I should remind you that you are expected at the village green for Hatching tomorrow. Any citizen who does not come to the green will be hung by the neck until dead. And any citizen caught with a blade any longer than their hand will also be executed. We will be an Empire of peace, by decree of Le Majest, our Imperial god and father."

His Swan Claws left with him in a storm of thudding boots and squeaking leather.

A hot tear spilled down my cheek the second the last one walked through the door. And I wasn't alone. The wails of the children began again in the dining room.

I swiped my angry tear away with the back of my hand and hurried to the door, not caring that my hand was still bleeding and in pain.

I peered out after them, wanting to be sure that they would actually leave. That they wouldn't be lurking in the shadows waiting to surprise us a second time.

The light of the door left a long golden beam across the darkened yard, illuminating a dark pile outside our door – the corpses of our dogs. That's why they hadn't barked.

The Claws had stacked them one on top of the other.

I gagged as my tears fell faster and hotter.

CHAPTER FOUR

Raquella wrapped my hand in a soft cloth bandage and a shrike feather for luck. I tried not to wince as she smiled tremulously at me.

"He missed the bone and the major blood vessels. You're lucky. It will heal fast," she said sweetly, talking under the loud voices of our older siblings.

"Still want to marry a prince someday?" I teased.

"Definitely not." Her dark eyes widened in horror.

Alect set the broken washbasin on the long table. There would be no repairing it despite the way he was trying to put the pieces in place. He looked lost.

The acrid smell of burning meat drifted in from the kitchen and Raquella cursed, dropping the bandage to hurry away. I gathered up the end of the bandage and continued winding it. She'd done a good job with the stitches. She'd always been good at needlework.

"We can't let them keep our weapons." Oska ran his tanned hand through his tangled curls. His expression was tight. "Only last week the

Forbidding nearly stole my best mare. I had to fight a pair of Forbidding bears tied together by tentacles of magic to set her free. A belt knife or a Hatchet wouldn't have been enough to stop them. I needed the speed and efficiency of my sword. What am I supposed to do without weapons? This is not a land for the peaceful or the unarmed."

"We should have fought." Awet hit the table and the dishes bounced loudly along the top of it. "Forbidding take us all, but we should have fought."

Anfrea clucked her tongue at him as she dabbed Royn's head with a wet cloth. He winced.

"Royn tried to fight," she reminded us, with a tight look on her face.

The children had been hustled up into the loft. I could hear the murmurs of my other sisters and sisters-in-law tucking them into bed with comforting sounds. Small sobs still escaped through the tender noises of mothers consoling their children.

"And then what?" my father asked with a sigh. He looked ten years older. The lines in his sunburned face were twice as deep as they'd been this morning. "Even if you hadn't been knocked down like Royn, would you have watched your children slaughtered? Or worse ... *stolen*? Have you forgotten Canaht?"

We all shivered.

Word had come of Canaht the same year my mother died. They'd defied the Empire and the Emperor had sent in his Claws. They took the children and executed anyone who got in the way, leaving the rest with the knowledge their little ones were being raised by other hands and taught to hate them from far away.

Canaht didn't dare rebel again. Not with their children held hostage. And every so often, the Empire sent them a small wooden box to bury. A reminder that even when they were good and submissive, the Empire was a fickle mistress and she killed as she pleased.

I'd met a man from Canaht when we took a trip to Far Port once. He'd kept his gaze down, shrinking back from anyone who tried to speak to him.

"They're beaten and broken, hardly men at all," my father had said when I'd asked him about the man. His eyes had been hard.

"I feel sorry for them," I'd said.

"Once your fight is gone, you're a dead man," my father had said sharply, and I wasn't sure if he was angry or afraid.

"We haven't forgotten Canaht," Royn said. He chewed on his lower lip, placing a hand gently on Anfrea's as tears filled her eyes. "And fighting would have done us no good, even if I'd managed it. They had four times our number with their swords already at our throats. We could have been killed on the spot, and our wives and children, too."

"So, what now?" Alect asked, pale-faced. He was clearing up the children's plates now, picking up scattered forks and broken pottery with trembling hands. "Can we get weapons from somewhere else? We should have hidden some in caches in the woods."

A look passed between my father and Abghar so quickly that I almost didn't catch it. *Did* they have something hidden?

I shouldn't ask.

Better not to know.

"The old plow can be beaten down and reshaped," Retger said quietly. "I can take it to Master Cuthern tomorrow."

Retger was the blacksmith journeyman for our town. His arms were already wider than my thighs from his work at the forge, little white scars dotted his forearms and neck from the work.

"A good sword isn't like a pot," Abghar muttered. "It takes craftsmanship."

"And you think I don't have what it takes to craft it?" Retger protested.

"No one is saying that," Oska said mildly. He was picking at the dining room table with his belt knife, carving what looked like a shrike into the surface of the fine table. If it had been any other time we would have been horrified at the disfigurement. It seemed fitting now.

I shifted in my seat, tightening the bandage. I felt like I might shake apart, the tension was so tight inside me. It was echoed in every strained word and worried look around the room.

"Not tomorrow," my father said. He held the large shrike totem that used to hang above our front door in his hands. It had been smashed into three pieces. He kept trying to fit them back together. "Tomorrow, we go to the Hatching. We keep our heads down. We don't draw attention. The Claws will leave after the feast. They've never been here before and they have no reason to stay. And then we'll go on our way, too, and make plans."

"We could go to Garbocco," Raquella said, coming in from the kitchen. She set the food down and fresh plates. No meat, though. It must really have burned in the oven. "Start a new life somewhere free."

Oska shook his head. "I heard from a trader last week. Le Majest has been talking about our long friendship with the islands of Garbocco. Last month, he threw a ball for their ambassador. Drank their local brew in his honor."

"Forbidding take it," Awet cursed.

I swallowed down a lump. That meant they'd be next. The Emperor always praised another country just before his armies marched. I'd seen it three times in my short lifetime.

"There's nowhere free to go," Royn said. "It's why my parents settled here – why you came here, Barran." He nodded to my father. "It was the last free place to live. A new continent with no high'uns, no Majests, no Wings, no Claws. Just land and work and freedom."

"Until now," Anfrea said miserably. "Let's eat something. We have food, at least. For now."

She began to help Raquella serve bowls to everyone, trying to mother us. Her eyes met mine and I gave her a tremulous smile.

"It will be all right, Aella," she said, her brown eyes meeting mine in kindness. She put a gentle hand on my shoulder. She had our mother's eyes. I'd thought so since I was five and she let me sleep in her bed after mother died of the Frost Fever.

"I don't know what we can do," I said. "Even if everyone agrees – all our friends and neighbors – then what? The Empire is too strong. Even here in Far Stones. And they have Wings with the power of their magic. Our whole family couldn't stand up to a Wing – and that's if we were armed. And what do we do when bandits come to our farm? Or Forbidding beasts? Or bears? What if the Forbidding Ghouls rise up like they did when I was a baby? We're defenseless now."

I didn't like giving up. It made me feel like I might be sick.

"Our fight's not gone yet," my father said, reaching for the bowl Anfrea gave him. "As long as we all stick together, they won't take more from us. We'll find a solution and we'll weather this storm. We'll find like-minded people. We'll use our heads. There has to be a way out of this mess. You know what I always say, Shrikeling."

He spared a smile for me – though it was tight and fraught with worry. I smiled back, trying to encourage him like he was encouraging me.

"The fight isn't over," I said. I knew his motto by now. "There's work to be done. Be Relentless."

We buried our dogs, and I fought back tears as I helped lay them in the earth.

And then I went to bed, tucked into the cot I was sharing with Helissa's six-year-old twins, with those words ringing in my ears, but it didn't feel like enough defense against what was pressing in on us.

I'd grown up on the edge of the Forbidding, feeling the way that the otherness of that place was always pressing in, always fighting to break down what was built up, to expel people from its eerie shores.

I was used to every task being a fight. I was used to doing without luxuries – or even necessities – out on the edge. But I wasn't used to feeling defenseless. I wasn't used to wondering if it was worth it or if we could ever see an end to the crushing work it took just to make it one day to the next.

The feeling ate at me, twisting me up inside until I was a tangle of thoughts and wishes and hopes. There had to be something I could do to get my family out of this mess – to keep them free and strong and *alive*.

If only I could figure out what that thing was.

I fell asleep dreaming that I was a shrike diving from the sky and Juste Montpetit was in the grip of my talons. I spit him on a huge thorn as my family watched, safe and well. As long as I had them, I had everything I needed.

Earlier in the Winged Empire

Vasyklo knew he had to keep his hands from shaking. His father looked on sharply with hands clasped behind his back, military uniform precisely outfitted, heavy brows pulled together over brown eyes. General Petren still had a patch over his eye from the taking of Dunit Hill. And he wore his military uniform, thick with white Swan embroidery rather than his Osprey House talismans even here – standing underneath their great family totem beside the sea.

The carved whitewood Osprey of the talisman looked down its long beak as if judging Vasyklo already.

"Cup your hands," the Imperial Wing instructed firmly. A translucent green hummingbird buzzed next to her left ear. She cocked her head to the side as the hummingbird echoed the motion exposing its red-tinged spirit throat.

Vasyklo swallowed and cupped his hands, pressing the edges of them firmly together to eliminate the shaking. He was ready.

General Petren gave a very slight nod of his head, his eyes narrowing. Vasyklo's family needed this – wanted it so badly that sweat shone on all their foreheads as they watched. They were lined up in military precision in two lines running parallel to the totem, the sea winds rushing up over the ragged rocks of the coast and tangling their hair and cloaks. No one in their line had Hatched in two generations.

And then there was his mother. Her death must not be for nothing. They only remembered her for accepting the sacrifice of her life for the chance to make him hatch, but Vasyklo remembered so much more. He would give up any chance at all just to have her back.

He swallowed down the memories and looked out over the blooming crocuses spilling across the rounded hilltop to the silver ocean beyond. Hundreds of masts dotted the horizon. Masts that needed Wings to help them defeat the enemies of the Winged Empire.

General Petren had taken him to see them yesterday and explained how vital it was to fill them with those who could control the manifestation of magic. He'd balanced him on the masthead – the place for a Wing at war.

"See the osprey flying near the shore, son?" he'd asked.

"I do."

"See how it swoops in to take the fish from the crest of the wave?"

Vasyklo had peered into the spray at the same moment that the bird wrenched a silver fish from the clawing sea.

"I do."

"Be the osprey, not the fish."

He must do this.

They were all counting on him.

He clenched his jaw, stared at the center of his palms, and summoned all his courage.

A large purplish-white egg formed in his hands.

"Hatch," he whispered, thinking of the powerful osprey.

Crack.

CHAPTER FIVE

"Stick close to me, Shrikeling," my father said as we approached the town of Far Reach.

We passed between the tall totems that stood watch over the road leading into the town of Far Reach. They were carved of whitewood, which bleached bright white in the sun. Owls were shaped on the top of the totems, reminding us that wisdom rules all. Ravens followed beneath the owls to remind us that the clever survive. Whiskey jacks came next to remind us that tenacity is the foundation of our lives here.

"We can protect ourselves if we stick together. We keep our heads down just for today and then we make a plan. There will be others who feel the same."

I was beside him as the village came into sight. Questions burned in my chest as we drew closer to the wide town gates formed out of two snowy owl sculptures, their wingtips meeting over the road to shelter travelers.

I couldn't help it. I found my questions spilling out at the sight of them.

"What do they care if we have weapons? They'll probably never see us again."

"People see other people's freedom as a threat to them," the old man said in a low voice. Today, his white curls were tucked carefully under his leather head strap. He looked as tidy and precise as I'd ever seen him with his shrike-feather belt strapped around his thick long-coat. "They think that if you have something – even if that's just air to breathe – that you owe it to them. That they have the right to take it from you and if you resist, they have the right to crush you. People will put more work into taking the results of your work from you than they will into working for that same thing themselves. It's human nature. That's why we stick together as a family. That's why we watch out for our own. We can help each other be a little more free and a little more able if we all work together."

He ruffled my hair and I smiled.

One more Hatching. One more feast. Then we'd go home and find a way to keep our homestead and our family safe.

"What if someone Hatches today?" Alect asked, looking nervous.

"No one will Hatch," my father said grimly. "Poor Amalia was the only one to ever have that honor in Far Reach. And before we came here, I only saw one other person Hatch in all my life on the main continent. It's rarer than you might think. You have to be born with the magic in you."

"Like you get it from your parents?" Alect asked. "Neither you nor mother had it."

"They say it's a gift from above." The old man sounded like he didn't believe what he was saying. "I say it's a mystery."

By the time we stepped past the first thatched roofs of Far Reach I was deep in thought about Amalia. What had her life been like since she Hatched? Did she serve in the Winged Court? Or on a ship? Or at an outpost somewhere?

I'd never really thought about what Imperial Wings *did*. They just were. Like Le Majest.

If one of *us* were a Wing, would we be able to stop what was happening all across the Far Stones? That Imperial Wing who had accompanied the crown prince could have stopped him last night. Those Claws wouldn't have been able to stand up to that massive bird. Of course, he'd been with them, helping with their dirty work.

He was just as to blame for taking our defenses from us as Juste Montpetit was.

But that wasn't the kind of Wing I would be if I Hatched. Not at all. I would find a way to defend my home and family. I would find a way to stop the injustices of the world. I'd use my power for good.

Was that possible?

I felt a flutter in my belly at the thought, but I pushed it down.

Today was not the day for nerves. Not with so much at risk. Besides, it wasn't going to happen.

We entered town with grave faces and watchful eyes.

Children too young to be tested to see if magic could Hatch in them waved down from the roofs as the scent of cinnamon rolls and candied nuts wafted up in the air. The streets were filled with adults, waiting as the young people of our town assembled on the green. You only needed to be tested once after you turned twelve. If you didn't Hatch a manifestation then, you wouldn't Hatch one at all.

But Wings didn't come to Far Reach very often, so people from twelve to nineteen would be tested this year.

Alect, Raquella and I were the only ones in my family who hadn't been put in the ring for the Hatching yet. I reached out to squeeze Raquella's hand with my uninjured one as she shot me a worried gaze.

It wasn't fair that the Winged Empire could make my sister feel like that. There had to be some path for us other than just going along with what they wanted all the time. Almost, I wished I could Hatch. Almost, I wished I had the power to save them all.

Frustration bubbled in me, like a pot at a slow boil. And I didn't know how to calm the pot or end the boil. I wasn't sure if I wanted to.

My father was distracted as we forced our way through the crowd, and I followed his gaze to see him exchanging worried looks with other men we knew. Old Aylmer looked like he was going to have a stroke with the vein in his neck throbbing like that. His hands never left the finch design on his belt buckle. He'd even tied a feather to the leather thong wrapped around his forehead. He waved urgently to my father but my father gave a tight shake of his head and made the sign of the bird respectfully, his clawed finger touching first one shoulder and then the other before tapping his forehead right where the leather band wrapped around it.

I saw men from nearby homesteads catching his eyes with tight expressions and angry shakes or nods of heads. He gave them all the same sign of respect.

He was waiting.

We were all waiting.

Bunting was hung from house to house over the street and the smell of roasting chickens made my mouth water, but under all the preparations for the feast was a feeling of tension, of worry. Like a bunched fist at your side. I felt my own fists forming and I flinched at the pain in my injured one. It would be fine. Tonight, I would bathe it in herb water and rewrap it.

When it healed, the scar would remind me not to trust the Winged Empire or the spoiled princes who made edicts for other people while hiding behind the protection of their Claws and Wings.

We pushed through the crowds of people, dodging laughing children, and avoiding knots of red-faced, tight-jawed men and women to find the village green. I stopped, frozen in place when we reached it.

The green was completely ringed by Swan Claws. There must have been two hundred of them or more. They wore their blue embroidered jackets and carried marked swords at their sides. Their chests swelled out, a look of smugness in their eyes that made my skin crawl.

Across the village green, Juste Montpetit stood – wearing a blue coat today with slashes of gold across the breast and heavy white embroidery depicting a pair of stylized swans across the shoulders of his coat, their wings meeting across his back and their tails dipping down his coat sleeves. His dark hair had been teased to curl and then waxed in place and a gold silk scarf was tied around his neck, under the high collar of his jacket. His glittering blue eyes found mine across the village green. I looked away hurriedly.

His smugness set my teeth on edge.

I watched as the villagers of Far Reach tried to press away from him and the Swan Claws as if Imperialness was an infection you could catch. As if he hadn't already done enough damage to our home and future.

Beside him, in a tight knot, were four Wings.

Four of them in one place.

I barely looked at them – only enough to notice their uniforms which were tight dark breeches, short colorful coats cut in sharp lines with emblems embroidered across the breast, feather-trimmed cloaks, and long leather bracers.

My attention was on the other-worldly birds they were manifesting. They were the reason we honored birds in the Empire – even here at the very farthest reaches of it. They were the reason for our house associations, for the talismans, for the sign of the bird. We were all born of the sky and would return to the sky one day. From the sky, we received the warmth of the sun and the blessing of rain. From the sky, came the stars to navigate and the moon to light the darkness.

As much as I despised the Empire, I felt drawn to those heavenly spirit birds and the mysteries they represented.

The tales we heard of them were unbelievable. Birds that ended wars with a single burst of their wings. Birds that flew all the way across the Great Emerald Sea. Birds that sang a song so sweet that people froze in place like statues, listening forever to the song until their bodies wasted away. Birds that plucked your sanity right from your mind and never returned it. Birds that imitated your words so that your nearest friend couldn't tell the difference. So many stories. Could any of them be true?

Power like that ... that could save us. Even from crown princes. Even from the Forbidding.

I wanted that.

I swallowed against the sudden desire. Wanting something like that was dangerous. Too dangerous at a time like this.

I studied the Wings out of the corner of my eye, trying not to be obvious.

Three women. One man.

One of the women was the one I'd seen when she came for Amalia – the fierce, dark-skinned Wing whose companion was a ghostly owl as tall as my arm was long. It glowed a faint white with a soft tan overtone. The Imperial Wing stood at her ease, seeming to lounge while standing straight, ready for anything that might come. She wore a deep maroon coat with the face of an owl stitched across the breast.

The other woman was pale-skinned and large-eyed. She bore a bluish-white swan the size of a small dog over her shoulder. It preened itself – its long neck curving beautifully in a way that seemed to enhance the soft blue glow it emitted. I shivered at the sight of it. I was starting to detest swans.

The youngest woman surprised me. She was about my age and she wore a dress of Imperial fashion rather than a uniform. In her cupped palms, she carried a tiny fluffy red chick that was more opaque than the other birds. It looked almost newly Hatched. She raised her nose proudly and frowned across the crowd as if daring any of the rest of us to Hatch like she had. She could go on waiting. None of us wanted that.

Except maybe me.

The male Wing was the one from last night – the young on who had come to our home with the crown prince. I could hardly keep a scowl from my face at the sight of him.

His eyes were on me again – still weighing, still considering. He leaned against a hitching post on the edge of the green, chewing a small white pick between his teeth. His purplish-white osprey fluttered behind him – so large it would dwarf a horse.

I gave him my most mulish look. He could go on looking all he wanted. I wasn't scared. I knew exactly who he was. A pawn in the hand of the crown prince. The killer of dogs.

I didn't even know him, and I hated him with all my heart.

My eyes drifted to his ghostly osprey. I didn't hate that.

It hovered there, wings outspread, its glittering eyes fixed on the crowd, constantly moving, constantly on the alert. A real bird that size could eat me for dinner. What could a spirit bird do? Something much worse?

I didn't know if the little chill I felt was a shiver or a thrill.

Goodwife Axelar pushed through the crowd, breaking my train of thought. She spoke in a hushed voice when she got to us. "Raquella,

Aella, Alect, hurry now. You're the last of those qualified for the Hatching." She looked over her shoulder and shivered. "There's a list this year and if we don't have you all ready by the time the bell rings, we've been told there will be ... consequences."

"Consequences?" my father asked in a tight voice, the muscle in his jaw popping as he ground his teeth together.

She leaned in close. "Take a look at Hunter's son Aledus."

I peered through people until I caught sight of Aledus in the circle. He could barely stand. He clutched his side with one hand and blood oozed through bandages wrapped around his head.

"He panicked," she whispered. "Tried to run." Her laugh was too high. Too nervous. "Shouldn't have bothered. It's not like anyone here has ever Hatched other than poor Amalia."

My father kissed Raquella's forehead and then mine. He squeezed Alect's shoulder.

"Just stay calm. Follow their instructions. Try not to be memorable. We'll all go home right after. No dallying. No looking for friends, yeah?"

We nodded and he smiled grimly, nodding to Goodwife Axelar.

She took Raquella's and Alect's hands and seemed sorry that she couldn't grab mine, too.

"You all look fine and healthy," she said nervously, hustling us to the ring. "Your mama would be proud to see you all grown up and strong."

Goodwife Axelar smiled encouragingly, smoothed down Alect's

collar, and then tucked a loose strand of hair behind my ear.

"We'll all be fine," she said as if she was trying to convince herself, and then she hurried off into the crowd again.

I swallowed and put my hands neatly behind my back. I was of House Shrike. I wouldn't flinch or tremble just because Imperial Claws were everywhere and there were four Wings here when usually one lone Wing was all that was needed.

But I couldn't help wondering if they were watching me. Would the osprey be watching, too?

I bit the inside of my cheek to try to distract myself from the pain in my hand and settled my mind with careful thoughts. If there were two hundred Claws here, they couldn't stay forever. There wasn't enough food for that many extra people and the mountain passes were too dangerous to cart up more food on a regular basis. They'd likely be gone by tomorrow. We just had to withstand this one last day.

That meant I needed to stop mooning over magic birds and imagining what it would be like to be one of them and start representing my family with quiet and honor.

A bell rang.

A Claw stepped out from the rest, ringing the bell over her head with rigorous precision. By the time she retreated again, the crowd had gone silent.

The Wing with the giant osprey was still looking at me. I glowered in return. He winked.

He could look all he wanted. One day, I'd have my revenge. And at least he'd recognize me when that happened.

I had expected one of the Wings to step forward, but instead, Juste Montpetit stepped into the ring, his face lit with a bright smile. His smiles were like pyrite in a stone – pretending to be real gold but just a trinket for children and fools.

"It is my honor to inform you, citizens of Far Reach, that you have been chosen specially for a new initiative. Something that as your lord and owner, Le Majest of the Winged Empire, it is my distinct pleasure to announce. Any Wing Hatched here today will have the honor of becoming the personal property of the Imperial family. When their training is complete, they will join me in the capital to further the peaceful ends of the Empire in the heart of our rule."

He smiled at us and my stomach tightened in fear and horror. I couldn't imagine anything worse than having to be near to Juste Montpetit for the rest of your life. To have to serve at his whim and stomach that nausea-inducing smile forever. I felt my face freeze as I fought to control my expression.

I take it back. I don't want to Hatch. Not even for the power that might free my people. Not if it meant being a slave to *him*.

It won't happen, Aella, I told myself. Not to you. Not to anyone here. No one here is going to Hatch.

But the way the osprey and owl were both staring at me, unblinking, was sending little chills up my spine.

CHAPTER SIX

One of the Imperial Wings stepped forward, confidence radiating from her. Her swan walked down her arm, wispy and ghostlike but with penetrating spirit eyes. It made me feel like I'd stepped into the cold on a winter morning. I tried to focus on the Wing to distract myself from my nerves. She was just past her middle years, her hair short and white and her skin so pale that it looked translucent. Her eyes were wide and delicate – but the look in them was anything but soft.

She strode to one end of the line and her eyes held a powerful authority that pinned us all in place as she checked each set of cupped hands. If anyone had the ability to manifest, their magic would bubble up in response to hers. Sometimes, I wondered what would happen if you had the ability to manifest but never met someone else who could. Maybe the magic would lie sleeping within you forever.

I gripped my hands behind my back, wincing in pain from the wound in my palm. I scanned the crowd for my father. He was watching us intently and when he caught my eye he nodded sharply.

Relentless. I had to be relentless. That's who we were in House Shrike.

There was no room for a lack of courage.

I took a deep breath, slowly letting it out as the first girl in line was dismissed curtly by the Wing. She fled the green, her orange oriole cloak flapping in the wind as she ran.

The swan adjusted his wings, turning his stately head back and forth, as he watched us with censure in his eyes.

I felt a shiver of anticipation.

The Wing moved on.

All eyes were on the next person in line to be tested. All eyes but mine – I was scanning faces, trying to gauge reactions. My gaze caught Juste Montpetit's. His cold royal eyes – bright blue in the morning sun – found mine and refused to look away. I felt like a bird, frozen in the gaze of a serpent. I was afraid to move in case he raised a finger and someone plunged a sword through my hand. I was afraid to blink in case I lost track of him and then he struck. He elicited feelings in me that I'd never felt before – revulsion, hatred, nausea. A creeping, wriggling feeling beneath my skin that demanded that I run as fast and hard as I could to get away from him.

What was he doing here? Why send the heir to the throne of the most powerful nation that existed to the fringes of civilization? Why send him here to agitate villagers and take swords? It didn't make any sense. It must be for a show of some kind. An action to cause a reaction somewhere else.

Maybe we were like those poor children from Canaht, innocent, killed only to make a point.

An advisor – a narrow, pinched fellow with a trimmed beard – leaned in to whisper to Juste and his gaze broke from mine.

I sagged with relief, only to catch the eyes of the Imperial Wing with the massive osprey at his back. He had witnessed our battle of gazes. Maybe he'd even seen the terror on my face. His blue eyes narrowed as he looked back and forth between us, chewing on that white sliver of wood speculatively.

I didn't like that he'd noticed me. He seemed far too intelligent with his taunting winks and ever-watching eyes – blue eyes just like the crown prince's.

My father had been right. We needed to keep our heads down and escape notice.

And now, I'd been so distracted that I hadn't noticed that the Wing had come all the way down the line of village youth. That they'd all been dismissed and all that were left were me and my siblings. I swallowed, but my throat was too dry. I had to cough to clear it.

The pale Wing's eyes flicked to me and I froze, suddenly tasting acid. I could see the tiniest tattoo of a swan feather sneaking out from the edge of her collar. One narrow eyebrow crept up on her perfect face and then she turned back to Alect.

"Hands," she said in a low voice.

Nervously, he cupped his hands before her, and she concentrated. The seconds seemed to stretch out. Had my heart always been so loud?

"You may go."

Her dismissal was so fast that I barely had time to share a nervous smile with Alect before he was darting away, as anxious to get away as I was.

Raquella had her hands cupped and held out immediately. She was always agreeable. Always ready to give people what they needed or wanted.

The Wing stared at them and so did I.

Please don't let there be anything. Please.

I breathed in and out, trying not to shake with nerves.

The minutes ticked out long and slow.

"Go," the Wing said eventually, her voice cold as Frost Season.

I let out a long breath as Raquella squeezed my arm and ran across the empty village green, plunging into the crowd to angle toward my father.

I'd be there with her in a moment. And then we'd go home and this part would be over. I could already taste the carrot soup Adigale had left over the hearth when we left.

So why did I feel a tinge of regret at the thought?

My stomach rumbled and the swan cocked his head to the side.

I looked up with all the bravery I could muster as the Wing settled in front of me. She was shorter than I was, but the swan made her seem much taller. And who needed so many belts and buckles? Most of them didn't even hold anything. They were just for show. All that metal and embroidered feathers with no purpose but display ...

"Hands," she barked.

I stuck my hands in front of me, cupping them slightly.

See? Nothing. I had no reason to be worried.

The swan adjusted his stance, leaning forward.

Had Raquella and Alect felt this strange tingling on their brow and a nervous warmth in their chest? I almost felt like I had the day I'd fainted at the village fair. I swallowed, wishing I had water to drink. I was just dehydrated. That was all.

Anticipation buzzed in my chest.

The Wing opened her mouth and I could already feel the relief flooding me mixed with a bitter strain of regret. It would have been nice to be powerful. It would have been good to have had a weapon to fight with now that all the rest had been taken.

But I hadn't Hatched. I'd be dismissed.

"Take the bandage off your palm. It interferes."

With a trembling hand, I unwound the bloody bandage, exposing my aching palm. I didn't dare look down the line at the man who put it there. Not because I was afraid he'd do it again, but because I wanted to show him what happened to pretty little soon-to-be-Emperor boys who stabbed people's hands – and I didn't dare let him see the hate in my heart. I didn't dare show him that I wanted to make him hurt like I hurt right now. I wanted to take his security and certainty like he'd taken ours.

I even wanted to take the confidence from this loathsome Imperial Wing and her solemn swan. She had walked past each of our young people, acting like they were worth less than the grass under her boots. What right did she have to treat us like that?

My nerves evaporated, leaving me trembling with frustration and anger.

The buzzing in my chest grew stronger.

"Cup your hands," the Wing said as the last winding of the bandage fell to the grass.

I cupped my hands. The flesh around my stitches was red and angry. They'd done that to me. I would make them pay for that.

I met her eyes defiantly. But where I had expected harsh arrogance, instead I saw surprise light her face.

I looked down.

A tiny golden glow rested in my hands like a trapped sun.

I gasped.

No! I shouldn't have thought about this. It was my own fault that it was happening now, and it was a bad idea.

Go away, little ball. Go away!

I tried to shove it away, my frustration building as the glow only grew stronger. I wasn't supposed to draw attention to myself. We were supposed to just ride this out.

"Speak to it," the Wing said, her voice almost seductive. Anticipation rolled off her like a wave. It lit her eyes and made them too large as her lips parted hungrily.

It was all I could do not to snarl. I wasn't a precious gem for her to find in a mine. I wasn't an unexpected strawberry found in a field. I wasn't something to be possessed and owned.

Oh, Forbidding take it! I would be *owned*. Juste Montpetit had promised it.

Panic flared in me and my breath came too quickly.

If this stupid ball of light Hatched, I'd be theirs forever, broken, owned, and made to serve – like one of my father's horses. Even one of those mysterious birds wouldn't be worth losing my freedom – my life.

I'd wished for the wrong thing. This was all my fault.

I gritted my teeth together.

"Speak!" the Wing barked, and I jammed my eyes closed and said the only words that made sense.

"Be relentless," I whispered.

There was no crack. No peep. No feeling of fluffy feathers on my hands.

There was only the angry buzzing in my chest and a whisper-soft caress against my fingers. Only the wind. Nothing magical at all.

I sighed in relief.

I let my eyelids crack open.

Above my palm, a translucent, golden bee hovered. Just one. Small and foreign.

I felt my mouth drop open. What in the ...

"Blasphemy," the Wing gasped.

And then the buzz got louder.

CHAPTER SEVEN

Bees poured from my hands like a river in the Spring, their buzzing ripping through the air. They sped out through the crowd, swirling in masses around the people of Far Reach, tearing through the armor of the soldiers, buzzing in the ears of the Wings. Screams filled the air, as the Claws broke ranks in panic. I caught the slightest glimpse of Juste Montpetit and felt a pang of satisfaction in the middle of my distress. He hopped from foot to foot like a child playing stones.

I stared at my own hands in horror as bees by the thousand poured from my palms. Were they ever going to stop? It was like a Forbiddingtale – like a story where everything someone touched turned to gold, or they had to weave moonlight into a rope to save a sister, or their tears made rivers when they cried. I tried to wave my hands, batting them away, but more bees poured out, surrounding me in a swarm.

My breath was coming too fast. They were in my eyes. On my face, crawling into my ears.

Ugh!

"Blasphemy," the Wing in front of me hissed again, grabbing my wrist and shaking it. It didn't stop the bees, but their buzz sounded even more irritated. "What is the meaning of this? Magic may only manifest itself as one of the great bird talismans. This is not possible."

I didn't know how to stop it.

"Seems pretty possible to me," I said through gritted teeth, my words buzzing with the bees.

I shoved my hands behind my back, but the buzzing continued. Glowing yellow bodies filled the air around me in such thick clouds that I couldn't see anything.

My head was spinning.

I couldn't breathe.

I clawed at my throat, gagging on what felt like a rag stuffed in it.

"Grab her! We ride," someone shouted. I dug my heels in. I wasn't going anywhere. I'd heard Juste Montpetit 's threat. I knew he wanted to make me his personal property. I'd rather die.

I gritted my teeth against the buzz that drowned out every sound around me. Shockingly, the bees didn't sting me, they simply surrounded me, their bodies and sounds blocking out everything else.

A dark shape emerged from the cloud and then my father was there, a sharpened stake in his hands that I recognized as one of the flag poles from the green.

"We'll get you out of here, Aella," he said. "Hold on, my Shrikeling. They aren't taking any daughter of mine."

I didn't know *how* to hold on or what to do as I saw Retger and Awet joining my father. Retger had a blacksmith's hammer and Awet a butcher's cleaver. They must have grabbed them in the chaos. They braced themselves in front of me with a cry of "Relentless!"

Blue-jacketed Swan Claws burst through the cloud of bees, fury on their faces and red welts springing up on their exposed skin. They threw themselves at my family, swords sweeping into clouds of golden bees as they lunged and slashed at my brothers and father.

Retger smashed a sword aside at the same moment as another blade found Awet's arm, slicing a nasty gash through the skin. He grunted, trying to parry the next blow with the cleaver, but it was too light a weapon. The Claw stepped in, triumph on his face as he swatted the cleaver out of Awet's hand. He raised his sword and my father jabbed his flagpole into the Claw's neck, stunning him. He choked, dropping the sword, his windpipe crushed by the blow.

"Back!" the old man roared.

"Don't!" I called over the buzzing as my brothers and father pushed me backward. I'd wanted to have a manifestation so I could help them – not to make them die defending me. "Don't risk yourselves for me. I'll go with them."

"No," my father said. His words held a grim finality. "They aren't taking you, too."

But the buzz of the bees was dimming, their golden bodies flickering out of sight as they vanished one by one. As my frustration melted into fear, they left me.

I gulped down air, finally able to breathe. I clung to my breath, trying to calm myself. I needed to think. I had a choice here if I could just take it.

"I'll come back as soon as I can," I said, tripping over my words in my hurry. "I'll help you fight. But not today. Not when it can get you killed."

As the bees left, I could see the ranks of Claws closing in on us and the knots of townspeople fighting the Claws. The bakery was on fire. The forge door was smashed in. People were screaming, rushing with buckets or improvised weapons. There were bodies on the ground in slumped heaps. Too many. Almost none of them in blue jackets. In the middle of a heap of tangled bodies, a small child was sobbing.

My pulse roared in my ears as my hands came up to cover my mouth.

Not Far Reach. Not my home.

In the distance, I caught a glimpse of Juste Montpetit, astride a great horned beast that looked like a bull. He was riding out of town with his advisor and a cluster of Claws, all mounted on similar beasts. The dust forming in clouds around them blew across the screaming, fleeing townsfolk trying to clear a path before they were trampled to death.

All this because of me.

No.

I shook my head in denial.

The last bee flickered out of existence.

My father's gaze caught mine and my dry lips wouldn't make a sound.

I mouthed, "I'm sorry."

Something yanked my waist, knocking my breath out of me and jerking me off my feet. My father's mouth opened in horror. He was smaller suddenly – the entire town growing small as I rose into the air.

A Claw leapt in from behind my father and he crumpled forward, a blade in his back. He roared, but I could hardly hear it. He was tiny now and growing smaller by the second. And so were my brothers, my friends, my whole town. I watched in shock as they scurried across the village green, fleeing, fighting, or desperately putting out fires.

No.

I closed my mouth, trying to catch a breath as the air beat against me.

No.

I looked down. It was an arm in a thick leather bracer that was holding me so tightly that it felt like a steel band.

A pair of feet were balanced below us, standing on the faintly purple, translucent back of a flying osprey the size of a large horse.

No.

I screamed, but my scream was snatched by the air as fast as it bubbled from my throat.

CHAPTER EIGHT

I felt a single hot tear smear across my face. But already, my town was nothing but a bubbly patch of tiny houses with a green patch in the center, surrounded by tumbling rocks all around. The dark, swirling mass of the Forbidding crowded in from one side, and from my new vantage point it looked like a tangled mass of writhing snakes clawing into the sky. The pale peaks of the Forbidding Mountains rose on the other side, the road to the narrow pass that cut through them marked by a growing cloud of dust that drifted out from the road like a wave on the shore.

I tried to catch my breath. It was coming too quickly. I was almost grateful for the crushing grip around me. My legs felt like water. I wouldn't be able to stand even if I was on the ground.

I'd never imagined myself flying. If I had, I would have expected exhilaration rather than the urgent need to be ill.

"No point fighting it," the Imperial Wing said. His voice was husky and his breath was warm against my neck. He sounded younger when he was this close – less the Imperial soldier with magic skills and more like a boy my own age. "There's never a point in fighting it. The magic will manifest. The Empire will take you for it. If you fight it, you'll just see the ones you love die for nothing. We call this the Winged Empire, but do you know what name they whisper in other lands? They call us the *Empire of War and Wings*. And that is what we are. Nothing but war and more war and wings that give us the power to wage that war."

I didn't say anything. I didn't know whether to thank him for taking me away before my brothers died with my father, or whether to curse him for being one of *them*.

It was hard to tell where we were from the air. I wouldn't have expected that. My heart was in my throat as he plunged toward a rocky peak on the edge of the Forbidding canyon. Blue rocks cut up into the air like jagged teeth. From where we were, the Far Stones looked like an uninhabited continent – nothing but trees and rocks and lakes and chaotic Forbidding. I felt smaller than I ever had before.

The bird below us stretched his wings and I gasped as I felt the brush of spirit feathers across my leg. It was like *Iri and the Great Bird* or *The Golden Eagle of Xi*. Like a story come to life. My breath caught as the Wing holding me leapt from the bird's back onto the light blue stone, carrying me with him.

The second his feet hit the ground he released me. I leapt away, pulling my belt knife.

"What do you want with me?" I asked in a low voice.

He pulled a small white pick from his sleeve and tucked it between his lips, considering me as he fiddled with it. He looked too refined to be standing on the rocks of Far Stones. And far too beautiful. He was nearly as handsome as the crown prince. Most boys in Far Reach had a broken nose by the time they were this age. It was no easy thing to fight for the ground you lived on day after day.

"Why did you steal me away?" I pressed.

"Did you want your family killed trying to defend you?" He sounded irritated. "Is that what you wanted? Because that's what you would have gotten, honey."

"Honey?" I asked warily. "You bring me up here – away from your friends and away from mine – and you start using endearments?"

He snorted. "Get over yourself. It was a reference to the bees." He pulled the toothpick from his mouth, shaking his head. "This isn't going the way I thought it would."

He ran a hand over his face, muttering and shaking his head as if he was arguing with himself about something.

"Am I going mad?" he asked aloud, eyes shut. "Is this my mind finally breaking?"

I held the knife out with a shaking hand. "If you try to touch me ..."

"I'm not going to kill you," he said in a pained voice, as if it hurt him to speak. His agony was exquisite on his planed, dark face. "And I'm not going to directly harm you, either. If I can help it."

He looked up finally, his face haunted. Maybe he was going mad.

"Not directly. That's rich." I laughed in disbelief, my mouth dry. "There are a lot of ways to die in the Far Stones and many of them are indirect."

"There are just as many ways to die in the Winged Empire. And just as many ways to be forced to kill." He closed his eyes for a moment as if he was trying to collect his patience. "You're from the furthest reach of the Winged Empire. So, you don't know how things work. Which means this is going to take more work than I'd hoped it would, isn't it?"

His superior attitude was only making me more irritated. I folded my arms over my chest refusing to play into his games. I studied him carefully, looking for a weakness.

He was well-groomed, his black hair carefully trimmed, his cheeks carrying only a day or two of stubble. His coat was finer than I'd first thought, edged with bottle green satin and trimmed with silver buttons worked with diving birds. Ospreys – like the spirit bird he bore. There were ospreys in an intricate pattern stamped into the leather of the thong tied around his forehead. His white shirt under the jacket was trimmed with soft feathers like lace. They spilled over his collar and out the sleeves of his coat like a light snow.

"Yes, it's going to be so frustrating for you. I feel terrible," I said dryly. "Your people just disarmed mine, made it impossible to defend ourselves, snatched me away, and stabbed my father in the back. But this is going to be hard for the pretty man in the feather-lined shirt. I'm practically weeping."

I was shaking, but it wasn't from fear. It was from everything – watching my father stabbed, watching my town in ruins, being snatched from them forever. It had to come out somewhere, so it came out in shudders up and down my body. I ran a hand through my brown curls to try to calm myself. I wouldn't be giving up the dagger just yet.

His eyes narrowed. "There's nothing wrong with decorative feathers."

"In Far Reach, even our women are too tough to decorate their everyday clothing," I said, giving him my best scornful look. But honestly, I didn't care. I just wanted to talk about something other than the fear and pain of what had just happened.

He leaned in close, his mouth making a lovely growl as he snatched my belt knife from my hand before I could stop him. My eyes widened in surprise. He was so fast. Faster than a Forbidding tentacle. I'd never seen hands that quick. I could feel his breath on my face and see how very long his dark eyelashes were. They made it look like someone had outlined his eyes with black charcoal.

"If you think being tough as old leather is something to brag about, go right on bragging. I've seen men dressed in pink silk slit throats faster than a farmer slaughters chickens. I've seen women dripping in layers of lace betray their own children. Strength and power don't come from a particular mode of dress. But you should know that I'm the one person who can save your skin – and maybe even some of your people, so either listen to me or waste our one chance to talk and your one chance for a life of anything but servitude ending in a grisly death."

"I thought Wings were glorious manifestors of magic, blessed by the heavens and precious to the Empire," I said as snidely as I could. I didn't want to play nice. I wanted to go home. There was a yawning pit of sadness and fear inside me at the very thought of home. I didn't want to think about it. I didn't want to wonder if my father was dead. If my brothers were dead. If their children ...

I pulled myself back from those thoughts. I had to deal with what was happening right in front of me.

"We're even better than that," he said with another one of those silky smiles. "But we aren't gods. And the weaker and more miserable people are, the easier it is for them to claw you from the sky."

"That sounds like something my father would say." I didn't manage to keep the sorrow from my tone.

"Smart man." He offered me my belt knife back. "Don't stab me with that. And stop making fun of my down feather linings. Don't you wear clothing to blend in around here?"

"Drabs for hunting?" I suggested and he nodded.

"I wear clothing to blend in, too," he said with a wink. It looked odd when combined with the deadly frown on his face. I had a feeling that his winks weren't playful things. They meant something else entirely.

"And if I don't stab you, what will you do?" I asked with a raised eyebrow.

"I will offer you something that no one else is going to offer for a very long time."

I took the belt knife and sheathed it. "And what is that?"

He stared off into the distance at the gathering dark clouds above us. "You can almost smell the revolution in the air in this strange continent. It's as if the land itself is restless."

"We just want to be free," I said. And those words felt as flimsy as cobwebs.

"That Forbidding doesn't help," he said, staring at where it bit the land at the base of the mountain we stood on. "It wants to eat everything up like a fire in the heat of midsummer."

"Which is why weapons would have been handy." I bit the words off hard. I needed to hear what he was going to say. "What are you offering me?"

He sighed and then shot me a slightly vulnerable, worried look.

"It's not easy. In order for me to make you my ally, I need to trust you. But I don't know you. And you lack judgment. You manifested clouds of angry bees, for the love of all that flies. Not just one. Swarms of them."

"Kiss dust!" I cursed. "You're going to judge me for that? Like I had any control of it."

"You have control now," he said. "And you're telling me to kiss dust. You're the worst choice for this."

He stood abruptly and jammed that white pick back into his mouth, chewing it violently as he looked to the horizon. He was muttering again and twitching agitatedly. There was something going on with him beyond what was happening here on this mountain.

"Then why choose me at all?" I asked, playing with the shrike feathers sewn into my belt. The talisman hadn't saved me at all. What was the point of it?

He turned from studying the horizon, his eyes furious with bright intensity. He clenched a muscle in his jaw and then shook his head.

"Because you manifested something other than a bird. For the first time in a thousand years." The toothpick wobbled as he spoke. "Most people didn't think it could happen. But we knew ... we knew. And we've been waiting." He seemed to realize what he was saying and he paused. "We don't have much time here. I'm just going to have to ...

Listen, I know you love that big family of yours."

"Yes."

Was he threatening them?

"That will have to be enough. We have a chance to end the Majest reign, end the injustices, end the wars, end the malevolent power of the Empire itself." He took a step toward me and he was vibrating with excitement. "You're the chance. I need you to promise to work with me. To help me put an end to them."

I hesitated. "And do what? What do you want me to do?"

"Whatever it takes." He spat out his mangled pick and drew another from a small pocket in his coat. "I need you to choose a side right now. I need to know I can trust you when I come to you with what's next."

"Aren't I owned now by Le Majest? The crown prince?" I hedged.

His upper lip curled. "Forget him. He's not what we're talking about here."

"I can't exactly forget that I'm owned by the Imperial family! He said he would claim whoever Hatched."

"But did you Hatch?" he asked with a smirk. "Do bees Hatch?"

I gave him a puzzled look.

"I didn't see an egg," he said persuasively. "And even if you did Hatch, wouldn't you rather work with me than with him? Wouldn't you rather find a way to give your people the freedom they want? The freedom to have their weapons back and defend themselves?" I froze. I *did* want that. "To have the ability to build up their towns and farms and resources without shipping off most of their wealth to a ruler across a sea? A ruler who doesn't know what they want or need? A ruler with his own agenda?"

I stared back into his fiery gaze. Of course, I wanted those things. He must know that I did. And he had baited the hook perfectly. How could I say no to that?

I swallowed.

And yet, I did not like being manipulated.

"Tell me you don't want that," he said leaning close again.

"I want it," I confessed.

"Tell me you don't want to be owned by a pretty prince who'd kiss a snake rather than let his people be free enough to threaten his sense of self."

I swallowed. "I don't want to be owned."

"Tell me you will be my ally. That you will do as I tell you – even without knowing why – for the sake of ending that rule."

It felt like a heavy burden was pressing on my shoulders. How could I say no? And yet, he clearly had his own motivations and he was pushing me into the path he wanted me to take.

"If you are so against those things, why did you help the crown prince disarm my family?" I challenged.

His cheeks flushed. "I am bound by chains you can't see. I can't do everything I might want to do."

"That's not a good enough answer."

"Maybe I'm not a good enough person for a good answer."

"Then why should I work with you at all?"

"Because I'm still the best hope you have. Trust me. Who else is offering you this?"

A long moment passed between us, and his eyes seemed to grow sharper and sharper as I stared into them.

"I just want out of this," I said. "I just don't want to do any of it. I want to go home."

"You don't have a home anymore."

"I want to go back to my family."

"You don't have a – "

"Will you shut up!"

We were halfway up a mountain, but I didn't care. I scrambled to the edge of the flat rock we stood on, trying to choose a path down. I had my belt knife and a flint. I was maybe two or three days walk from home up here. I could get back. Maybe.

I slipped on the stone, skidding down a few feet until I managed to catch myself on a scrubby tree.

"What are you doing?" he asked.

"Going home."

He snorted. "Do you honestly think I'm going to let you do that?"

I ignored him, careful with my balance as I picked a careful path down the loose rock to the next stub of a tree. I could do this. One step at a time.

"You're an idiot."

I could hear the rocks tumbling behind me as he followed me. It just made me move faster. I slipped, skidding down the rocks. I felt them scrape my thigh. It was going to leave a mark. My breath hitched for a moment, but I kept going. I didn't believe him that he had some kind of plan to fix things. Though I also didn't know why he'd try to trap me with such an obvious lie. Maybe they did that to everyone and if you said yes they killed you on the mountain and left you there for the birds.

"You're going to break your own neck."

I wasn't going to be able to lose him on the mountainside. There was nowhere to hide and I couldn't go any faster.

A hand caught my arm. I tried to jerk away but his hand was strong as steel. He twisted me toward him and though I fought his grip, he didn't budge and he barely seemed to be exerting himself. His expression was grim.

"It's getting late and if we take too long people will be suspicious. You can't run away from this. You can't go home. But I also can't keep you here right now trying to convince you. The other Wings will wonder what kept me and they will take out any suspicions on you."

"There's nothing to suspect," I said.

"They'll take you in hand. They have their own ways of training Hatchlings. You need to think about deciding to work with me. It's you best hope no matter what I must say or do before the eyes of others."

I snorted. "So, you're going to pretend that you're indifferent to me even if they beat me or torture me and you still expect that I'll want to work with you toward some goal you haven't explained?"

He nodded, sincerity in his eyes. "I can explain it now, if you like."

"I don't want to hear it."

"Think about what you want."

He stepped forward and wrapped an arm around me so suddenly that my breath caught. His bright osprey popped into sight in front of me and he stepped on its back smoothly.

"Be fast as wind and light as a feather," he whispered so softly that I could barely hear the words. "Bear all my hopes and dreams and do not fail me."

The osprey flashed bursts of lavender across its white wings as if something was exciting it. It seemed more opaque than before, more alive as it dove through the clouds to the world beneath.

My heart was in my throat and my belly rolled every time I let myself think about where I was as we sped down the side of the mountain to the high pines below. It was easier to keep my eyes on the horizon instead of dwelling on the steady roll and heave of the bird beneath us flapping his wings, or even worse, the fluid roll and tip when he soared in wide circles.

I was going to be sick if I wasn't careful.

I swallowed, looking down for long enough to watch the mighty osprey beneath my feet, it twisted its head so that one steely eye fixed itself on me and my heart sped up until I was afraid I would pass out. The magic pulsing through it was almost palpable. I fixed my gaze carefully to the horizon again, sucking in air through my nose and blowing it out my lips to try to calm myself.

The Wing spat and his white pick tumbled toward the earth. I watched it as it grew so small that my head hurt from watching and I blinked back a new wave of tears. My family was far down there somewhere – whichever of them still lived.

"We're flying down to camp," he said and his voice sounded troubled again. "So, remember this advice. Trust no one. Don't draw any more attention to your family back there. Don't mention them. Don't cry for them. Try to make the Empire forget you ever had a family. It's the best way you can protect them right now. Don't try to escape. They'll only kill your family – one member at a time – if you do something that stupid. Just work hard and focus on mastering those bees, and we'll talk again soon."

"There's nothing to talk about."

We were both silent as he began to circle lower and lower toward a camp of white tents set up in the foothills of the Forbidding Mountains.

"Make sure to call me Osprey if you address me," he said when we neared the ground. "It's my title."

I was too focused on flying to be worried about what I was going to call him.

I dreaded the thought of landing. What was waiting down there with the other Wings and the son of the Emperor? Would he be able to tell that I was plotting to flee? I had never been very good at disguising my purposes, but I was going to have to learn to be.

CHAPTER NINE

We sailed down into the camp as the sun was setting. It shone off the spirit wings of the osprey as they curled up on either side of us. I found it impossible not to be impressed by how beautiful and magical those wings were. Even harder not to be curious if anything like that would ever be possible for me when what had Hatched in me was a furious cloud of bees.

I fought those thoughts. I needed to remember that this world was against me and that they were a threat to everything I loved. This was not my home and it never could be. These were not my friends and they never would be. Not even Osprey – or whatever he called himself. Even if I mastered this new strange magic and found a way to use it against the Winged Empire – to carve out freedom from them like a quarryman carving rock. Even then, I would only be proving how much of an enemy to them I was. And I wasn't planning to stick around long enough to do that.

They'd laid their camp next to the Great Forbidding Bridge that spanned the chasm over Snipesnake Canyon. I'd traveled over it, but I'd never seen it from the air before – never seen how the breathtaking white bridge spanned over the canyon with flawless grace, the sides arching up as if they were wings of a great white heron. But they were not designed to look like wings as everything from the Empire was. They were from the time before when the Forbidding crawled across all this land and a mysterious and elusive people had built such magnificent structures. And, like everything they had created, this was a bridge of snakes and winding roots, of vines and flowers and lurking asps. Someone had taken the better half of their adulthood carving these winding patterns into the ribs and floor of the bridge, marking it forever as a part of a civilization long vanished.

"Snakes everywhere," Osprey muttered. "Why does this land love snakes so much?"

"We don't," I replied, but my voice sounded foreign to me, like it did the morning after my mother died when I spent the night crying. "We found them here. Everywhere. Whoever lived here before the Forbidding took this land carved everything with snakes. Every bridge, every rock, every cliff face. They were obsessed with them. My father said that when he landed here with the first ship to bring settlers, there were snakes on the rocks in the cove."

"Maybe that's why the land writhes the way it does."

"The Forbidding isn't a snake," I said scornfully. "If it was only a snake, it could be destroyed for good."

"Does anyone know what it is? I checked the Imperial libraries before we left for Far Stones. Scholars, it seems, had little to say about the matter. All I found were a few dispatches detailing the settling of Far Stones thirty years ago. Nothing about the origin of the strange magic here. Nothing about how to deal with it."

"Like most things, you have to deal with it as it comes," I said shortly. If he didn't know how to fight the Forbidding, then that wasn't my problem. I had to keep my eyes out for what was my problem – escape.

The great spirit osprey spiraled twice around the encampment, giving me a good look at the pavilions. They were made of overlapping feathers to keep the rain out and to add an air of drama and wealth. Who could afford to sew tents all over with overlapping rows of colorful bird feathers anyway? Some were striped, with a row of red feathers followed by stark white, others were made of purple and green iridescent patterns, still others were completely black with a single tuft of yellow at the peak of the roof. I watched them in awe. Our village wasn't as spectacular as this single encampment managed to be. Someone had even set up small man-height totems outside some of the larger tents. One – beside a pure white tent – depicted a swan in flight. I shivered at that one. It was ringed by Swan Guard and there was no doubt whose tent that was.

The double lap also gave me a chance to see the Claws surrounding the encampment in a solid ring, their powerful bull-like carabao mounts tied along a picket on the side of camp farthest from the canyon. I swallowed. The camp looked impregnable. There would be no escape tonight for me – even if I ignored Osprey's advice and chose to put my family at risk.

When we were only inches from the ground, Osprey stepped lightly from the back of the bird and landed on the soft earth just outside of the camp. It was the first moment in a while that an arm hadn't been wrapped tightly around my middle and with the loss of it, a massive wave of insecurity washed over me. I pressed my hands to my own middle to try to keep my emotions in – trying not to think of the moment when my father had been struck from behind, of the look in my brother's eyes when he was pushed back, of the terrified faces of my nieces and nephews. The only way I could be relentless was if I refused to cave in to fear and anxiety.

Come on, Aella. Don't let them see how strange this all seems to you. Don't let them see how terrified you really are.

The nearest tent had a warm glow lighting the pale feathers from within so that they glowed a golden orange. A luxurious woven carpet with a winged design patterned into it spilled from the mouth of the tent. A pair of folding chairs made of a light segmented wood and canvas cloth stitched with peacock feathers were set up in front of it, though they were empty right now.

"Come," Osprey said, taking a new pick from his pocket and jamming it between his teeth. He moved with a kind of purpose that made him always seem about to leap in any direction, and his eyes glittered as they took in his surroundings like the osprey he was named for. I didn't think he missed a thing.

He wrapped a gloved hand around my arm, surprising me with how rough his grip suddenly was. When I glanced at him, he raised an eyebrow. Apparently, he wasn't lying when he said he was going to pretend that he hadn't spoken to me.

"You don't need to hold me like I might fly away," I said dryly. "I don't have wings."

"We'll see about that." He paused, looked around furtively, and leaned in close. "Listen, it won't help you if I appear to care. But if you want to live, you should try to tame that tongue. You won't be much of an ally to me if you're dead."

"I haven't agreed to be your ally at all."

"You will. Eventually. When you calm down and start thinking rationally."

He straightened, adjusted his toothpick and his careful frown, and then marched me toward the glowing tent, while I was still trying to catch my breath. They'd threatened me and practically chosen me as a slave, and they'd threatened my family, but no one had said anything about killing me until now. I gritted my teeth. For some reason, the idea of it made me more angry than afraid.

A figure emerged from around the side of the tent, his brow furrowed with worry.

"Ah, Osprey. You're here." It was the advisor I'd seen whispering at the village green. "We expected you hours ago and he is worried. Have you forgotten your duty?"

"You know I never forget my duty, Butiez," Osprey said, rolling one of his shoulders irritably. Standing beside the advisor, he suddenly looked more lean, more muscled, even taller. The glitter in his eyes turned from intense to charming. "It is my constant companion, my shadow, the bedfellow who wakes me in the night to remind me of my place in this world."

"Is it now?" Butiez said suspiciously.

"You know how tightly I'm chained. If he'd wrapped ropes around my viscera he couldn't have me more tightly bound." His words elicited a cruel smile on the face of the advisor and I watched them both intently. This felt more like a sparring match than a conversation. "But I also have some other small duties to attend. Personal hygiene." He flicked the light feather down at the edge of his sleeve. "And oh, I have this Hatchling to deliver to the other Wings."

He looked at me idly as if I was of no more concern than downy feathers.

"Be quick about it." The advisor looked in either direction. "Guardians should not long leave those they protect."

"Are you thinking of changing your feathers, Butiez?" he asked, taking the pick out of his mouth and looking the advisor up and down like he might be judging a horse he was about to buy. "I didn't know you hankered after protection detail but if you can get a little more muscle on those bones, I could try recommending you to the Black Swan when we return to the continent."

The advisor snorted angrily, spinning on his heels and striding away. Osprey winked at me before he flung back the tent flap, ducked his head, and drew me after him into the golden light.

I swallowed. What had that all meant? It felt important – as if Osprey was trying to show me something by provoking that advisor. What had been revealed in that brief battle of wills? Was it merely that the advisor was a pompous fool, or had he been trying to show me more than that?

Later, Aella. You can sort it out later. I felt my mouth growing dry as Osprey stepped out from in front of me, giving me a clear view of the tent.

The pale Wing with the swan manifestation sat on one of those folding chairs behind a small desk, her swan rested on a blackwood perch behind her desk, peering over her shoulder. Both of them stared at me with the same intense gaze.

I could hear her voice in my head as if she were still yelling it at me. *Abomination.*

That's what she thought of me.

"You're late," she snapped. "Don't tell me you're getting soft, Osprey."

He flinched.

Her eyebrow raised and her lips twisted with an expression I couldn't read. "Does your name chafe so soon? I would have thought you'd still be preening like a cockatoo at earning it. So few are chosen to protect – and never any as young as you. What an honor."

He picked at his teeth with the white stick and made a sound out of the side of his mouth that sounded like "*tsk.*" It reminded me, somehow, of my brother Retger when he was trying to hold his temper.

"I thought I'd let the dust settle before I landed," he said mildly. He sounded nothing like the intense young man who had spoken to me on the mountain. "You know I'm above petty squabbles."

"Are you?" she asked sardonically. "You can leave the girl here. Essana or I will take her until we get to Astar Harbor."

"And then?" he asked mildly.

"And then it will be none of your concern who we give her to. She's an aberration. A disgrace. Only Far Reach would give us *bees.*" She practically buzzed with fury and I felt an answering buzz deep in my chest.

What was wrong with my bees? They certainly seemed to get people's attention, didn't they? Perversely, I felt the immediate instinct to *want* bees over birds. Everything this woman said made me want to say the opposite.

"Essana might be a good fit," he suggested casually. "Maybe she would take on the task of Guide?"

"Don't tell me you care, Osprey." Her eyes narrowed and he shoved me to my knees with his grip on my arm.

I grunted, shooting him a furious look. He was pushing my patience too far. I would not be cowed. I did not kneel to anyone. Well, except when they were threatening my family and I had no choice. I pushed up against his hand, trying to fight the pressure and he shoved me forward. I caught my fall with both hands on the woven carpet. I should have made him promise more when I swore to him. Our deal was far too one-sided.

"Of course not. Take her," he said, storming out of the tent.

My eyes followed him as he left me with the woman who clearly despised me.

He's not your friend, Aella. Don't forget that.

"Never in all my days have I seen such a stir," the Swan Wing said coolly. "And all over what I'm sure will prove to be the most useless of the Hatched we've ever seen. *Bees. Bees!*"

"What's so offensive about bees?" I asked, standing up and crossing my arms over my chest. The buzz in my chest was getting stronger.

She gave me a cool look before dipping her quill in ink and slowly writing something across the parchment as she spoke.

"Your family caused quite a stir. You should know that stir was quelled. By force."

I said nothing, but I swallowed down worry and the sharp hatred swelling in my chest. She spoke so coolly about violence done to my family as if they weren't even worth her regard. Maybe she needed a little violence done to her. Maybe I should be the one to do it. My fingers twitched for my sword, but it had been taken. Everything had been taken.

"If that makes you angry," she said with a taunting lilt to her voice, "by all means run out of this tent and throw yourself off that canyon. Trust me, it will be the simplest result here. Otherwise, prepare yourself to be brutally trained. Le Majest has expressed to me that it is my role to see you changed from a manifestor of *bees* into a manifestor of some kind of bird by the time we get to Astar Harbor and I will see it done."

"Is that possible?" I asked. The way Osprey had talked it made it sound like he'd picked me for an ally *because* of these bees. He must not have thought they could be changed.

She merely narrowed her eyes at me.

"We left Claws in Far Reach. And I have fast pigeons."

That was worrying.

"Have you ever seen a crucifixion?" she asked mildly, dipping her quill again.

"What?" I asked, surprised by the question. I felt a chill spike through my veins. That was an oddly specific question.

"I'll spare you the tortuous details. But know this. Balk at any order or request from me, and all it will take is one little scrap of paper sent to the town of Far Reach with my order and they'll use your family to decorate the roadside in the most grisly fashion. The crosses they use make lovely perches for birds. I'm more delighted by bird imagery myself but I will use horror instead if it suits the purpose."

"I thought Wings were supposed to be like their bird manifestations in temperament," I said, barely choking down my sudden horror. I felt like I was going to be ill. Images of my family in agony, dying slowly, flooded my mind and it was all I could do to choke down my terror.

She smiled this time, a secretive, dark smile. "You heard correctly, child. Were you fool enough to think that swans were kind? Clearly, you've never encountered one. Majestic, they may be, but with that comes equal levels of cruelty. Do not mistake my graces for compassion. I will break you down to your base elements if I must."

She waited, watching me as her words settled in.

There would be no escape. There was no way out. I would have to endure whatever she sent my way or risk my family. Even here, a day's ride from them, they were not safe. My actions could still mean their deaths. I tried to prevent the shiver that rose at her words, but I couldn't stop it. She smiled as I shook under her gaze.

"You understand. That is good. Stupidity would only have made this harder. You will sleep in the tent of my apprentice. Any attempt to escape or attack us will be met with a tiny note sent to Far Reach. You understand?"

I nodded, speechless as the swan leapt from its perch and flew past me and out the tent door. One of its wings passed through me, leaving me ice-cold inside. My skin crawled at its touch – at the touch of this extension of the Wing.

"Yes," I said breathlessly.

"We begin your training tomorrow. I care not if you sleep or simply lie shivering in fear, but do not disturb my rest." She flicked a wrist, looking toward the tent flap. "Come."

I looked behind me to see the swan returning, leading a girl about my age into the tent. Her eyes were dark and hooded, as if her face was a rock wall protecting her from the outside world. Her glossy hair hung in a smooth curtain and she wore an Imperial court dress, complete with small puffs at the top of her sleeves. In her hand, she carried a tiny red glowing chick. I gasped as I realized she'd been at the Hatching, too. She sailed across the rug like a ship at sea, making the sign of the bird across her chest.

"Take this child to your tent, Zayana," the Wing ordered. "And do not let her presence distract you from your exercises."

The girl bowed and motioned to me to follow her out of the tent. It felt like an escape – but not for long because leaving the tent meant entering the encampment of my enemies. None of them would flinch at my death or the deaths of those I loved. And no one was coming to save me – not even Osprey with his talk of allegiance. I could only save myself.

CHAPTER TEN

Zayana, it would seem, was not my friend either.

She kept her nose in the air as she led me through the camp, lighting our way through the twilight with her glowing red bird. She held her fancy court dress out of the dust, her tiny feet stepping gracefully over stones or small dips in the ground like a heron stepping through a marsh.

She led me to a tent made of grey and white feathers that looked like they'd come from a partridge. The edges fluttered slightly as if the tent might fly away and I ached inside with the desire to fly away with it.

We marched in over a thick rug of bear hides sewn together. There were pallets of blankets on either side of the tent on small, puffy down mattresses, a washbasin, and a large wooden chest.

"Don't touch my things," Zayana said sharply, kicking off her shoes and settling onto her pallet with a huff.

She whispered something to her bird and it winked out before I could find my way to my own pallet. I crawled to it in the darkness and kicked off my boots, staying silent until Zayana's breath slowed and lengthened.

I felt like I had run a thousand miles. My muscles and even my bones ached, and yet I could not sleep.

I eased myself from the mattress and crept to the edge of the tent.

This was a bad idea.

Wing Xectare had warned me what she would do to my family if I escaped. But that was assuming they hadn't fled already. I knew my family. If they had survived – and I knew in my heart that I would feel it if they had died – then they would already be establishing a plan to keep themselves safe. They would flee or they would build defenses. They would not be easy for the Claws to slaughter – even without weapons and I thought they might have some of those hidden. Which meant that if I was really fast, I could get to them and warn them and we could all escape together.

I drew a long breath and snuck out of the tent and into the night.

I'd spent my whole life dodging the Forbidding, keeping my wits about me so it didn't take me by surprise, sneaking through the woods after wild mustangs. I'd spent my whole life in training for this. There was a watch posted, of course. The Claws efficiently marched around the perimeter, guarding their mounts, keeping watch on every angle into the camp. But they weren't watching for someone sneaking out. Or at least, not very well.

I didn't try to look around camp for a weapon, or where the crown prince was staying, or to steal a mount. I wasn't letting anything distract me from my goal.

Not even my pounding pulse.

I waited for my moment – right when the nearest guard was steps away from the cook fire – that tiny instant when his vision would just be a bit less sharp with the light in his eyes.

I stepped lightly behind him, passing into the night.

The forest embraced me, the soft rustling of mice in the grass and night owls in the leaves covering the tiny sounds of my entrance. I breathed a long sigh. It would be a long walk home and I needed to start immediately. I didn't dare leave the road in the darkness. That was an easy way to find yourself entwined in the Forbidding. I would creep around the edges until I could safely meet it.

I took a step. And then another.

I was free.

Joy seized my heart as I scrambled through the dark woods, guided only by the moonlight. I gave the camp a wide berth, circling to the road. I didn't leave the trees until camp was out of sight. Hope flooded through me. It had been easier than I'd thought. Perhaps their threats were meaningless after all. I started to jog, speeding down the dirt road. If I was fast enough, I could cover enough ground on the road that I could afford to take a tougher route when the sun rose – the kind of route that would keep me out of sight from the sky in case one of the Wings came looking for me.

I looked up at the mood, veiled by the clouds racing across the night sky. They were edged in silver where the moonlight kissed them. I had time.

A hand closed over my mouth, the force of it pulling me backward. It was all I could do not to scream. I bit the hand instead. My captor whispered a curse.

Osprey?

"Bite me again and I'll bite you back," he whispered, his mouth so close to my ear that I could feel the warmth of his breath. "I tried to warn you about escape."

I struggled against his arm. It had me pinned to his rock-hard chest. I tried a kick to his ankle, but he stepped smartly out of the way.

"I grow impatient with how slow you learn, Aella of House Shrike." He'd learned my proper name. "Or did you think I was lying when I said that running from this would only bring danger to your family?"

I might have responded if he didn't have his hand clamped over my mouth.

"Did you think you were sneaky enough to go unseen?"

I bit my own lip, frustration filling me. I had thought that, yes. But I wouldn't give him the pleasure of agreement.

"Did you think you think that you were fast enough to outrun me?"

This time I did nod. I still thought I was fast enough to outrun him. He was just lucky this time. Sure, his osprey was faster – but it would have to find me to catch me.

His next words came through gritted teeth. "You're impossible. I'm going to loosen my hand and hope you aren't stupid enough to draw attention to us. I already told you that I don't want to kill you. Why are you making it so hard for me?"

He eased his hand and I spun, face to face with him in the moonlight. He was holding a drawn short sword.

"I don't want to be part of this."

"None of us does." There was sadness in his voice.

"Then why can't you just let me go."

"I'm bound with cords you don't understand. I thought you'd realize that from what Butiez said. But since you are stubborn as one of these Far Reach rocks, let me explain this again. There will be no escape for you."

"I'm going to keep trying," I whispered.

"Then you're a bigger fool than I thought. Work with me. Be my ally."

I shook my head.

He sighed, scratching unhappily at his tired jaw. His fancy clothes were in disarray, his hair mussed, as if he'd been half asleep when he'd come after me.

"I had a sister," he said quietly. "We were not raised together. Our mothers are not the same, but I met her once. She had large kind eyes. That's what I remember most about her, the kindness in her eyes. No one else in my family ever looked at me like that."

I tilted my head, imagining Raquella. Imagining her kind eyes and then imagining how they would widen if the Claws returned and ripped my family apart. A stab of guilt rippled through me.

"I only met her on that day. The day that they dragged her before me to teach me a lesson. She had been given in marriage to a man of the Garbocco Islands. A chance for a family alliance. She had tried to flee the marriage. 'I just want to go home,' she'd said, just like you. I stood there helpless while they taught her that there was no home to return to. Watched as her own mother spat in her eye. Watched as they slit her throat."

I gasped, hands clenching in response to the depths of emotion in his voice.

"Do you want me to have to watch as they slit your throat? Do you want me to be the one to do it?" He scrubbed a hand over his face. "I don't want that. In a minute, I'm going to try to sneak you back into camp. I don't want you to say anything. Not to the guards and not even to me. I just want you to think for tonight. Think about how much life you have left to live. Think about how you could join me in opposing the kind of Empire that slaughters young girls just because they're homesick. Think about how much good you could do that family of yours if you let the Empire train you to use that bee magic and then you unleashed it on them. Just think about what your options really are. Because it isn't a choice between freedom and servitude for you. Not right now. Right now, it's a choice between servitude or the death of everyone you love. I know what I would have chosen if anyone had ever given me a choice. Maybe you didn't believe me about that before, but I'm begging you to believe me now."

He was true to his word. He didn't say anything else as he led me back to camp at sword point one hand gripping my upper arm. He sheathed the sword silently as we came in sight of the guards around the camp, catching my eye and lifting a brow in warning as we stepped through the perimeter ring.

"Claw Fadrus," he said with a nod.

"Wing Osprey," the Claw acknowledged, making a stiff sign of the bird. Interesting. They didn't seem to care about him coming or going, thought he Claw's eyes narrowed when they caught sight of me.

I thought Osprey might say more but the Claw stiffened suddenly and came to full attention, his sign of the bird was sharp and precise.

"Out for a moonlit stroll?" the velvet words slipped through the night and I stiffened. Osprey's grip around my upper arm tightened to the point that it hurt but I was too nervous to wince at the pain.

"You know I rarely sleep, Le Majest," Osprey said lightly. "Even more so in this land. I feel like any moment the strange dark magic that binds this place will descend on us."

We turned as he spoke, his grip on arm never loosening. Juste Montpetit's eyes lit with excitement.

"Dismissed," Juste murmured to the guard. "I wouldn't worry too much about the Forbidding, Osprey. It hasn't bothered us yet. I'm sure the locals like to use it to keep strangers on edge with all their legends. I've already heard of how it was once snakes that were turned by an evil ruler into one being to defend their land, only for the snakes to turn on them and drive them from this place. Someone else claimed the Forbidding was fed by nightmares and that he could procure an elixir to keep me from dreaming while I was here and feeding the darkness. Still another claimed it is the manifestation of our sins, paying upon us what we deserve in suffering. Entertaining tales, but hardly worth worrying over. Or is that why you've brought this rock-born girl with you into the night? Is she here to offer her expertise on the matter?"

"She got lost," Osprey said tightly.

"On her way to meet you?" Juste Montpetit seemed pleased by the idea.

"On her way skies only knows where. Likely to find the jakes," Osprey said wryly.

"Or perhaps to escape." Juste Montpetit stepped closer, reaching out faster than I imagined he could and snatching my jaw between his fingers, forcing me to stare into my eyes. "Perhaps you were too excited to listen when I gave my speech in your pathetic little dump of a village. I'll admit, I have given that speech so many times in so many little villages that I forget it myself. We've tested every half-grown youth on this continent and found a total of one other Hatchling – a boy in Astar Harbor – and you, an aberration. I'm claiming both of you for the Imperial family as my personal property. Isn't that right, Osprey?"

There was a hit of satisfaction in how his lip curled up and now I did flinch from it. Property. Owned. I hated the very words. Osprey's hand was clamped so tightly around my arm that tears began to form in the corners of my eyes. But I refused to give them the satisfaction of seeing me cry.

"As you say, Le Majest," Osprey said coolly, taking one of those white picks from his sleeve and picking at his teeth with it as if he was hardly paying attention to the conversation.

"Perhaps I should mark you, property, so that you know you are mine," Juste Montpetit whispered, drawing a knife from his belt.

A tremor ran down my spine at the thought of being marked – in any way at all – by him. Did he mean to cut me up with that blade?

Osprey's grip was so tight that I almost cried out.

"Can it wait until morning?" his voice ended in a yawn, so calm and sleepy compared to the frantic grip on my arm. "Even I am growing tired of this."

"Do you have a soft spot for this Hatchling, Osprey?" Juste asked with a hint of a smile. His smiles were worse than most men's frowns. If he was like this in his late teens, what would he be like when he was fully matured?

"I have a soft spot for my pillow, and I wish to return to it," Osprey said, yawning a second time.

Le Majest regarded us for so long that I was certain he was going to draw his dagger and mark me right there. Eventually, his smile widened.

"You're right, Guardian. These things are better done in the light of day."

He turned and strode gracefully into the night but I didn't relax until the sound of his passing faded into the night.

Osprey's grip relaxed, but he didn't say a word as he led me to Zayana's tent.

"Think," he whispered and then he was gone.

I crept back into my bed, stinging at my foiled escape attempt, trembling at the memory of Le'Majest saying he would mark me. I lay there long into the night, shivering and worrying about my parents and my family. If I had imagined where my life was going, I would never have guessed it was heading here. But Osprey was right.

I couldn't run. He'd proven that. And his story chilled me to the bone. So did the meeting with Le Majest. Those weren't just empty threats. That was a real girl who had died. And that was really the crown prince of our nation threatening to mark me. If I wanted to keep my sister safe – my whole family safe – then I needed to shelter them from these people who kept threatening their lives. This was about more than just me. This was about my little nieces and nephews, about Alect and Raquella, about all of them.

Oh, sweet skies, I hoped my father had survived. Was that possible with the blow he'd taken? I felt ill as I thought about that strike from behind, over and over, and over.

I wasn't going to be Osprey's ally. That was just as risky as running. But maybe he wasn't all wrong. Maybe I could learn to use my magic for my family's sake.

I cupped my hands together in the dark, trying to find the buzz of the bees, but though I tried again and again as the night wore on long and dark, nothing happened. The only buzz was inside me and it was growing more and more agitated.

CHAPTER ELEVEN

Zayana woke before dawn, lighting her red bird. I guessed they didn't need lamps when they had those around.

"If you want to escape punishment, you'd best get up quickly," she said to me, shrugging her court dress back on and beginning to brush her long black hair.

"That's a pretty dress," I said, trying to straighten my own clothing and pallet. I hadn't slept, but I also hadn't removed my clothing. I shrugged my boots on, trying to ignore how my hands shook – still painful and exhausted. The encounter in the night with Le Majest had shaken me more than I'd thought it would.

Zayana huffed from her cross-legged seat on her pallet. "If we were anywhere but an encampment in the far back of beyond, you would never be granted access to anywhere I stayed, commoner. I am House Cardinal, one of the great families of Kestrel City."

I swallowed. But in Far Reach, you didn't take an insult like that silently. Those who couldn't stand up for themselves soon found that no one else was planning to stand up for them, either.

"I think that since we'll both be Wings someday, I'll probably end up in all the same places you are," I said giving her my best bold face. "So, that makes me your equal, doesn't it?"

"Wing? Ha! I saw those ridiculous bees. Do you think the gods above will bless you when you're so obviously a blasphemy?" She sniffed loudly. "I knew there would be a problem that morning. I saw three ravens and a strand of red thread that hadn't been trimmed."

"What does that have to do with anything?" I asked scornfully, trying to tame the tangle of my brown curls.

The shocked look on her face was priceless. "Don't you backwater fools follow the omens of the Black Crane?"

I raised a single eyebrow. "We follow common sense and self-determination."

She snorted. "Go ahead and tell yourself that. Your days of 'self-determination' are long gone – if they ever existed at all. We are all owned by Le Majest and it is Le Majest who determines our course."

"By the crown prince?"

She rolled her eyes. "If you don't know that all of the Imperial family is referred to as *Le Majest*, then you don't know much, do you?"

"Of course, I know that." It was going to be hard to keep my temper around her. She reminded me of my sister Adigale – always picking at any loose thread in something you said.

"Then you know that our lives are not our own."

My path wasn't determined by anyone. Certainly not Le Majest

– whether that was the crown prince or the whole lot of stinking Imperials.

“For all your fancy dress, you sure have common ideals,” I said, standing up.

She opened her mouth, her face flushing, but it snapped shut when a figure burst into our tent. It was the Wing with the owl.

“Wing Essana!” Zayana looked horrified at being caught arguing with me.

Wing Essana’s mouth formed a grim line. “I can hear you Hatchlings arguing all over the camp. The Empire’s Wing does not tolerate childishness. Stretch out your hands.”

Zayana held her palm out reluctantly, her bird winking out of existence. I followed her example, confused.

Like lightning striking, Essana pulled a switch from her belt, striking our raised palms. I bit back a yelp, pain flaring through my palms. I blinked away the sting, but I couldn’t blink back the frustration and anger at being struck. Were any of these rules even written anywhere?

It made me feel like a misbehaving child.

“What is the first rule of the Empire’s Wings, Zayana?” Essana asked calmly.

Zayana’s answer was stiff. At least I wasn’t the only one stinging.

“Words have power.”

"That is correct. Go and report to Wing Xectare. We are packing up camp and your service is required. I will deal with this Hatchling."

Zayana made the sign of the bird respectfully and left the tent. I stared at Essana, refusing to make any sign of respect. I wouldn't pretend. Not even to save myself a switching.

"Words have power," Wing Essana said with grim authority. "You will learn that under our care. You must guard your words. Any slip and you will be physically punished. You will use your words to wake your manifestation and feed it. What we manifest can be influenced ... maybe even changed in those early stages. They feed off what is in our hearts and what we say to them. Choose what you say wisely."

She stared at me and her owl appeared out of nowhere, clutched in her arms. She cooed to it in a low voice, whispering something I couldn't make out. It seemed to glow brighter.

"The words you speak determine how large and strong your manifestation can grow. The best of us would stun you with what they can manifest."

"The osprey is as big as a horse," I agreed.

Essana's eyes narrowed even further. I was definitely not getting into her good books. "Size is not everything. Nor is gaining a name. Loyalty to the empire is what is important."

Well, now I knew what she valued ... or at least what she was good at.

"You will prove your loyalty by changing your manifestation to a majestic bird from those dreadful bees. You shall ride with me today while I teach you."

"We aren't going to fly?"

Her cheeks flushed dark and a muscle in her jaw jumped as she said in a tight voice. "Not all of us waste our power on childish stunts."

Interesting. So, both Essana and Xectare were jealous of Osprey. And neither of them were named after a bird, which apparently, was a big deal.

Perhaps, this journey could be about more than just becoming powerful. Perhaps I could learn things about the Wings and our Empire beyond what we knew in Far Reach. Perhaps we could use that information to finally gain our freedom. I felt like I could breathe for the first time since the bee manifested. I had a reason to be here. A purpose.

I smiled.

"Don't smile," Wing Essana said. "We will be riding a carabao. You will not enjoy the experience. Come along."

The carabao was one of the huge horned oxen that the Claws and Wings all rode. Compared to a horse they were both slow and bulky, but they pulled large carts and their horns made them powerful weapons when ridden by a warrior.

Wing Essana's carabao had a high pommeled saddle with a narrow shelf behind it where I was told to ride. Her tent and other trappings had already been loaded onto a cart behind a pack carabao by Zayana who shot me a dark look as we passed her – bent and sweating – while she packed Xectare's things into the same cart.

I ignored her look. As much as she despised me, I despised them all.

I settled myself in the saddle as Wing Essana found her place close to the front of the caravan forming up. A vanguard of Claws formed ahead of us, blades out and ready as they prepared to cross the Forbidding Bridge. I still found their grand uniforms and fierce expressions intimidating. But I needed to get over that. They were tools of a cruel Empire. I couldn't afford to regard them with fear if I was going to fight that Empire.

They had drawn their swords to march across the bridge and I felt my mouth twist in a sneer. The safety they had stolen from our people was what they could rely on now to protect themselves. The frustration in me bubbled hotter at the sight of that and so did the hot buzz in my chest. It had spread now to my belly.

I tried to keep my eyes watching for Osprey or Juste Montpetit, but neither of them were in sight.

"Attend now," Essana said. "Each Hatchling is given over to a full Wing for training. That Wing is the Guide to the Hatchling. You are *not* assigned to Xectare or to me. We have our own apprentices. Mine are waiting for me at Karatua. Xectare has Zayana. Neither of us is prepared to take on more burdens, so you will be given to a spare Wing when we arrive at the port. Until then, you must mind us. If you listen well and do as we say, perhaps we will find you a Wing for your Guide. If you are stubborn and difficult, you may find there is no one to train you." She looked back at me. "Don't look so hopeful. Those who have Hatched but are untrainable are a liability to the Empire. We decorate our ship masts with their heads. With all that mass of hair, it will be easy to string yours from the top of a mast, hmm?"

And with that, my first lesson in magic began.

CHAPTER TWELVE

"When you are adept at this," Wing Essana said, "You will be able to call your manifestation easily. Some speak a word. Others whistle bird song. Some can even think, and their bird appears. But it takes work to call up your manifestation."

She made a deep call in the back of her throat and her owl fluttered down, its strange eyes flickering slightly as it watched me. I leaned back as it settled on the neck of the carabao in front of her. Even with Wing Essana between us, the owl made me nervous.

"I didn't even want it the last time," I said, my eyes trying to take in everything around us. "How was that any kind of work?"

The camp was completely packed already and loaded into carts pulled behind more carabaos. These people were clearly used to this routine and no wonder if they'd already traveled to most of the towns of Far Stones looking for Hatchlings – and confiscating everyone's weapons while they were at it.

"The first time is the easiest. All that magic was building up in you, waiting for a release. Although you likely can feel the results of it now. Are you in pain down to the bones? Do you feel weak and tired? That is the cost of what you did."

She leaned forward and began to caress her owl. It hooted, leaning into the caress.

"Will that happen every time?"

"The cost is equal to the energy expended. To be frank, I'm surprised you did not faint from so much energy lost all at once, but perhaps it did not strongly effect you that first time."

My eyes weren't on Essana – though I'd only be looking at her fine coat and the back of her head if they were. I was scanning the crowd looking for Juste Montpetit. At last, I caught a glimpse of him at the back of the camp, his head leaning in close to Counsellor Butiez. The Counsellor scratched his short beard and looked in my direction with a considering expression. My gaze snapped away.

"Why do the birds seem like they are spirit at one moment and then they are substantial enough to touch the next moment?" I asked, trying to pretend I hadn't been staring at the crown prince.

I did not succeed.

"Don't let your eyes linger on those whose station is as far above yours as the sun is above the earth," Essana said sharply but then her tone returned to teaching. "How substantial or how large a manifestation is depends on the manifestor. All birds appear to flicker from substantiality to insubstantiality, but whether they will let a hand pass through or be so solid that you may stroke and tease them – that will depend on what words you use to invoke them. A manifestor may choose to invoke their bird to any size from very small to the largest they can manifest, though larger manifestations take more energy. Sometimes, we may choose to keep them small to preserve our strength."

"Where did all the magic come from?" I asked.

Wing Essana kicked up her mount, and she was quiet for a moment as she maneuvered him. He ran with a jostling pace that jarred my bones and made me long for my father's horses. I gritted my teeth as she switched him to make him hurry toward the front of the group. We fell in behind the first guards as they approached the bridge, small creatures and songbirds kicking up around us with screeches and cries.

The sun was coming up in a light golden haze, burning mist off the bridge. My breath caught as the fog rolled over the twisted structure. I'd only been on this bridge a few times and it made me nervous every time. It felt like it was too much from another world. Like it wasn't real. Like it might melt away under our mount's feet. Or, perhaps, I might cross from this side only to end up in another world completely when my feet hit the ground on the other.

"The great powers that emanate from the bones of the earth manifest themselves in those who provide a conduit to that power. Some of us, favored by gods or fate, have access to the edges of that great power. Without any effort on our part, this power slowly accumulates within us. You burned yours off yesterday. Given enough time, it will accumulate again. But we don't have years to wait. And if we left you to wait to accumulate again, the consequences could be deadly."

"How deadly?" I asked, curious. Perhaps I could *be* the weapon my people needed. Perhaps if I could accumulate enough power, I could shake the Empire itself.

Wind blew across the carabao's back as his feet hit the tangled mass of carvings, and he took his first step onto the bridge. He snorted, tossing his horned head.

"Why is it always snakes?" Essana sawed the reins and then flicked her fingers at the carabao's head. The owl appeared on Essana's shoulder and then swooped forward, flying right in front of the carabao's face as if leading him forward. She settled back in the saddle again. Neat trick.

She carried on lecturing as if she spent every day lecturing from the back of a horned bull. "You would be dangerous enough to destroy your village if you weren't found by us. Those bees of yours did damage already. If it had not been for my owl and Xectare's swan, you might have killed everyone on that village green." I didn't believe that. Somehow, the bees felt friendly. They'd attacked my enemies. Not my friends. "You should be grateful that your bees are more of an annoyance than, say, an eagle, might have been. I've watched an eagle manifestation tear the throats out of seasoned warriors, and a great frigate bird swoop down and pluck whole ships from the waves."

"But they manifested as chicks, didn't they? Someone newly Hatched ... even if they'd been waiting for years ... wouldn't have that kind of power right now."

She grunted and my eyes narrowed. She was hiding something from me behind this talk. But what? Was it because my magic was so different? Or did she fear the power of an entire swarm of bees where other magic manifested as fluffy chicks?

"Has anyone else ever manifested something other than a bird before?" I asked, trying to find my way to what she was hiding.

"Not in the Winged Empire. Who knows what madness rages on other shores," she said with a sniff. But that also felt like a lie. Why would she hate something so much if she'd never experienced it before?

"Wouldn't we know?" I asked as I watched the Claws before us tromping over the long white bridge. It was so long that as we moved into single-file to cross, the Claws at the very front grew invisible. Only their bright blue banners, embroidered with a white swan could be seen waving above them. Sweat pricked my brow as our carabao's hooves echoed dully on the bridge. It was too long to be human-built and too delicate. It shouldn't be able to hold our weight – and yet it did. "The Empire's Claws have been all over the world in conquest."

She sniffed again. "Such knowledge is not for Hatchlings."

"Maybe if we knew how they handled their manifestations, it could help with mine," I pressed.

"Hush, child," she said but she didn't sound as certain as she had before. "We will simply hope that you are so freshly Hatched that you can change the manifestation. Our ranks dwindle as the years pass and I'm loathe to lose a Hatchling – even one from a troublesome frontier town with a rebellious family."

I clamped my lips tightly at those words. My town was not troublesome and my family were not rebels – though if I was being honest, I wanted to be both. I scratched at where my belt dug into my waist. Without a change of clothes or any possessions other than my belt knife and flint, I felt more like a slave than a Hatchling. Although, maybe Hatchlings were slaves. After all, Zayana didn't seem much more in control of her fate than I did.

"Which is why you must concentrate. Every moment of this journey, you must pour every ounce of yourself into your magic and into correcting this lack. I will teach you how we do it with birds and you will do that with these bees until one of them grows a beak and is a proper winged manifestation. You must put all your heart into it, child. I don't crave your death, but I will not stop it if there are still bees around you by the time we reach Astar Harbor."

Which seemed silly, since bees could be valuable, too. Why kill someone who could be a potential tool? But I had to admit that as I watched her owl wistfully, it was all I could do not to wish for something great and glorious like that, rather than a swarm of insects. I could imagine a huge bird – bigger than Osprey's – slashing through ranks of Swan Claws with its talons extended and beak snapping. Surely, that would be better than bees – wouldn't it?

I sighed.

Maybe I should try to change my manifestation like she suggested. If I was going to keep my family safe, I would need to be powerful. The buzz in my torso grew stronger.

"No sighing. Attend," Wing Essana snapped. "You will cup your palms and blow on them and think of all the things you want.

I cupped my palms, trying to ignore the jostling of the powerful carabao and trying to pretend I wasn't suspended over a rocky canyon, hundreds of fathoms deep. I thought about what I wanted.

Freedom. Family. Loyalty. Something worth fighting to protect.

I thought of what I must be. Determined. Relentless.

A soft golden glow began in my palms. Relief filled me. I still had the spark.

"Now, speak to it."

"Hatch. Be a bird," I said.

Nothing happened.

"Try your house bird. Sometimes that's a good focus. We are naturally in tune with our house birds."

"Be a shrike."

Nothing happened. I looked furtively behind me, but all I could see were the Claws pressing in behind us in this long single-file line.

"If we fall from the bridge, can your owl catch us like Osprey's bird did?" I asked.

"No." Wing Essana's reply was sharp. Had I offended her? "Try speaking to your manifestation again. Tell it what to be."

"Be relentless," I whispered. A golden bee, small as a housefly, appeared in my hand. I shot a glance at Wing Essana, but she was focused on driving the carabao. She couldn't be looking behind her at me all the time. I hissed at the bee. "Go away!"

It started to buzz, flying around my cupped hands and banging into my thumb and fingers in a way that was incredibly cute. I was not interested in cute bees. I needed a bird.

"Each night, a good Wing feeds their bird on words and hopes. You will tell it your dreams in the lonely dark of night. You will whisper who you are."

But if I did any of that, I would likely be punished by this Empire that hated me and mine. The little bee buzzed in sympathy.

"Each morning, your manifestation is made new – a tiny shade different than it was the day before, for good or for ill. Weaker or stronger, faster or slower, better at diving, further seeing, more wise. Who can say? It is your job to groom it, to grow it, to slowly seduce it into your power with the words that you say and the way you caress and tend to it."

I had a hard time imagining Osprey caressing that purplish-white bird the size of a shed. Did he really run his hands all over its feathers and tell it his dreams? Did his lace brush its feathers? Did it like it?

Did Essana, whose face looked like she chewed rocks to keep her teeth sharp, whisper sweet nothings to her owl? What about Xectare and her acid tongue? It was hard to believe that she spoke her hopes to her swan. This seemed to be the job for someone kind and big hearted. Someone like my sister Raquella.

I felt a burst of worry at the thought of my sister. Had she escaped what happened in my town? Maybe she was tending my father at home, nursing him back to health. He had to still be alive. He had to.

There was a strange sound like a strangled scream from behind us.

"What was that?" I asked.

"Nothing." Essana's words were hard as flint. "Focus."

"Protect my family," I whispered to the little bee, careful to be quiet enough that Essana couldn't hear me. Which seemed silly, since what could one bee do? The bee buzzed, rubbing gently against my thumb.

The other side of the bridge was finally visible as the last of the mist burned away and the road up through the mountains appeared. I knew from the few times I had traveled this way that it was a grim and forbidding path. And I had nothing with me except this little bee to face that.

But I did not dare let myself despair. If I did, I wouldn't be able to do even the small things that I could. I had to keep hoping this would work out. I had to.

I focused on the little bee as Wing Essana's words drifted over me.

"Seduce it. Charm it. Form it with your encouragements – we call that blessing Invocation. Then you prune what you do not like out of it with sharp words and harsh scolding. We call that cursing Forbidding. You have the power of both in your hands. Use it and shape that manifestation into something fit for Le Majest. You have fourteen days."

"Be a bird," I pled with the little bee in my hand. "Please, be a bird."

But as our carabao's hooves hit the rocky road on the other side of the bridge, the bee stayed stubbornly exactly the same and as my frustration filled me, he only vibrated louder and louder in perfect synchronization with the buzzing in my chest.

The osprey above us screeched and I glanced up to see it circling overhead, its Wing riding on its back. I could have sworn it winked at me.

CHAPTER THIRTEEN

I spent the rest of the day trying to speak to that Forbidding-taken bee and trying to hide it in my closed hand when anyone looked at me. It stung me twice – something I thought must be impossible when it was only made of spirit. And because bees generally lost their stinger when they stung. But the sting and the pain in my hand were real enough.

"What are you thinking?" I whispered to it when we stopped so Essana could follow nature's call. "I need something strong enough to save my family. I need something powerful and pervasive, something relentless and brave. Something to save a whole continent from an Empire. I like you, you fluffy adorable bee, but you are *not* what I need."

What were you supposed to do with magic that did nothing but hurt and enrage you? Magic that had drawn you into the most precarious spot of your life? That threatened everything you were and loved? If Essana thought that would make me charming and sweet to draw the best out of it, she could think again.

If only the bee was like the horses I'd helped gentle. But with horses, the goal was simple – convince them to join you in purpose. You could look them in the eye. You could ride on their backs – but how could you do any of that with a bee?

"Be better," I growled at it, frustrated to the point of tears. "Be what I need. No, be what my *family* needs."

I had just finished speaking when Osprey flew past, his icy eyes locking on me, full of concern. He saw the bee, looked relieved for a moment, and then winked, shooting back up into the sky as if nothing had happened. Irritating man. He was worse than the bees. Frustration buzzed in my chest as Essana returned.

"Was that Osprey?" she asked.

"He flew by," I said. "He didn't stop."

"I suppose even Le Majest's Guardian longs to see you with anything other than an insect in your palm," she said scornfully.

I swallowed. She'd seen the bee. There was no hiding that I'd failed at my first task.

By nightfall, we had reached a part of the road where the side of one mountain hung over the pass, giving a little protection from the endless blast of the wind. It widened enough for a camp, though one side was rocky and steep and we couldn't pitch our tents too close to it for fear of someone stumbling over the side in the dark. My limbs trembled from a long day of riding combined with the bone-deep exhaustion of my first touch with the bees and my night of sleepless worry. I felt like a cloth that had been wrung out.

I watched as the wagons settled, the carabao around them lowing in a way that sounded more angry than hungry or sad. From the wagons, strange sounds emerged like strangled groans. Essana made a face at the sounds and hurried our carabao to the other side of the camp.

"Was that a moan from the covered wagon?" I asked her.

"Just the healing wagon," she said with compressed lips, turning the carabao so that I lost track of which of the identical wagons had contained the moan.

There were five covered wagons. I'd thought they were full of supplies. They were tall, smooth-sided squares with canvas wrapped around everything except a wooden door at the back. A good place to protect perishables from the rain. I hadn't considered that one might be used as a medical wagon. Had people come in and out of it? I didn't remember. I'd been too caught up in my own distress to pay attention. Which was stupid. I needed to keep my eyes open.

"We stop here," Wing Essana announced as a pair of pigeons fluttered down and landed on her hand.

I fell from the ledge behind her saddle, my bottom aching from the rough ride.

"You'll help Zayana set up the tents," she announced as she unwound the little scraps of paper and stored the pigeons in small woven baskets she pulled out from the saddlebags. "She knows how it must be done. Make do with what supplies you have until we get to Astar Harbor. If you live longer than that, the Wing who takes you in will fit you for the next leg of the journey and will procure clothing or bedding as required. Hop to it, now."

I stood on my tiptoes, searching for Zayana at the same time that the advisor with the short beard – Butiez – came rushing up to Wing Essana. He was slight of build, dressed in silk robes with cranes painted on them. Highly impractical. Though perhaps that was the point. Anyone who could afford to be that impractical must be wealthy. A robe like that was worth more than a barn. More than I could earn in two years if I lived for free with family and was cared for by them. And it was dusty with a singe mark on it from a fire. Likely, he could replace it on a whim. I ground my teeth at the thought.

"What do the missives say, Wing?" he demanded.

"Counsellor Butiez," Wing Essana acknowledged, making the sign of the bird. I still hadn't spotted Zayana, but I made a show of looking for her as I eavesdropped. "One is from Far Reach. They have quelled the riot. Ten were executed for disruption of the peace. Others have fled into the Forbidding. Our Claws hunt them."

My heart seized in my chest. Ten. All from my village.

"Grim news. We will lose men to this."

"Mm," she said noncommittally. "The other is from the south. There has been some kind of incursion outside Portua Town. The Claw Regiment begs Le Majest to hurry and end his grand tour. The Regiment wishes to secure his person more fully."

The counsellor nodded before noticing me. "Begone with you, Hatchling. These words are not for your ears."

I started to hurry away but he grabbed me by the collar, pulling me so close that I could feel his belly rub against me through his thin silk robe. I shuddered.

"Must I remind you that you are property? We have already executed ten of your kind. More deaths can be arranged if that's what you require."

I shook my head, trying not to let my anxiety about those deaths show. I forced only my hate and defiance into my eyes.

Who had died? Was it my father? My brothers? Worse ... was it my little nieces and nephews?

I wanted to threaten his life. I wanted to kill him myself. But I didn't dare. Osprey's words echoed in my mind. *Don't let them see you care.* I didn't want to be the reason my family died. I kept my tongue still, even though it took all my willpower.

He released me, but I felt so sick from the thought of him ordering the deaths of my family – the thought of who might already be dead – that I could hardly keep myself from vomiting. I stumbled through the camp as it was set up, looking for Zayana, battling nausea so strong that it made my belly roll and doubled me over more than once. My bee buzzed around my head and my head seemed to buzz with it, too full of distraction and distress to form clear thoughts.

Claws worked quickly to erect tents and gather tinder – but I passed a knot of them packed so tightly together that I couldn't see what was in their ring of bodies. What I heard was enough to make me want to shy away. Agonized moans rolled out, interlaced with harsh curses and sounds I couldn't identify. One of the Claws met my eyes and pointed aggressively away from their ring.

Perhaps one of them had been injured in the fight with my bees. Perhaps they were trying to tend his wounds. If they were, then he'd not be excited to see my face. Not when I was the cause of his injury.

I scanned the encampment for Juste Montpetit, but while I saw Claws erecting his tent, I saw no sign of the pretty prince. Where had he been hiding this whole time?

Another Claw from the knot of their ranks turned and stared at me, his hand moving the hilt of his sword.

I half-stumbled away in my hurry. No need to provoke them over nothing.

I took two more false turns before I found where Zayana was unloading a cart. I ignored her haughty looks as I fought to keep my head enough not to collapse. I could never forget these people were my enemies. They might be of the same Empire, they might want to teach me new skills, but they were no friends of mine. My friends were far away, and they needed my help. And I needed to hold it together if I was going to help them.

With all the grit I had, I forced myself to work, following Zayana's curt instructions to set up the tents, unroll the rugs, open folding chairs and cart desks and trunks to their correct positions. I almost had my rolling belly and buzzing head under control by the time we were close to finished.

A purplish-white streak shot by as we set the final stake. Something white tumbled through the air and landed at my feet.

A toothpick.

I followed the streak to see Osprey standing beside a fire, preening his spirit bird. It was taller than he was and I could have sworn it winked at me again as he caressed it, whispering something as his dark brown hands ran over its sleek feathers. I tore my eyes away. The scene looked almost too intimate to be allowed to watch. The way he leaned his forehead in to touch the bird's was almost sweet. The bird budged back, his head burrowing into Osprey's chest. I felt myself flushing and I looked away.

I picked up the toothpick and put it in my pocket. Which was silly. Who cared what happened to a piece of garbage? And what right did I have to care what happened to something of his?

“Don’t even think about it,” Zayana said from the edge of the tent where she was fussing with the folding chair.

“Think about what?” I countered.

She rolled her eyes. “He might be nearly as pretty as the crown prince, but he’s also nearly as untouchable. Just because they’re close to our age doesn’t mean we have the right to even look at them. Before he earned that name, Osprey was Vasyklo Petren, son of Klavov Petren, Lord General of the Claws. I knew him. We danced at balls together.”

“The Lord General?” I asked dryly. “Wasn’t he a bit old for you?”

She sneered. “You know who I meant. Osprey. And now he’s too high for even someone of my social standing to be near.”

“How nice,” I said. Like I cared about balls. Or dancing.

“You’re so far below him that you aren’t worthy of the flies he crushes under his boots.”

“What kind words. I can see that you’ll be amazing at charming that chick of yours into a beautiful bird,” I said, refusing to back down. I didn’t care about Osprey or how high up he was in a society I hated. I didn’t care about dances or who was someone and who wasn’t. I didn’t care if Zayana thought I was beneath her. I was worried about my father. Worried about my family. Didn’t she have anything worthwhile to worry about?

I clenched a fist and received a sharp sting in response. Great. The manifestation was turning on me again. My frustration bubbled up like a geyser and I gritted my teeth, opening my hand.

There were three bees in it now, buzzing around like they were trapped under an invisible jar.

I cursed and closed my hand again.

"You have no idea what you're doing or who you're talking to," Zayana said coolly, brushing off her dark green court dress. "And I doubt you'll live long enough for it to matter."

"Even if I die tomorrow, I'll have had more of a life than you," I shot back. But I was too overwhelmed by everything. My voice was far weaker than I wanted it to be. If only I could figure any part of this out. But it was all foreign and opaque to me.

I stalked off to the edge of the camp and sat down on the nearest rock, looking out over the steep drop and grateful for a moment without anyone watching me. I opened my hands, pretending to speak to my manifestation, but all I was doing was thinking about how Le Majest had stolen me from my home and family and now he had killed people from my own. Maybe my own family.

He was far from home with only these few Claws and Wings protecting him. He'd traveled all this way to bring misery to other people. But that also meant he was uniquely vulnerable in a way he may never be again. Maybe it wouldn't be the worst idea to take advantage of that. Maybe someone like me should take down the Emperor's son and save us all from another generation of their oppression.

People always talked like that, Oh, if I ever saw him, I would kill him for what he's done, they'd say. But no one ever actually did it. Perhaps it was just because they were too afraid to try.

I glowered at my bees, letting dark thoughts fill my mind until a husky voice spoke low and deep from behind me.

CHAPTER FOURTEEN

"I'm of House Shrike," I objected as I looked to see Vasyklo Petren – Osprey – leaning out from behind a huge rock. Had he been there all along? He seemed to come and go almost magically. And yet he'd said he was chained. He made no sense.

He crooked a finger and winked at me. I stood, hurrying to join him behind the shelter of the huge standing rock.

There was a better view here. The steep slope beside the pass rolled out before us, swathed in shadow as the sun set between the mountain peaks.

"Apidae is the bee family. Whatever house you had before, I think that's a fitting title for you." He had a dimple in one cheek when he smiled. It gave him a mischievous look but the glint in his eye looked dangerous.

"They're torturing someone in the camp," I said in a brittle voice. There was something about Vasyklo that made me confess things I shouldn't. "I'm trying to decide what to do about it."

He shot me a sharp look, twisting the white pick in his mouth. His black brows knit together.

"Who are they torturing?" he asked carefully.

"Does it matter?"

His expression softened slightly. "I'm here with a warning. When you hear the names of those who died in your town. Don't react. Don't flinch. Even if it's the name of someone you love. Trust me."

"And what if I do react?" I demanded. "What if I do flinch and scream and fight? You can't force me to be submissive and accepting. I haven't even agreed to this alliance you want between us."

"Shhh." He looked from side to side worriedly, his lips parted as he listened. "Someone will hear you."

I crossed my arms over my chest, flinching when the bee stung my palm again. I didn't want to look at him. I knew there would be fear in my eyes. And that was the last thing I wanted anyone to see. Rage, I was happy to share with them, but my fears were my own.

He reached out quickly and took my hand in his, wrapping it around my fist and pulling it toward him. Reluctantly, I let him, but I kept my eyes lowered. There were hot tears stinging them and I didn't dare let anyone see them – especially Vasyklo Petren with his perfect osprey and powerful life. I blinked them back, relishing their sting as if that tiny bit of physical pain could help ease the emotional pain and frustration tormenting me. Whose names would they read? Would one of them be my family? Would all of them be my family? I didn't know if I could bear that.

"Show me," he whispered, holding my fist in one hand while he gently unfurled my fingers with the other. His face was so close to mine as he bent his dark head over my hand that I saw a tiny tattoo behind his ear. It was a symbol that looked a little like a single wing. Odd.

The bee buzzed furiously in my palm, its pale-gold glow all too bright in the descending dark.

I didn't know if the sound Osprey made was a delighted gasp or a horrified hiss. I didn't try to see which it was. I didn't care what he thought. What any of them thought. My bee was just fine. It didn't deserve to be eradicated just for existing. And neither did I.

"Are those stings on your palm, House Apidae?"

"Yes," I admitted.

He gave a low chuckle. "Your magic is so violent it even stings *you*. You know they say your bird reflects your temperament? I'd say yours is a perfect fit."

I looked up, finally, meeting his gaze with my determination. "You mistake defiance for violence. This bee refuses to be caged – and so do I."

"I'm not trying to cage you," he said, his gaze never leaving mine. He chewed his toothpick furiously.

"You're trying to trick me into serving you, just like your crown prince is forcing me to serve him. But none of you know who I truly am or what I can do."

"What can you do?" One of his eyebrows quirked upward.

I shrugged, swiping a tear away.

He dropped my hand. "You are mistaken. You think compassion is manipulation and allegiance is servitude. You Far Reachers are so hard, it's like the rocks of this place have worked their way under your skin and into your spines."

"Maybe being stubborn is a good thing."

He shook his head, dimples gone now and fire in his eyes. "It's dangerous. If you want to survive, you have to use your brain, but you Far Reachers strike out like wild tigers, always ready to rip off the arm that feeds you."

His blue eyes bored into me. I crossed my arms over my chest defiantly.

"Why did you want me for an ally if you think so little of us?"

He chewed the toothpick again and it spun between his wry lips. "I told you already. It's because of the bees. You can be a symbol of a new age in a way that we can't be in an Empire where everything is woven through with birds. Please don't lose that. Don't change that bee into a bird." He paused. "And, House Apidae? You should learn to be more polite to your only ally."

"I haven't agreed to be your ally yet."

He chuckled. "But *I* have agreed to be yours."

I let the silence hang between us.

It was pierced by a haunting scream.

"What was that?" I asked.

He peeked around the rock, shoving me behind his back as he drew a sword the length of his forearm from his belt. It was decorated on the hilt with an inlaid ivory osprey. Bitterness flared in me at the memory of my shrike-marked sword. It had been stolen from me just like everything else.

“Stay behind me.” His voice was pitched low. He whispered into the dark, “Come, Os.”

And his osprey flickered to life beside him. It tilted its head and at a new whisper it shrank to normal bird size. With a single flap of its wings, it settled on Osprey’s shoulder.

“Is that his name?” I asked.

A second scream rang out from the far side of the camp.

Osprey began to run and I fell in behind him. I didn’t have anything more than a bee and a belt knife to fight with – and neither was very useful – but I felt safer behind my “ally” and his manifestation.

The camp was in chaos. Claws ran in every direction. Screams tore through the night. Someone kicked one of the fires and sparks shot up into the sky.

Xectare burst from her tent, her swan skimming out overhead, racing ahead of her. Her hair was wet as if she had been bathing.

We sprinted toward the edge of the camp that faced the part of the pass we would travel tomorrow – the South. We were not the only ones. Around us, blue-coated figures sprinted toward the screams, weapons at the ready. Weapons that might have been stolen from my people. I glanced at every hilt looking for a shrike.

Another blood-curdling scream rent the air ahead of us and Osprey snapped his fingers in response. His bird leapt from his shoulder and dove ahead of him. He jumped – higher than I thought possible – spun into a front flip and landed on the osprey's back just as it flapped its wings and plunged forward.

I was left far behind, looking after him in shock. He might wear soft white feathers at the ends of his shirt sleeves, but what he'd just done took any notion of him being too soft from my mind. I wanted that. I wanted to ride on the back of a bird into battle just like that, with my hair flowing in the wind and my sword ready. Ridiculous, Aella. That's something that will never happen.

A pair of Claws shoved past me, weapons in hand, their eyes focused and muscles straining as they sprinted forward. I hesitated. I could join them and run toward the attack.

Or.

I could go find out what they'd hidden in that wagon they'd been circling before.

Heart in my throat, I ducked behind the nearest tent. It wasn't far from here. Smoke swirled through the air, baskets rolled over the ground and pots boiled over on the sides of the campfires. Everything was left unattended. That would be, too. I was sure of it. I swallowed, hoping no one saw me as I made my way through the camp, running from tent to tent.

There! The covered wagons. I sprinted toward them, heart in my throat. I didn't know what I would find there. I only knew that I hoped it wouldn't be what I feared – prisoners. What would I do if they had captured someone and were holding them against their will?

What if they really were torturing them as I suspected? What if it was someone I knew?

My legs trembled as I drew close.

And my gaze landed on a wooden cage hitched behind a carabao – the cage the Swan Claws had been in a circle around only minutes before.

The cage with its canvas cover ripped off and tossed aside.

The cage that held my father, bloody and broken, his neck and hands bound in wicked stocks.

CHAPTER FIFTEEN

"Father. You're alive." I rushed to the cage. I hadn't watched him die after all. He was still alive. There was time to save him if I hurried. My pulse was racing so fast it was hard to concentrate.

The old man looked up at me, craning his neck to bring it up high enough from his bent position in the stocks. One of his eyes was missing.

"No!" My hand flew up to my mouth and the bees darted out, buzzing agitatedly as they swirled around me. The buzzing in my chest grew hot and loud.

"Shrikeling," he gasped and the ghost of a smile flickered over his lips. "You live. I feared they had killed you because of the bees."

I bit my lip, glancing around. No one was looking. "There has to be a way to get you out of these stocks."

He grunted. "Stabbed in the back. I'm not sure I could escape. Not even sure I could stand if I wasn't held in place."

My stomach lurched at his words. Against all odds, he was here where I could help. I couldn't let this chance pass.

"What happened to your eye?" I asked. There was no key close, but there was a barrel of water. I filled the dipper and offered it to him with a shaking hand.

He lapped it up gratefully.

"They took it last night."

I felt my head getting light. "I would have heard. I would have ..."

"No. They kept me gagged. Hard to hear screams through a gag of magic."

My eyes stung. It felt hard to breathe. They'd done this. While I lay quietly in Zayana's tent, they'd done this to him.

"Magic," I echoed stupidly. That meant one of the Wings. Xectare. Or Essana. Or Osprey. "Who did it?"

Could it have been Osprey? I thought of his worried face when he'd told me to pretend not to care when I heard the names of the dead. Had he expected my father's name to be added to that list? Ice shot through my chest.

My father shook his head. "Too many faces. That prince was there."

"I'm going to find a tool to open these stocks," I said, searching around us. There was nothing nearby. Not a hammer, not a prybar. I wanted to scream as the buzzing grew so loud it was hard to think of anything else. What useless magic. If I'd had a bird like Osprey's I could have torn the cage to bits and freed him. Instead, all I had was this useless buzzing.

"Shrikeling." It was almost a moan.

Hot tears streaked down my cheeks as I knelt so I could look into his single, burning eye. I bit my lip to keep from sobbing. I needed to help him. I needed to save him so bad that it burned through me like a fire.

"Father."

"No more tears," he said gently. "No tools. Don't try to help me. Think about this. Clever fox is the one who hides in the coop during the day and when the chickens come in at night, he has his choice of them. Be the fox for us. Wait in the coop."

"No," I gasped.

"There are others like us," he said in a hushed tone. "Others who want freedom. Watch for the sign of the single wing."

"I don't care about others," I said, fighting a sob that stuck in my throat. "I just want you."

"Use your head and the stone in your spine, girl, and not your sweet heart," he said gently. "Look at my feet."

A sticky, dark stain surrounded him and as I watched, a trickle of red joined the pool.

"I won't last the night. Maybe not the hour," he said in a burred voice that I was sure disguised his agony. "Try to save me and they'll make you pay. I don't want that for you. I want you to keep living. To thrive. To be the fox and to be relentless. You've always been my courageous little Shrikeling. Be that now. Listen. This is important." He coughed and more blood poured to the ground. The scent of it filled my nose and made the buzzing in my head louder.

"I can't leave you like this." My words seemed ridiculous. But I grabbed my belt knife and jammed it into the lock on the cage, twisting it as I tried to break the lock.

"Go," he muttered, head hanging. His voice was weak now. "I love you, Shrikeling. Go and be free."

"Please hold on," I begged. I couldn't let him die like this. I wouldn't.

My knife tip snapped in the lock.

Behind me, an Imperial drawl startled me into stillness.

"Trying to steal from me, are you, property?"

Juste Montpetit. My heart sped to dizzying speeds. This was his work. His fault.

"I'm glad you came. It reminds me that I own you and I haven't even told you yet what that means. I taught your father what it meant last night when I took his eye."

A furious snarl bubbled up in my throat and I fumbled with the knife, turning to put the jagged, broken point between myself and the crown prince. In the background, more screams rang out with the sounds of metal clashing.

If I acted now, no one would know it was me. And he probably had the key to free my father. Now, Aella! Do it.

But now I understood why people so often failed to murder

evil people even when they were right before them and vulnerable. Something inside me resisted. Something inside me insisted that he was human and that I couldn't just kill him.

It was wrong. I pushed against the feeling as the buzzing in my chest became painful.

Juste Montpetit smirked at the knife wobbling in my hand.

The smirk was enough.

I lunged toward him with the knife and he caught my hand, his beautiful face not even showing strain as he wrenched the knife from my hand and threw me to the ground.

"On your knees," he said in a low voice. The triumph on his face made me ill. "Kneel before me. No, here."

He directed me to right in front of him so that I was so close I could have reached forward and touched him. Everything inside me rebelled. I should not have to kneel to the man who did this to my family. Tears poured down my face – tears of frustration and rage. The emotions tearing through me shook me. I hated him with every nerve of my body, with every beat of my heart, with every breath I drew in. I pushed all that hate into my defiant stare.

"Do you love your father, property?"

I looked at my father.

"Be relentless," he whispered as blood dripped from his lips. His head slumped forward.

"Oh look, he has passed out again. Shall I take one of his hands to wake him up?"

"No," I gasped, terror making me shudder.

"Then you'll repeat after me, property. And make it convincing. Or I'll take the hand."

"Please," I begged, almost choking on the sob crawling up my throat.

"Repeat after me!" His voice was like a whip crack.

I swallowed the sob down.

"Say, 'I am the property of the Winged Empire.'"

I kept my mouth shut.

"You must not believe I can take the hand," Juste Montpetit said, drawing the sword from his scabbard. A pair of Claws rushed by, coated in soot. Smoke poured across the camp, black and acrid, but my eyes never left Juste Montpetit. "One more chance. Say the words."

"I am the property of the Winged Empire," I said, staring at him in fury. I hated myself for saying it. But I hated him more.

"I am nothing. I was born nothing. I will never be anything but the property of Le Majest, Juste Montpetit, and I will fulfill his every wish or die trying."

I hesitated. Words were powerful. Saying that about myself – well, it couldn't be unsaid. But it was that or my father's hand.

I opened my mouth.

A roar came from the other side of the camp and I turned my head to look at the flames rushing from tent to tent. The carabaos had broken loose from their picket and screams followed their furious charge.

A brutal, wet sound pulled my attention back to Juste Montpetit. I screamed as he pulled his sword back out of my father's neck. Red blood poured out over the floor of the cage, soaking the ground where I kneeled.

"No," I said, stupidly, shaking like a leaf at my father's head lolling lifelessly to the side. A prayer poured out of me instinctually. "Fly him to the great beyond on the wings of the dawn. Shelter him under your wings"

I clutched my chest with my fist full of bees. I couldn't seem to catch my breath.

"Next time, you will speak without hesitation," Juste Montpetit said. "You never know when the punishment might be worse than what was promised."

He killed my father on a whim. He treated him like he was not even human, like he wasn't the man I'd loved all my life. What kind of a monster did that?

My mouth hung open in horrified grief. I sucked in a long, shuddering breath. The buzzing in my head was so loud that I couldn't hear what he was saying. And I didn't care.

Something inside me seemed to reach a crescendo. Warmth flooded my body.

I turned back to Juste Montpetit. I was on my feet and rushing at him before I even stopped to think.

Like a dam breaking, the warmth and buzzing left me. Bees swarmed around me, angry and humming. And I was angry along with them. I felt stings on my hands as I grabbed Juste around the throat, trying to throttle him. I didn't care.

His screech was high-pitched and satisfying. I tightened my grip. I would take his life. A life for a life. That was the old way my father had taught me. An eye for an eye. I would take one of his. I would tear him to pieces until they couldn't tell what was him and what was dust.

Strong hands grabbed me around the waist and ripped me free of him. I screamed, kicking back at whoever dragged me aside.

"Ah, there you are?" Le Majest said to whoever gripped me in his arms. He seemed pleased though he was swatting at the bees swarming him, his face already red with stings. "I thought that you'd be keeping a better eye on things than this." His eyes were full of fire despite the hungry look in them and there was a dark mark blossoming on his neck and it made my heart soar. "Take this creature away until those bees are gone." He paused and then leaned in, his voice low and threatening. "If she escapes it will be her head. And I don't think you'll like carrying out that order, will you?"

CHAPTER SIXTEEN

I tried to twist to see who had me in his grip, but my arm was jammed back, twisting painfully. I bit back the pain, channeling it into rage.

Juste Montpetit killed my father. And before that, he'd tortured him.

My father.

He'd ordered the deaths of ten people in my town. And I'd hesitated when I had my chance to kill him. That half-second had cost me my opportunity. It had cost my father his life.

And it was all my fault.

My heart felt like it was breaking in half I gulped in gasps of air as my bees hummed all around us. Not like this. It shouldn't have been like this.

I struggled in the arms of the soldier holding me – whoever he was – not caring that tears blurred my vision, not caring that my fury burned so hot that I was close to vomiting. Not even caring that the bees around me had swelled to a monstrous cloud.

A streak of light shot by – hard to see easily through my glassy eyes – and then the soldier holding me jumped and we were sailing through the air.

I gasped.

I'd thought I was angry before.

That didn't even compare to how I felt now.

Osprey.

I struggled twice as hard, encouraged by the low curses that came from behind me, fast and steady.

It was one thing to be betrayed by your enemy. It was another thing entirely to be betrayed by someone who had made you swear in blood to be their ally. He should have told me about my father. He should have helped me save him before it was too late.

We sped out from under the rock ceiling and up into the night, leaving the burning tents, billowing smoke, and clashes of forces as we climbed ever higher.

The smell of burning flesh and feathers mixed with the scent of blood on my hands, leaving me ill. It was my father's blood. And maybe some of Le Majest's. The thought of it on my hands made me want to be sick – for two very different reasons.

I tried to focus on my surroundings to steady myself. It was harder to breathe up here. It was colder, too.

"Have you calmed enough not to kill me if I set you down

somewhere?" Osprey's breath on my neck was surprisingly warm in the cold air.

"Maybe I *should* kill you. You're just as bad as Juste Montpetit. Maybe I should kill all of you Wings. Maybe that would be the best thing for this world."

He sighed and then we landed on a ledge. He stepped off the osprey, dragging me with him. I tried to aim a stomp at his instep, but he adjusted his stance, moving his foot out of the way.

"Easy. Stop fighting like a dust-kissed tiger. I *will* bite back if I have to." His words were muffled slightly as he dodged my elbow strike.

"He killed my father," I said and the words seemed to rip something out of my heart. "Right in front of me."

"I saw." His tone was too mild. He shouldn't be allowed to be so calm.

"He tortured him last night. And you knew, didn't you? You knew that when I said I was trying to decide what to do about the person they were torturing. You *knew* that was my father." I tried to turn around, but he kept me pinned against him with that iron forearm. He was all tight, hard muscles and I couldn't get them to give enough to hit him. "Le Majest called you his Guardian. Is that what you are? A protector of that monster? A bodyguard?"

"Yes."

"I hate you," I breathed, feeling the truth of that right down to my bones. I trembled at the force of the fury rocketing through me. It made me lightheaded and made it hard to think. But I didn't care. I wanted more and more of it. I wanted it to make me powerful enough to smash all my enemies.

"Understandable." There was a tightness to his tone.

He let go of me and I spun, striking out with my fist. I hit his jaw in an explosion of pain up my knuckles and into my forearm. I wanted to hurt him like he hurt me. I wanted to hear his voice panicked and broken. Not calm and measured. I struck out again, but this time, he caught my fist in his palm, shoving me back so that I stumbled.

His lip was bloody from my punch. He spat to the side.

"Does it feel good to prey on people you've disarmed? Does it make you feel powerful to take their weapons and then smash their bodies like dropped eggs?"

"No." There was pain in his voice mixing with guilt. Good. He *should* feel guilty.

"Really? I think I'd like to try that for myself. Why don't you hand me those swords and let me push you off this ledge and I'll see how good it feels."

I charged toward him, but his spirit bird was there, leaping between us, its wings fluttering powerfully as it held me back from him. I battered at the bird, my hands striking nothing but light and something that sizzled over my skin like the scrape of nettles. My hands should go right through the flickering bird, and yet it was solid as a wall.

I stepped back, panting. I expected him to lunge at me, but instead, as I raised my fists again, he jumped onto the back of his osprey. The osprey flew slow, sloping circles right above my head in a ring around me.

I leapt, trying to grab hold of a feather, but my hands left with nothing in them but light.

At least Osprey was damaged. His face and the exposed skin around his neck were red with stings. His lip was swollen and bloody. And my bees were still around me, throbbing with our shared anger.

Bees were the right choice for me. The perfect choice. I would buzz in the ear of the empire. I would sting them over and over as relentlessly as a bee. I was small, perhaps. But size had no matter when it came to inflicting pain.

"You think your fury can make a difference," he said calmly, but a muscled bunched in his jaw – as if he was having trouble controlling his emotions.

"It could have. If you hadn't pulled me off Le Majest, it *would* have." I spat the words.

"Really? Don't forget, I've been to your home."

"I remember." I let those words fill with my hate.

"I saw little children there. Babies." He paused and his face twisted with something that looked like agony. "Do you like them?"

"What are you saying? Are you *threatening* them?"

His voice was low and tense. "If you had succeeded, foolish House Apidae, and if the crown prince was dead in that mountain pass, it wouldn't just be your father who was executed. Or your brothers. It would be your entire family. The Swan Claws would march back and hunt them down and butcher every one of them, and I would have been blood-bound to do it with them. Can you really blame me for wanting to spare myself the horror of that?"

I could blame him for *everything*. And I certainly wanted to. The bees buzzed louder, swirling around me quicker and quicker.

"You didn't spare yourself the horror of my father's death." I wanted to make him feel this pain. He was well-dressed and cultured and arrogant. He had no idea what it was like to watch his protection stolen or his father murdered and he thought he could lecture me on how to feel about it. He was wrong.

"If you want your revenge, House Apidae, you need to learn how to calm yourself. Your rage is out of control."

"Do you expect me just to sit here meekly while they kill my family?" I asked, frustrated by the way my voice came out high-pitched. I was on the edge of tears. And I hated that, too. "While *you* threaten them?"

"No, I don't. I expect you to work with me. I expect you to finally accept the alliance I've been offering you. One angry girl can't overthrow a government. That takes a plan and patience."

"And a lack of morals," I said bitterly. "A willingness to go along with evil while you wait for your precious plan to play out."

He leapt from the bird and stalked across the rock, leaning in so close that I could see his chest heaving as he breathed. The purplish-white light of his osprey was the only light here on the mountain and it set his dark features in stark relief.

"Do you know that this is the final stop of Le Majest's Grand Tour? He went through the continent first, visiting each province of the Empire. Then he went to the islands and the conquered lands, one by one. Last of all, he came here to the Far Stones – the dark continent. And do you know how many people rose up and defied his order? There were none on the main continent. They had parades where they brought out all their weapons and handed them to the waiting hands of the Claws. There were balls. I watched the nobles collect their swords and halberds and dance in the streets of the new era of peace and unity. I watched the people of Canaht give up the last of their weapons with hollow eyes. They'd already been ground into the dust. This was the last nail in the coffin of their self-respect. One island tried to fight. Fareesha. Have you heard of them before? You won't now. They've been wiped off the map and it is now against the law to speak their name. I killed so many of them that I smelled like blood for a week."

"And this is supposed to make me want to *stop* fighting? Hearing that the rest of the Empire is just kneeling before him? That's supposed to make me sorry that I tried to kill him?" My lower lip trembled uncontrollably.

He swallowed before he spoke, clenching his jaw as he leaned in so close that all I could see were his piercing eyes. "It's supposed to make you stop for a moment and think. The chance of ever opposing the Winged Empire is shrinking. The opportunity to find allies – to find armaments – to gather what is needed for revolution is getting smaller every day, and if you end up dead or do something stupid, you might doom our chances forever. Can you understand that? Now is not the time for out-of-control passion and stupidity. Now is the time for precise strikes."

"And what? You want me to kneel? I will not bow before evil."

He made a frustrated sound in the back of his throat and closed his eyes, his lips moving silently as if he was praying. Os settled onto the ledge, preening his wings as Osprey drew another pick from his sleeve and jammed it into his ruined mouth. Red stained the white pick.

"You will be the death of me, House Apidae." Eventually, he opened his eyes and met my defiance with a cool expression. "Ally with me and we will drive the Winged Empire from the shores of Far Stones together."

"How?"

"Words have power. You've been told that is the first lesson and it's not wrong. So. Learn the power of words and master your magic. Learn their power so you can oppose evil. Learn them so you can rally allies and for the love of freedom, keep your stupid mouth shut until you can be useful."

I felt like I was crumpling as the tears broke free and shame settled on my shoulders. "He killed my dad and I couldn't stop him."

He grabbed my upper arms, crouching so that I had to look in his eyes as he spoke, slow and sure. "The Empire has killed thousands. And the people are complicit. They believe the false words and the story of peace and prosperity. They repeat his empty words again and again. 'Peace and unity.' they say, but there is no peace for those who think differently. There is no freedom for anyone who won't bow."

"Is that why you bow?" I said, sharply. "How can you talk about defying them and fighting for freedom when you are on your knees?"

His face flushed hot. "I'm bound by oath and honor, by the ties of a magic that goes bone-deep. I cannot directly defy his orders. I cannot directly threaten his life or allow another to do so. I'm bound by chains you cannot see. But you still can do all those things. That's why I need you. I have a plan, but I can't carry out that plan alone."

He spat his white pick to the side, droplets of blood spraying out with it. He watched me as he continued to grip my arms. I felt like I was being assessed. Who was Osprey under his strict rules and clever plans?

"And my father?" I wasn't willing to let that go.

"He will have justice eventually and you will have vengeance. If you'll just trust me for a little while longer."

I swallowed, studying him. How could I trust him when he served them? What other option did I have?

I nodded curtly and he sagged with relief.

"I'll do it," I said a little breathlessly. "I'll be your ally."

"I want a blood oath," he said and I shivered. "Draw your knife."

I drew my knife – hesitant, uncertain.

He drew his belt knife, slicing his palm and offering it to me.

"I, Vasyklo Petren, Osprey of the Winged Empire take your loyalty and allegiance in the coming struggle. In return, I will give you what allegiance I may, I will endeavor not to kill you, and I will attempt to help you work for the sake of the revolution."

I still hesitated. "This is a revolution?"

"Nothing short of revolution can save us now."

"That's it? All you're swearing is that you will endeavor not to kill me?"

"It's the most I can promise."

Reluctantly, I cut my palm.

His smile was sad as he pressed his bleeding palm to mine, sealing us as his hot, weathered palm gripped my painful one. "Pledge your loyalty."

"I, Aella Svoboda of the House of Shrikes pledge my loyalty to you. Together, we will fight for the freedom of my people."

He reached into a small belt pouch and produced a light grey scarf. "Bind your hand."

He was already done wrapping his own wound with a handkerchief by the time I was done wrapping the scarf around my palm.

"We're bound in blood now and you will have your revenge. Work hard on getting your bees under control," he said. "At mastering your words."

I nodded again, realizing that my bees had diminished to just one. It perched on my shoulder, buzzing innocently.

"And I promise you, we will have our freedom."

"Tell me how you are bound to Le Majest," I demanded.

"What?" He shoved a new white pick in his mouth, chewing it furiously while he peered deep into my eyes.

"I've sworn to you. If you want me to trust you," I said, planting my hands on my hips, "then you need to tell me how you are bound. You keep saying that you will help kill my family if he orders you to. That you want to bring Juste Montpetit to his knees. That you have killed for him – so many people that you smelled of their deaths for a week." I shuddered. "Tell me why I shouldn't think you are a monster for that. Tell me, and I'll trust you."

He swallowed and his hands shook as he dropped his grip on my shoulders. There was something raw in his eyes. The toothpick migrated from one corner of his lips to the other before he finally took it out and looked at me for a very long moment.

"I can't tell you that. But if you want your father avenged, you're going to have to trust me anyway."

BOOK TWO: BREAKING

A song to sing the sad to sleep,

A song to creep, a song to weep,

Tuck them in their slumbering beds,

Steal their years, twist their heads.

Sing to them of peace and love,

Soar in like the wing'ed dove.

They'll never know to run in fear.

They'll give you every sword and spear.

You'll take their future, steal their past,

You'll make their hard times last and last,

And in the end they'll be your toy,

And all their labors bring you joy,

And your harsh laugh will be the last.

And a long shadow you will cast.

-Songs of the Winged Ones

CHAPTER SEVENTEEN

I was still crying angry, bitter tears when he offered me a hand. I didn't want to take it. My lip trembled. I was close to breaking down. I stared at it, everything in me refusing to go back. Refusing to budge.

He sighed again. "I'm not your enemy. You just think I am."

"You aren't my friend either."

He shook his head like he was out of patience and spat his toothpick. "If you don't go back, what do you think Le Majest will do? Do you think he might remember that you have other family members who also have insulted him?"

I took his hand reluctantly, memories of my family flickering through my mind – Oska taming a wild horse, being bucked around with a look of fierce determination on his face. Aghar rushing in to tell us Delia had accepted his proposal, his eyes alight. Raquella brushing my hair while singing her favorite song about hummingbirds.

"I can't promise you much," Osprey said as he stepped behind me and wrapped an arm around my waist. "But at least I can promise you that what we do now will keep them safer than if you ran or if you'd killed Le Majest."

It didn't feel like enough.

I choked down a sob as we stepped onto the back of his osprey – a marvelous thing that was beginning to feel almost normal – and the osprey flapped its wings, sailing up into the sky.

"Fly, Os," he whispered to it, producing a new toothpick from his pocket and jamming it between his teeth. He seemed to have an endless supply of them.

We drew near enough that dark forms could finally be seen, holding lanterns high above their heads as they battled tangles of the Forbidding. It reached into the camp from the pass, bits of ground and rock reaching out like tentacles toward the Claws who fought it.

"They're fighting it the wrong way," I whispered. No one had set a fire. No one had found the heart of whatever had attacked. They were hacking and slashing at only the tangled tentacles. Around this edge of otherness that clawed across the ground, bodies lay in heaps. Claws. Dead by the strangling, striking tangles.

"Then it might be a good time to show us how it's done," Osprey said. I couldn't tell if he was amused or irritated.

"I'd need a sword to do that."

"You can borrow one of mine."

I twisted enough to look back at him as we dove toward the tangled mass. He was serious. I could tell by the way his eyes were narrowed on our target and his finely carved face was sharp with concentration.

I clutched at Osprey's arm, my breath in my throat.

"Take a breath," he whispered. "By the time we land you must be in control of yourself."

We landed in the night between fallen bodies and Osprey drew both his swords, handing one to me. I moved it through a form, checking the balance. It was a short sword for him, but just a touch longer than I was used to using. Not a problem. This was sized like Alect's swords, and I had experience using those when I needed to.

Essana emerged from the darkness, running fast, her owl behind her. It dove low and snatched up a strand of Forbidding that was following her through the night. The owl wrestled it in the darkness, bright silver light shedding from its wings as it rolled and flapped, trying to fight the Forbidding tentacle.

"We need to find the heart," I told Osprey, stealing a glance toward him. "You set a fire there and it will bring the whole thing down."

He held the sword like he knew how to use it, but the look he gave me was skeptical.

I patted my belt pouch. I hadn't made a fire since I left home, but I had the tools for it in the pouch. I looked toward the Forbidding, steeling myself to fight as a Claw was thrown past, screaming, his hands clawing at the air.

Sorrow hit me in the chest like a punch. I'd just seen my father die. Did I really want to risk myself fighting the Forbidding to keep the people who had held and tortured him safe? I didn't. Not really.

"This is your land," Osprey said from beside me. "This terrible place with a thousand ways to die is your home. But only if you fight to keep it."

I swallowed and dove toward the darkness, grateful as the bee buzzed over my head with just enough golden light to keep me from tripping. A moment later, Os soared overhead, lighting the way.

The tangle here was intense – made worse by the slain Claws on every side. Men lay on the ground with empty eyes and tangled strands of Forbidding clawing through their chests or around their necks. They'd fought this all wrong.

"Did no one tell them how to fight?" I asked in horror.

"They're the best warriors of our Empire, House Apidae. If they have not succeeded, you will –" Osprey's words cut off as he leapt over a clawing strand of twisting Forbidding. A man-thick strand tried to knock his legs out from under him. He landed on it, keeping his balance as it writhed and slashed side to side. I stabbed at it, having to move with lightning reflexes to avoid the flicking end. Osprey rode it, balanced in a low crouch as he stabbed it again and again.

"Fighting the strands is only a temporary solution," I gasped as I fought. "We have to find the heart."

In the distance, I saw a burst of white light and the faint outline of a Swan. Xectare must be in the darkness there. Where would the heart be in a mass of Forbidding like this one? It wasn't a tree with an obvious trunk, or a bear with a heart. This was something else.

I tried to think as Osprey hacked off the ribbon of Forbidding and leapt from it, slashing and stabbing as the severed end kept fighting.

Above him, his Osprey flared, shooting up suddenly and extending its wings long enough to bathe the area in a bright purplish-white light. In that flash, I tried to see everything at once.

The Forbidding tangle seemed centered on a tall standing rock that had been carved with serpents at one point. It was set on one side of the pass just outside our camp. Tendrils of rock and sky broke from it like ribbons and arced out from the rock toward us and into the camp.

There were heaps of dead.

Xectare stood outlined in the light, her swan above her as she fought one strand of the evil twisting. Zayana was not with her.

Essana had rallied and was rushing forward again, owl high and screeching.

A knot of Swan Claws pressed forward toward the standing stone, Le Majest in their center, his narrow sword raised and at the ready. That was surprising. I didn't think he ever got his hands dirty.

There were hundreds of tentacles of all sizes reaching out from the rock, everything from spiderweb-thin to man-thick. But I could see a way through the maze of them to the heart and the Swan Claws clearly didn't realize that's what you had to do.

"This way," I called to Osprey. "Cover me."

He made an irritated sound in the back of his throat, but he followed. The bright light overhead concentrated as Os ducked down, following us. His light was our only chance to fight. In the darkness, even seeing the tentacles was too difficult.

I rolled under a snatching tentacle, popping up on the other side and dancing backward, balanced on the ball of my foot as I narrowly avoided a swipe near my midsection. I tensed and hopped, stepping on the clawing tendril and using the momentum to launch me between two more and into a gap on the other side.

"You are mad, House Apidae," I heard Osprey cry from behind me.

I chuckled darkly. I wasn't mad. I was experienced. If a fire wasn't lit soon, this Forbidding manifestation would expand and kill us all. Maybe. Or maybe it would just kill me and Le Majest and the Claws would return to my home and kill my family. I couldn't allow that.

The little bee buzzed around my head as I made a daring dart under a waving tentacle and reached the standing rock.

If only he was bigger. I could barely see to find my flint. I fumbled in my belt pouch and dropped it.

Forbidding take it!

I fell to the ground, searching for it. There was a bird above me. I twisted up to see Os locked in a battle with one of the tentacles. It shook him, spraying spirit feathers in every direction – and with them enough light to see the flint. I snatched it up in my fist and was knocked back by another tentacle. I heard Osprey curse.

"Next time you fight with me you don't go off on your own like a warrior in her first battle. You're too independent, House Apidae."

"I know how to fight the Forbidding," I said, snatching a ball of fire-starter from my belt pouch.

Out of nowhere, a strand of Forbidding struck toward me. I ducked and Osprey cursed. I heard his sword strike as the strand wrapped around my neck with the speed of a snake. I tried to slash it with the sword, but my arm was equally pinned.

The tangled manifestation twisted me so I faced upward. Above me, I saw Os snarled in the strands. He screamed with a bird voice, ripping with talons, but irreversibly caught.

Osprey screamed with him.

We were all caught.

This was it.

I let my heart drift toward the heavens as my vision narrowed and my lungs burned. I was going to go meet my father in the skies beyond. A shudder of fear filled me, but I was surprised by the relief that came with it. No more guessing. No more wondering if I could trust. No more fear. I could join him there. I gasped, trying to suck in a breath but nothing came.

Gold light flooded the sky above me. Perhaps it was the light of the sky beyond.

But no. It was a golden eagle. His golden feathers flashed bright and searing. He was like light come to life, like a dawn in feathered form. Unlike a real bird, his feathers seemed to have a pattern woven in them in gold and white light. He was almost too beautiful to exist.

My eyes widened as he descended with a shriek, and someone dropped off his back into the tangle beside me.

"No, get her first," I heard Osprey grunt as the eagle ripped at the shreds of Forbidding encircling Os.

There was the wet sound of hacking and then suddenly I could breathe. Strong hand pulled me from the tangle and I looked up to see a man in his late middle years, wearing two crossed belts over his chest instead of a shirt. His long brown hair swirled in the air behind him, bound only by the leather lashing around his brow. He was grizzled, his rippling muscles so covered in scars that it was hard to tell what color his skin had started as.

"Truth, justice, and the Imperial way will get them every time," he announced, his voice loud and hearty. "No manifestations stand a chance when old Wing Ivo arrives."

I tried to speak, but my words came out as a hoarse groan as I tried to catch my breath.

"Is this who you called me for, Osprey? This little bee?"

"Keep your voice down," Osprey said, his voice roughened from the attack.

"The heart," I managed to gasp out. "We need to set a fire at the heart to kill it."

"No need," Wing Ivo said quietly. He pulled me up by the back of my coat, steadying me on my trembling legs. "Le Majest used a different method."

He was right. The Forbidding was recoiling back in on itself. I gaped at it. I'd never seen it do that. I would have gone on gaping, but a voice cut through my thoughts, sparking fury and a stab of misery.

"Who gave my property a sword?" Le Majest said in a blade-sharp tone. His eyes were fixed on me, hatred brimming in them that almost matched mine for him. The shadows around his head seemed to almost move.

Just the sight of him brought back the memory of his sword plunged into the back of my father's neck. I gritted my teeth as the sound of buzzing filled my ears. Little golden spots swirled up from my hands into the sky. One of them sped to Juste Montpetit, but he swatted it away with cold indifference.

At the crown prince's feet, a Claw lay dead, his throat ripped open so tidily that it almost looked like the slash of a sword. However he'd died had been bloody. I swallowed down bile at the sight of the gore surrounding him.

"My apologies, Le Majest," Osprey said from beside me, making the sign of the bird. He snatched his sword from my hand. "I recruited her in removing this disturbance."

My bees grew louder as my sorrow grew. He'd killed him and mocked him as if my father didn't matter. As if the old man was nothing more than a tool or toy to be used as he pleased.

"Did you? You trusted her with your own blade."

Le Majest looked at the standing stone and then around him at the bodies lying in heaps. Their blood soaked into the ground all the way to the standing stone. I hadn't realized it before, but more Claws had died on their way toward the stone, following the path I'd taken. He'd lost at least fifty of his Claws to this single manifestation. Which seemed crazy, since we rarely lost so many at home to such a small incursion. I frowned. They didn't even look like they'd been killed by the Forbidding. Their wounds weren't from being strangled or stabbed, but from something that had slashed them, opening their veins.

What had stopped it? I thought that only fire was effective. And yet, it had shrunk in on itself again. I swallowed, made nervous by what I didn't understand.

I was shaking all over, humming with the bees and with the strange mix of despair and fury that swirled in my heart.

Le Majest turned his attention from me and I slumped with relief. "And you have returned, Wing Ivo. Why is that?"

"I was sent to help aid you in this last leg of your journey back to Karkatua, a week's ride south by road, Le Majest," he said, but his bold flare from before seemed guarded now.

"I know where our destination is, Wing. We shall speak in the morning. Clean this place up."

He spun in place and his guard went with him, leaving me gaping.

That was it? He lost all those people and almost lost his own life and his only response was a complaint and an order to clean up?

I made a scoffing sound.

"What?" Osprey whispered in my ear. When had he snuck up behind me?

"Before you came to my town, I'd never seen so much beauty and horror as I've seen now."

"So soon?" he asked, and his words seemed to echo as if he was saying them more than once.

I shook my head. What did I know anymore? My father was dead and my heart was broken. The man who claimed to own me was cruelty and indolence incarnate and I was only allied with Osprey because the alternative was even worse – facing this with no goal at all.

But my goal was different than his in one small way. He may have asked me to join him for the sake of a grand revolution, but I had only one goal in mind – destroying Juste Montpetit. My eyes followed his retreat as if they could burn him alive.

Essana stumbled forward, wiping dust from her weary face. Her owl was half it's usual size and she hugged it to her chest protectively.

"Where were you?" she demanded of me, but I barely noticed her I was so intent on the crown prince.

In the distance, someone moaned. Everything suddenly seemed very quiet. There were no more screams or cries. There were no more bellows or howls. Just the subdued sounds of moaning and of people beating out fires. And all those extra bodies that shouldn't be dead at all.

"I was here, fighting," I replied. "Were you fighting with Le Majest."

She nodded. "It is an honor to serve. You should be proud to have survived and you should give us a proper bird for these battles."

As if that mattered. Somewhere in the middle of camp, my father's body needed burying. My heart stuttered in my chest at the thought. And all she could think about were my bees.

"You always make an entrance, Wing Ivo," Essana said to the man with the golden eagle. "Are you staying with us this time, or do you have secret business to attend once again?"

"Who is this?" the Wing asked. I hadn't realized that he still had the back of my jacket gripped in his fist. I didn't care what they told him. I was wondering if Le Majest would stop me if I tried to bury my father. My heart was singing a long sad song, an endlessly weeping cadence.

"Just a Hatched, Wing Ivo. We picked her up along the border with the Forbidding," Essana said. "Le Majest has claimed her as his personal property once she's trained – provided she can manifest a bird instead of those dreadful bees."

I looked up at him, practically quivering with all the emotions ricocheting through me. I was keeping the bees. This decided it. They were as angry and frustrated as I was. They were the symbol of my defiance and how I would never bend to this empire. I raised my chin and crossed my arms at the same time that Wing Ivo chuckled.

"I'll take her," he announced.

"What?" Essana sounded shocked.

"As my apprentice," Wing Ivo said, smiling at me. No. Smiling at the bee on my shoulder. "I like difficult things."

"But you haven't taken an apprentice in thirty years," Essana's owl flapped unhappily.

"Well, then it's high time I did. Come along, Hatchling. We have a mess to clean here. My apprentices work long, hard hours. You'll get used to it."

I gaped at him and he snapped his fingers at me – three times in quick succession.

I shook myself and followed, too stunned to object. I shot one look at Osprey who offered me a stony-faced wink. I was going to have to ask him what those winks meant – they were not playful at all. I was going to have to ask him a lot of things when I got a chance again.

"We start with the wounded," Wing Ivo said, "then move to the dead. I hope you're used to hard work because it's a long night ahead of us. Not easy to bury bodies on stony ground, and of course we'll have to keep an eye out in case that rock decides it's not beat."

Was he serious? I shot Osprey a questioning glance as he strode past, Os shrunk down to the size of a normal bird and shrieking irritably on his shoulder. The look he sent in my direction looked torn, as if something about me hurt him.

"Message received," Wing Ivo told him quietly as he passed, his eyes far away as if he wasn't talking to Osprey at all, and then we were moving away at the speed of his long strides. What kind of a message had Osprey sent to Wing Ivo? And how had he done it?

"Ever buried the dead before?" he asked me.

"Yes," I said tiredly as I tucked my flint and fire starter back into my pouch. "And I've fought the Forbidding before, too. Both death and that dark magic are equally unforgiving."

He laughed but there was a note of approval in his laugh that I found I rather liked. Perhaps, if I had to be claimed by some Wing, this brash one wouldn't be so bad.

CHAPTER EIGHTEEN

We worked through the night – long past when tents were found for Juste Montpetit. I saw his scalding gaze piercing the darkness toward me while he waited for the Swan Claws to erect his tent. He toyed with the hilt of his dagger, running the edge of his thumb along his lip as he looked at me. I tried to ignore him. The other Wings – Essana, Xectare, and Osprey had already gathered around him for an after-battle report and they were safe behind a ring of Claws. I'd made a scoffing sound under my breath and gone back to work. He could watch me all he wanted. One day, I would cut out his eye like he cut out my father's.

Juste whispered to a Claw and then the man was running out to where I was working with Ivo. He gave us the sign of the bird when he arrived, still catching his breath.

"Le Majest wishes the service of the Hatched for tonight," he said.

My heart fell to my belly. What did he plan to do to me? He'd taken my father's eye and then his life. I didn't doubt that he'd be happy to take those from me, too.

"Tell the crown prince that he has my compliments," Wing Ivo said, "and I'll be keeping my apprentice close tonight. There's too much work to be done here."

The Claw looked horrified, but when he returned to Juste Montpetit, the man's eyes simply followed me, his expression still opaque and confident.

"Crisis averted," Wing Ivo said when Juste eventually looked away. "Now, let's get back to work."

"He's not going to be pleased," I said.

"Did they not tell you that the Guide has ultimate say in what his Hatched may or may not do and not even Le Majest himself can change that?" he asked me.

"No," I said, wide-eyed.

"Didn't think so," he said with a self-satisfied grin.

"He still won't like it," I warned. "Can't he order you around?"

"He can try. That would be its own kind of fun," he said with a laugh, turning me toward the path out of the pass. He must be very confident in his own abilities to defy the crown prince like that. Or maybe there was no one he loved enough to be fearful for. "Start there. We'll have to deal with the dead in the old way. Stone cairns."

He watched me as he spoke, the light of his golden eagle illuminating both our faces. The eagle was perched on his shoulder now, and whenever I looked at him, it was staring at me.

"Why did you choose me as an apprentice?" I asked, warily.

"I like challenges. I'm a hard-working, go-getting, fly-by-night, magic-smagic, get-er-going kind of Wing."

I watched him in semi-fascinated horror every time he spoke like that. It was like he was trying to whip up a crowd, but he was only talking to me.

"Have you taken apprentices before?"

"Sure. I've taken on apprentices, and hangers-on, treasure-hunters, wannabe Claws, even a wife once. The beautiful Jamaile, Queen of the Sea."

Perhaps he meant to be shocking. He certainly seemed shocking to me. I nodded along with wide eyes because I didn't know what else to do.

"Go find the dead and when you find one, stand there," he ordered. "I'll see the glow of that bee and send old Harpy here to get the body. It will be more respectful than the two of us dragging the poor victim. Isn't that right, Harpy, hmmm?"

"You named your eagle Harpy?" Hopefully he couldn't see my raised eyebrows in the dark.

"You betcha. He's the death on two wings, he's the eight-taloned terror of the skies, the light in the darkness, the pride and fury of my heart."

The eagle seemed to swell with his words and I swallowed. If they thought I was going to talk like that and mean it when I spoke to my bees ... well, that just wasn't my way.

"Go find the dead, Apprentice."

I nodded and hurried through the dark. We started on the edge of the battle where the fighting had been the thickest and slowly worked our way out across the trail. The dead were strewn here and there across the path.

I studied the first body I found – a Claw in a bright blue coat. I shut his eyes gently, whispering a prayer over him as my bee buzzed gently. Would they allow me to do the same for my father when we reached him?

I moved from body to body, my heart breaking at all these lost lives. It felt strange to feel like that about people who would kill my family on a whim. And yet, what a terrible waste. None of these people would hug their loved ones again. None of them would watch a sunset or hear the birds sing. It made my heart weep inside, adding a layer of sadness over the bone-deep grief for my father as I sent them off with the eagle, one by one.

And almost every one of them had been killed so strangely. I found two that had been strangled. One still had roots wrapped around his neck which I was forced to cut with my belt knife. That was expected and normal. One poor Claw had his chest caved in from a blow. I'd seen that before, too, when I was travelling with my father. We'd buried the poor soul and brought his belt to the nearest town to be given to his family. All of that – tragic as it was – was an expected thing when it came to the Forbidding. I'd seen people pierced with those tendrils, too. Sometimes they struck so fast that they stuck right through a person. The old man had gotten one through the leg last spring and he'd been cranky for weeks while it healed. One winter, Oska had been hit in the side and he'd spent weeks fighting the infection and fever that came after.

But I'd never seen a throat slashed as if by a knife. And the piercing wounds on these men were small and neat, like a sword blade, not like the larger, rougher wounds made by a Forbidding tentacle.

Something was wrong here.

And it didn't make any sense. Why would someone in this camp kill their own people? And what would they do to someone who pointed this out? Especially if I was wrong? I'd seen what they did to my father just for existing.

I kept my lips sealed shut as I noted the wounds and counted the dead. I'd better keep this to myself for now.

"Bring it in," Ivo called to me, probably waking half the sleeping camp as I hurried from the last body on the trail and began to work my way inward in a slow, back-and-forth sweep.

There were bodies here, too. Men dead of the strange puncture wounds. Men dead with more normal crushed skulls.

The weight of grief pressed down on me as the night wore on, and my legs got heavier. I had begun to think longingly of sleep when I stumbled across the cage and all thoughts of sleep vanished.

I fell to my knees – almost in the same place where I'd knelt before, hoping that by kneeling I could save my father's life. Now, I pressed my forehead to the cage bars and whispered, "I'm sorry."

They'd left him where he'd been killed. He didn't look like my father anymore. But that didn't mean he wasn't. That didn't mean they had the right to treat him like this. I sucked in a long breath, trembling. Wishing I could bring him back. If I'd just been faster. If I'd just been less defiant. None of this should have happened.

I whispered the old prayer again. "Fly him to the great beyond on the wings of the dawn. Shelter him under your wings."

"Who is that?" Ivo's voice startled me. I turned to see him standing over me, arms crossed over his chest. There was no point in lying to him.

"It's my father." My voice sounded dead.

His arms uncrossed and he knelt down on the earth beside me. I startled as his eagle lifted onto the cage, resting its wings downward as if kneeling with us.

He was silent for a long moment and then he cleared his throat.

"I'll finish up. And I'll see him suitably buried. I set up a tent on the edge of the trail. Harpy will lead you to it. I won't have time to sleep tonight. It is yours until dawn."

"I should bury him," I said, my voice thick with tears.

"Not like this, girl." His voice was low and gentle as he set a hand on my shoulder. "You've said your goodbye. Now, go and sleep."

I opened my mouth to thank him, but he was already gone, walking firmly through the dark. His eagle hovered over me and then flew through the night toward the road out of the pass. I reached into the cage, put a hand on my father's head, and let myself weep for long moments before I followed the eagle through the night.

CHAPTER NINETEEN

I woke to whispering on the other side of the tent wall. I could barely force my eyes open. Perhaps it was grief, or perhaps it was all the magic I'd used yesterday in calling my bees, but I felt like I could barely lift my head.

"She's in there?" That sounded like Osprey.

"Yes, sleeping." And that was Ivo. "When I found her father ... You should have warned me."

"And how would I have done that? Our only hope is that no one knows that I sent for you," Osprey hissed. His voice had a vulnerable quality to it that made it seem younger than usual. I could almost believe the truth – that he was only a hair older than I was.

"No, our only hope is that the histories are right. That Fernius sent us in the right direction. That we're not new puppies chasing our tails. That's our hope. You should have sent for me sooner."

"Sooner than when she Hatched? What am I supposed to be, clairvoyant?"

Ivo snorted. "Don't tell me you couldn't feel it in her before that ceremony. I could feel it when I set down in that tangled Forbidding. The power of that manifestation ... it's almost too much."

"But what can she do with bees?"

"Who knows? How could any of us know? But we know this is our chance and we have to take it. Now. While the Emperor is distracted by his new prize and his heir is dancing around the territories like a peacock in breeding season."

"You know as well as I do that this isn't simple. It's not just a matter of lopping off the head of the snake. The people are behind him."

"The people wouldn't know common sense if it bit them in the ever-loving, bright-shining, fat-gathering – "

"Nevertheless," Osprey cut him off. "We can't end one reign without another reign ready to start."

Ivo sounded wry when he said, "The son of a general makes for an interesting choice."

"No one loves war or the sons of war, Ivo," Osprey said tiredly. "And I'm bound. You know that. I nearly had to kill her father myself." I gasped. He'd done *what?* "You know how I'm bound. What my limitations are. But there are others who aren't. And that's what the people need. They need hope. They need the promise of a future. They need a different kind of dream."

"I still think you're aiming too big. Aim small, miss small."

"Aim big and maybe you'll still hit something. And now I need to get back to my post. I've been missing too often lately."

"Keep your head down and no more contact with the girl or with me unless you can't help it. Send the bird if you must. Is this Forbidding going to be a problem? I only saw it twice on the roads here and it wasn't as formidable as it was last night. That was some display it showed me when I arrived. Makes a man rethink a few things."

"The crown prince doesn't take it seriously," Osprey said dryly. "Not even when it claims the lives of his Claws. Another reminder of why he's unfit to rule a teapot, nevermind the Empire."

"That smacks of bitterness, Osprey which is not a good emotion to feed your bird. But it's also another reminder of why you and I will spill every drop of our blood to save a scrap of the world from him. My vow to you was true. I will be faithful in this."

There was a sound like a clasp of hands and then the rustle of wings taking flight.

I sat up. A single bee buzzed around my head, but to my surprise, there were no welts left from the stings I'd gotten yesterday. I looked at the bee and concentrated on it.

"I refuse to give you up," I whispered to the bee. "Together, we will be relentless."

I could have sworn I heard it buzzing louder. Was it buzzing inside my mind? It sounded pleased with itself as if it liked the fact that I'd decided to keep it. I watched it for a few minutes, letting myself marvel for the first time at the wonder of it. The bee was so delicate, every hair glowing and golden, its meandering flight almost playful and happy. Perhaps it had come for a reason. Perhaps it was exactly what I needed. I shrugged, straightened myself, and then came out of the tent.

"They tell me you have nothing of your own," Ivo said as I emerged. He was crouched beside a small fire, a pipe clenched between his teeth, his hands warming over the flames. There was a twinkle in his eye as if he suspected I'd been eavesdropping. Sounds of the camp being packed up rolled out across the crisp morning. "No tent, no pack, no weapon, no clothing but what you wear."

"I have this bee," I said, opening my palm to the buzzing bee. It seemed almost cheerful this morning. And searing across the endless washing waves of sadness in my mind, was a little hum of happiness.

"Yes you do. You can pack up that tent for me. Did they tell you that they'll kill you if you don't manifest something other than bees before we get to the main city?"

"Yes."

He snorted. "Well, don't listen to them. The first thing you need is some kind of control, not wishing what you have away. We can't have you manifesting rogue bees every time you lose your temper, as amusing as that may be. Osprey tells me that their stings don't last, so they aren't even handy as a weapon. Until you get control, they never will be. So. We teach you. First lesson. Figure out what you want."

"I already know what I want," I said grimly.

His laugh was nasty as he flicked out the ash from his pipe into his little fire. "Revenge? That doesn't last, girl." He paused, sobering. "Okay, instead, figure out what you can do that will make your life meaningful."

"I know that, too. I'm going to kill Juste Monpetit," I said, staring him in the eyes and daring him to do something about it.

He shook his head, snorting.

"Dust-kissing fool. You don't announce a thing like that to the world. Besides, it's the wrong answer. So, you kill him? Then what? That's the question. You can't live for something that small – you can die for it, but not live for it. So, by tonight I want you to tell me what you want to live for. What the great purpose of your suffering and your hard work and dreaming is going to be. Okay? You're going to suffer. You already have, and you will suffer more. That's life. It's as inevitable as it is tragic. The key is to accept that and then find meaning despite it. Or maybe because of it. Give me an answer about what kind of purpose could make all of that worth something."

"That doesn't help me with controlling my bees," I said, worried now.

He snorted. "Have you ever taught someone magic?"

"No," I said.

"Then why don't you let me do the teaching and you do the learning, okay? Now. Pack the tent and then go find that other Hatchling they have around here. You'll walk with her today. Ask her how she controls her bird. What does she say to stir it up and wind it down?"

"Do you think she can teach me something that would help?" I asked hopefully.

"No, but she can get you out of my hair for the day."

I felt myself frowning as I turned to the tent, but he had more to say.

"Oh, and girl?"

"Yes?" I met his eyes. There was genuine pity there. "I gave your father an honest burial. Made his cairn high. Sang over it." He nodded fiercely. "It was the burial of a great warrior."

"He *was* a great warrior," I said, not even knowing if I was telling the truth.

"Then you should be one, too." He paused. "Okay. There's work to be done."

"That's something my father always said."

"Indeed." He reached up to scratch at his hair and I saw he had a tiny tattoo behind his ear. If I got close enough to see it, would it match the one behind Osprey's? My eyes narrowed. "And one more thing. Don't kill Juste Montpetit. Not today. The timing is all wrong and it won't help you. I want your promise on that."

"Not today," I agreed reluctantly. I needed time to plan, anyway. Attacking on a whim hadn't worked and if I tried it again, Osprey would just be there to snatch me away like he had last time.

Ivo watched me for a beat and then nodded sharply and strode away.

CHAPTER TWENTY

I turned my attention to packing his things in a large leather bag he had laid out for the purpose. There wasn't much, so it didn't take long. I was striding toward Zayana before she was finished loading the carabao cart with Essana and Xectare's things.

"Back so soon, bees?" she asked, the sting of bitterness sharp in her voice. There was an angry gash along one of her cheeks.

"What happened to your cheek?" I gasped.

"Nothing," she said, but she was blinking back tears.

"I think it needs stitches," I said, helping her load the last of the things into the wagon. I put Ivo's pack in there, too.

"There's no one to stitch them," she said sharply.

I looked around. The remaining Claws were still packing the camp and putting out the night's fires.

"If you have thread and we're fast, I can stitch," I said.

"Are you some kind of maid?" she asked scornfully, but she pulled a needle and thread from a belt pouch.

“Come on,” I said, guiding her to sit on a chest in the cart. I licked the thread and threaded the needle quickly. We didn’t have much time. “It’s going to hurt.”

“I might not be some rube on the edge of society with a history of stitching wounds, but even I know that,” she said sharply, hissing as I dug the needle in for the first stitch. I flinched on her behalf as I set the it.

“I’m supposed to stay with you today and learn how you call your bird and what you say to it,” I said as I worked.

She gave a refined sniff. “You really must be terrible at this if they’re asking me to teach you. I only Hatched the week before we set sail across the sea.”

I paused, tying the stitch. “What was the journey like?”

She sniffed. “Hard. They killed my father before I left, of course.”

“What?” I couldn’t keep my horror from my lips. “Why would they do that?”

“You really don’t know anything.” Her tone was bitter. “Imperial birds sing stronger when the bloodline is narrowed. A rube like you wouldn’t need your father killed. You won’t have any power anyway. But my father put his own head on the block. He was the last of our line other than me. He did not Hatch. But now all his power is condensed in my blood.”

“That’s barbaric.” I spat as I tied the next stitch.

"What do you know about it?" she asked, but I was close enough to see her eyes glass over as she blinked her tears away. That had only been a few weeks ago. Her loss was nearly as fresh as mine.

"They killed my father last night," I said quietly as I worked.

She turned so sharply that it was all I could do to let go of the thread so I didn't pull on the wound. Her eyes met mine in something like sympathy mixed with fury.

"Xectare beat me last night because my bird could not fight. That's how I hurt my cheek."

I sucked in a sharp breath.

"What's a little bird like that supposed to do?" I asked, realizing that she was cradling it protectively against her chest. That was new, wasn't it? I hadn't noticed before. I'd been too obsessed with my own pain.

She leaned into her bird, whispering to it. "Be stronger. We need to show them we aren't afraid. We need to remember the flames in the bowl of the Beligran, the red feathers of the cardinal, the soaring winds of Zephira. I danced the dance of a thousand steps on the white marble there and the Emperor himself gave me a notice feather. I wore it in my hair for the Hatching when you arrived, little flame. Don't fail me now. We shall be strong together."

Her words made me blink back tears. I hadn't realized that she was so much like me. Obviously, we came from totally different places. She was a high'un – from a High House – and I was a Far Reacher. Her history was full of singing and dancing and fine dresses and mine was of breaking horses and fighting the Forbidding with my big family. And yet, we were similar at heart. I finished the last stitch.

"Is that the kind of thing you always say to the bird?" I asked.

"It's an invocation. I tell the bird my memories and hopes, the images that matter to me, what I need from it and every morning it is made new again – a little closer to what was invoked. The thing is, negative words have equal consequences. Forbiddings can curtail the bird. That's probably what you should use on your bees. You should forbid them from being bees."

That was ridiculous. The bees couldn't be birds any more than I could. We were all what we'd been made to be. We could only shape that.

I handed the thread back to her. "I don't think I can bandage the wound, but you should try to keep it clean."

She nodded stiffly and hopped off the cart. Together we began to follow the carabao. It was moving to follow the others like it as they formed a line.

"Do you have to guide the carabao?" I asked.

"No. It follows the others. Isn't that strange? On the continent, they are known for being the most vicious beasts imaginable. But they can be trained to be as docile as a lamb."

"How do they make them docile?" I asked.

"They cut the tips off their horns," she said and I followed her eye to see she was right. "And they make them walk through the bodies of other carabaos that have been slaughtered. It breaks their spirits."

Just like they were trying to break mine. Just like they were trying to break all of Far Reach by stealing our defense and ripping us apart. They could think again. I would not be broken. *We* would not be broken.

A hum began in my mind and I looked down at the bee in my hand, buzzing away like a little ball of happiness. I hated it for being so happy when I felt so broken. And at the same time, I didn't want to forbid that. I wanted to grow it until I could taste that happiness again, too.

We followed the carabaos toward the back of the line. Up at the front, I saw Juste Montpetit riding a black carabao, his weedy advisor on one side of him and Osprey on the other. I couldn't help the resentment that formed in my chest at the sight of my supposed ally standing beside the man who had murdered my father. What chains bound him? Or was he lying about that?

"I thought you liked him," Zayana said, following my gaze. "Which would have been stupid. I mean, even though they're both hardly older than we are – the crown prince is twenty and Osprey is nineteen – they're out of reach and we all know what happens to lovers of the royal family. But it's even stupider to hate him like that."

"What?" I asked. I didn't know what happened to lovers of the royal family and I didn't care. I wanted to murder Juste, not kiss him.

"Didn't you notice how large Osprey's bird is? I've rarely seen a bird so large. Xectare's and Essana's are more average in size. It doesn't change what the bird can do – but it can do it on a more massive scale. He can even ride his, as I'm sure you've seen. That's not an enemy you want to have."

I grunted noncommittally holding my little bee up to my lips and whispering, "Revenge."

"He has a title, too. Osprey. It's what binds a named Wing like that to the crown prince. It usually means his family made blood oath. They will pay in kind for any harm that befalls the crown prince. An eye for an eye. A tooth for a tooth. That's not someone you want to provoke with angry stares."

"A blood oath?" I asked.

She shook her head, looking at me sadly. "I thought it was bad enough to come here where there are no Daja dresses, no compella makers, no proper porcelain cups, or actual mirrors, with your fashions twenty years behind the times and everyone wearing a sword at their hip." She shuddered. "I had no idea how truly backward this place is." She shook her head. "The best of the Wings are sometimes selected by the Emperor for a special task. They lose their given name and are called only by the name of their bird – and thus their house – from that moment on. Everyone they love is brought to the Great Nest and bound by blood and magic. Osprey has the name, so that's what must have happened to him, too. If he fails to protect the crown prince, his family will suffer. If he refuses an order, they will die. The magic will know. They will be eating breakfast or in the bath, or dancing at a ball, and then they'll crumple as if from an unseen blow. Or lose the sight in an eye. Or fall stone dead. An eye for an eye."

My breath caught in my chest.

And suddenly the events of last night made a lot more sense.

"For how long?"

She smiled wryly at me as if trying to educate a child. "Forever. The Empire doesn't ever give a reprieve. The Winged Empire is not kind. Only the harsh will soar. Only the sharp survive."

CHAPTER TWENTY-ONE

I watched the shadows with careful eyes all day. If the Forbidding had crept up into the pass, I expected more patches of it than a single aberration. No one spoke about the fallen as we passed the cairns Captain Ivo had set up. No one so much as paused. Those men had worked side by side with them and all they did was make the sign of the bird as they passed.

It was all I could do not to break down when we passed a lone cairn set aside from the rest. I paused before it, noticing that someone had scratched something into one of the rocks laid upon it. It looked like a single wing. I looked up in shock and caught Osprey staring back at me as if he couldn't help himself. The second my eyes met his he looked away, bowing his head.

Beside him, Juste Montpetit looked from Osprey to me, eyes glittering.

"Don't linger," Zayana warned me quietly. "We don't pause for the dead. It will cause ill winds."

I looked at her in disbelief. "You didn't mourn your father?"

"I mourned in my heart."

The Wings were busy around Juste Montpetit and any attempt we made to draw closer to them was quickly rebuffed. I heard snippets of chatter whenever we came close – speculations about the Forbidding. The Wings, like everyone else, were wondering what it was, how it was formed, how it could be destroyed. As if they could solve a question we'd all been asking for longer than I'd been alive. No one knew. No one had answers. Some things in life just *were*.

"Hatchlings ride with the supplies," Essana said sharply when Zayana tried to stride up beside her. "Off with you."

But despite her warning, I found two sets of eyes looking back at us often. Juste Montpetit, his lip curling as he spoke, and Osprey whose eyes were fraught with worry.

We paused to give the carabao a break at noon, eating a quick meal of dried meat and flatbread. There was no source for water and our skins were mostly empty.

"There's a river on the other side of the pass," I told Zayana when she watched me with worry as I took a swallow from her skin.

"I hope so." She sounded like she didn't believe me.

The sudden time sitting still brought my grief back to the forefront, and I hurried away to hide behind a cleft in the rock and weep silently into my hands. My body rocked with silent sobs. I just kept thinking of my father staring at me with just one eye and mouthing the word, 'Relentless.' How could I be relentless when my grief threatened to drown me?

I kept thinking of his hand on my shoulder while he smiled at me warmly, of watching him sprawled in his favorite chair while he talked with us about his plans for the horses, of watching him select a horse from a wild herd and then carefully plan out how to draw it in and break it. He'd always been infinitely strong, always had answers to all my problems, always been so certain of himself.

And now he was gone. I drew in a long, shuddering breath, trying to calm myself. I needed to return to the group with dry eyes and a calm face but right now that felt more unattainable than anything else could.

I heard a grunt outside the cleft of rock I was hiding in and froze. Had someone else come out here seeking privacy? I bit my lip and crept forward just enough to peer out through the crack. Osprey looked furtively over his shoulder as if he was afraid of being seen. His coat was unbuttoned and his tunic unlaced and spread wide, showing the hard planes of his chest and stomach. On the left side of his chest above his heart, something glowed. It looked like a smoke-white feather curled in a ring just under his skin. It was lit faintly, like a feather from a spirit bird, and around the curl of the feather, the skin was red and irritated, bubbled like he had been burned.

He studied it as if he was worried it might get worse before grunting as he closed his tunic again.

His bird fluttered down and landed behind him.

"Os," he gasped, reaching for his bird and leaning his dark head against of the bright feathers of the bird. He closed his eyes, clutching the bird as he gasped in long breaths. It flickered in and out of sight, cooing gently to him.

I ducked back behind the rock. This moment was too private to watch. I didn't realize that Wings were so very close to their birds. Were they real entities outside themselves or a further extension of the Wing?

And what in the world could that glowing feather be? Did it have something to do with these chains of magic he kept talking about?

I trembled as I waited to hear him leave. When, eventually, I heard the crunch of boots on rock, I took five long breaths and then scurried out from behind the rock and back out to where the carabaos were starting to move again. I barely managed to catch up to Zayana before anyone realized I was missing.

She took one look at my puffy eyes and shook her head in warning. I avoided her eyes. I could grieve if I wanted to. I *would* grieve, because my father deserved it.

I faced forward and my gaze caught on Osprey looking back at me from his mount beside the crown prince. His face seemed pale, as if he had seen which way I came from. I looked away sharply, keeping my eyes fixed on the rocks around us. Someone should be watching for the Forbidding. Was I the only one with sense?

When I returned to Zayana, Wing Xectare chose to ride with us to give a lesson for the rest of the afternoon. I'd thought I was tired from the bees sapping my strength, but nothing sapped your spirit like Wing Xectare.

"Palms out," she said, sniffing loudly when we showed her our manifestations. "Today we speak of the eight pinions of the Wings. All fully matured Wings have a proper bird manifestation," she said looking at me with a cruel twist to her mouth. "And just as all manifestations grant their manifestor different skills and powers, still those powers and strengths find natural groupings. We call these groupings pinions in honor of the feathers in the wing of a bird. Can you name the eight pinions, Zayana?"

Zayana pursed her lips. "Hummingbird."

"Which represents?" Xectare prodded.

"Artists, dancers, singers, and musicians," Zayana said promptly.

"Yes. And?"

"Ravens for merchants, traders, and finance. Kingfisher for envoys, messengers, and advisors. Tern for the navy, sailors, and ports. Swallow for common work – building, farming, and such management. Snowy Owl for alchemists, assassins, watchmakers, glassblowers, and the other high callings. Eagle for the Claws, guards, and all kinds of warriors. White Heron for the Emperor's House, the high houses, the imperial workers, and the governing of the Emperor's social callings."

"Adequate," Xectare said. "You will teach Aella these things for the rest of the afternoon."

She kicked her carabao and hurried forward as if glad to be rid of us.

Zayana and I exchanged a look. What was she supposed to teach me? After all, my bee fit none of those categories.

"Perhaps there is a ninth pinion," she suggested quietly. "Perhaps you will show us what it represents."

By nightfall, we were through the mountain pass. We set up a ragged camp on the side of the mountain. I did not like how the shadows seemed darker and more alive than usual. My hand drifted often to my empty belt, longing for a weapon against the Forbidding. I could hear the hissing of our old enemy on the edges of my hearing, there but not there. Exhausted from constant vigilance and the hollow feeling of sadness, I clung to the bee, hoping some of its warmth and golden light would expel my fears, but they only grew greater as the darkness progressed.

I'd been told to spend the night in Zayana's tent and I sank gratefully under her spare blanket as she whispered to her bird in the dark.

"Sleep, my sweet Flame. Sleep and wake born anew. Wake as a strong and brave bird with bright eyes to see farther than my eyes can see. Wake to fly stronger than a bird your size could imagine. Wake to be so bound to me that you do not stray."

Her whispers carried on into the night and I found myself thinking about what Ivo had said. What goal did I have that would make this suffering worth it? What goal could be worth living for? I wanted to protect my family. But killing Juste Montpetit would not be enough to ensure their safety. Osprey had convinced me of that. Just being silent and compliant would not save them either. Zayana's predicament taught me that. In time, they would be killed by this heartless empire – just like my father and hers. Or they would be taxed into poverty. Or they would be rendered defenseless and overrun by the Forbidding.

What they needed was somewhere to be free. They could only be safe when they could make their own choices without a heartless empire deciding for them. When they could defend themselves from danger. When they could hold on to what they loved. But how could I give them that?

My longings mixed with the never-ending ache of my heart as my tears flowed down either side of my face and sank into the pallet.

Eventually, I fell into a troubled sleep and woke before dawn to the sound of someone whispering through the tent wall.

“Are you in there, girl?”

My eyes snapped open just in time to see a golden eagle crawl under the edge of the tent. It hissed at me, its huge talons clawing at the blanket.

I gasped as it hopped onto my chest, glaring down into my eyes, its razor-sharp, glowing beak as dangerous as any sword.

From the other side of the tent wall, Ivo said, “Oh good, you’re awake. Practice time.”

The eagle hopped off my chest and I rolled over, shaking from the encounter. I swallowed against a dry throat and snuck out of the tent, leaving Zayana asleep. I’d be envious of her sleep, except that I’d seen what her mentor did when she failed. At least the eagle hadn’t ripped my face apart.

Ivo caught me as I stumbled out of the tent, and pulled me along behind him. “Quiet, or you’ll wake the whole camp.”

“It’s not even dawn,” I said through a yawn.

“Shh.”

He hadn’t been kidding about not wanting to wake the camp. He pulled me through the darkness until the camp was so far away that I could barely see the glow of the campfires. A smaller fire was set here, and his small tent was pitched beside it.

I froze. What did he want with me all the way out here?

“Stop shrinking and check the kettle. We’ll both be wanting tea,” he said.

I relaxed a little as he produced a pair of battered tin mugs from the tent. The steaming kettle was on the rocks beside the fire. I carefully poured it into the cups he had ready, breathing in the clean scent of green tea with gratitude. It was the same kind my sister Adigale favored. Would I ever see her again?

"Did you find a purpose?" he asked quietly.

"Do you always wake your apprentices in the middle of the night?"

He snorted. "I do when I have to pretend to be uninterested in their success."

I froze with my mug halfway to my lips.

"Just the facts, girl," he said, shaking his head. "The only friends you can have right now are secret friends. The princeling wants you to fail. You represent everything that he hates – the independent minds of the outer reaches. The chance that they might rise up against him someday. Those bees."

"What about the bees?" I asked warily.

"Well, I'm guessing your people have to work hard to keep alive in a rocky land like this," he said, nodding with me. "Which means you probably don't spend a lot of time on poetry."

I nodded again.

"There's a poem that some think is a prophecy."

"And is it?"

"Well, that's the thing about words. They're powerful. Even if it's not a prophecy, if you say it like it is ... well, it might become one."

I sipped the tea, gathering my courage.

"Is the poem about me somehow? That seems a little far-fetched."

"You tell me," he said, and then his voice changed as he quoted it from memory.

"Slither, scale, bend, squeeze,

The dark tangles the land,

The blood of the brave freeze,

New conquerors come on the sand.

Soar, swoop, fly free,

The bird dives to the land,

The wing crosses the sea,

The bright leaves a brand.

Buzz, cluster, group, sting,

The bees drive back the rest,

The bells of freedom ring,

They conquer and they best."

I cleared my throat. "That sounds whimsical."

He laughed. "You think it's only a rhyme. Most do. But I do not."

"You think it's a prophecy. A prophecy about conquering and besting."

"Mmm." The sound committed to nothing. "What did you decide was worth suffering for?"

I looked at the tea, my stomach suddenly feeling queasy. The words tasted like acid on my tongue, but I said them anyway.

"The only way to protect my family is to give them a place to be free. But there are no places like that left."

"Which means?" he prompted. I looked up, searching his eyes. Hoping I'd judged him properly.

"That I must carve one."

"Hmmm." This time he sounded pleased. "That's good. You can live for that. Here's your next lesson. The closer you can get to the truth, the stronger your manifestation will become. Some people can't tell the truth. Not even close. It means their manifestations remain small. And even those who can get close to it have a hard time really speaking what is true. You think you do – but you don't. You can't believe the truth, so you don't tell it. Or it hurts. Or it's embarrassing. Or it changes you in ways you don't want to be changed. I don't expect you to tell the truth right away."

"Then why ask?" My voice was wry but he ignored me.

"Start by just refusing to lie. Learn what lies you tell yourself and stop telling them. Learn what is true and start to line your life up to that."

"What does that have to do with magic and freedom?"

"Everything," he said, sipping his tea. "The truth is the only power there is. It's the only way to ever be free."

His golden eagle sailed down in a circle around us, searing a bright gold against the black sky before settling behind him.

"I guess I should feel lucky that you swooped in out of nowhere to be my Guide," I said, testing him.

"I didn't come out of nowhere," he said. "If you think that then you aren't the intelligent girl I thought you were. I came because someone I trust sent for me."

"Osprey," I said.

"It's only because of him that you're alive."

I didn't answer that because I didn't know what to say. My thoughts about Osprey were tangled. He was both enemy and ally. Both hope and the obstacle to everything I wanted.

Ivo caressed the eagle and it preened delightedly as he whispered in its ear. I swallowed bitter tea. It was easy to imagine that a bird had thoughts and emotions, that it could understand you and grow and thrive. It was much harder to believe that bees could amount to anything at all.

I opened my hand and stared at the buzzing bee in my palm.

"I wish you had some sort of personality," I whispered to the bee. It felt so true that for once the taste in my mouth was as sweet as honey. "I wish you cared about the things I care about."

"That's a worrying invocation," Ivo said, not looking at me. "Sometimes the things we care about are the wrong things. Or we care too much."

"Do you care too much?" I asked, letting my mind rest on the buzz of the bee. At least it was steady. Nothing else about my life seemed steady right now.

"Absolutely," he said, his eyes meeting mine. "And so do you. And that's why we'll carve our freedom from the face of these rocks and challenge anyone to defy us. I have a vision of a wonderful land full of free, independent people speaking the truth and living life to the fullest. I can already imagine the banks of this place teeming with ships and boat, of hauls of fish being pulled into boats in the gleaming sun, of rolling farms and apple-scented orchards, of glowing smithies and the crash of industry. I can imagine a people swelling strong and proud in a place where each man and woman can walk with head held high and provide for their families. That's what I imagine. And it's what I'll see come to pass."

CHAPTER TWENTY-TWO

Maybe there was something more than herbs in that green tea because I felt more hopeful than I had before as I helped Ivo pack his things into his bag and then stumbled back into camp.

"Freedom," I whispered to the bee in my palm. I could almost believe that he swelled bigger.

The golden ball of the rising sun lit the silhouettes of the trees with bright silver as it reflected off the dew gathered overnight, and I let my heart feel hope for just a moment – hope tinged with deep regret. If only I'd known about my father being in the camp earlier. I might have been able to save him. If only I could fly to the sun and let it burn away all my regrets.

But I hadn't saved him. And now I could only see one way forward – I would carve out a place of freedom away from the Winged Empire. I'd make that poem into a prophecy. I'd do it with my bees.

"Relentless," I whispered to the bee. "We will be relentless."

It hummed happily to me.

I passed the ring of perimeter guards, sliding through the sleeping tents with ease. They kept a guard on the outside ring, but no guard at the tent of Juste Montpetit. How odd. There was just Counsellor Butiez sitting outside the tent writing at a collapsible travel desk, his brow furrowed in concentration.

I felt my feet drawing me toward the crown prince's tent before I realized I was making the decision to go.

Don't do it, Aella. This can't end well. Osprey said that if they caught you hurting him, they'd kill your whole family.

But I just needed to see him. He'd been slinking along in the group like he'd done nothing wrong, like he was a grand and glorious prince and not the horrific creature that had plunged a sword into my father's neck.

I swallowed. My heart was racing.

What would I do when I got there? Did it matter? Perhaps if his death looked like an accident, then no one would blame me and they wouldn't take revenge on my family. Or maybe it would just mean we had to carve out our freedom that much faster. We could deal with that when it happened. So, how did I kill him and make it look accidental?

And what would happen if I got in there and froze again, like when I tried to kill him last time? I gritted my teeth. I'd just been horrified at the idea of taking a life last time. I hadn't had tie to process what it would mean *not* to take it. Every day that the crown prince lived was another day that he brought suffering to others. Surely, that justified his death.

There had to be a way to do this and get away with it. Despite all my promises about carving out a new future, I just had to try.

If I went in ready to commit the act, I wouldn't hesitate. I just had to be ready. I clecnched my jaw harder, formed my hands into fists and took a deep breath. This time, I wouldn't hesitate.

I strode purposely past the counsellor, refusing to look at him in case my face gave me away. He didn't even look up as his pen scratched and scratched across the paper.

Made of black and white layered feathers, the tent was heavy and thick. That should disguise most of the noise – if I was careful. I parted the heavy feather- sewn canvas.

The moment the tent flap parted, my hand was on the hilt of my knife. I drew it in a single determined motion. Courage, Aella. Do not falter.

The inside of the tent was darker than I'd expected. After the bright light of morning, it was almost too much for my eyes to adjust, but I didn't dare hesitate. I blinked hard at the silhouette of a young man leaning over a chest at the foot of the bed. His head and arms were inside the chest as he rummaged through it, his back to me. He was shirtless, at ease in his own tent.

I could barely make him out in the darkness. I blinked hard, glancing quickly in either direction. Fancy furniture and trinkets filled the space with uncommon luxury, but there was no one else in the tent to stay my hand.

I didn't dare hesitate. I slipped across the layered rugs, my footsteps soundless, and at the last step I sprang toward him, wrapping my arm around his throat, knife positioned for the kill.

He was so fast he made lightning look slow. A crushing grip stopped my hand, clamping down so tightly that the knife dropped from my hand. I refused to gasp in surprise. I tried to pull my hand back but his hold on me was too powerful. My breath hitched in my throat as he thrust his hips back into mine, knocking my feet out from under me as he tugged my arm forward.

I flew through the air over his back and landed on the bed, the breath knocked out of me. I clutched at my throat but he was already scrambling on top of me, straddling me with one hand on my throat. He leaned in close with a growl and then startled as if he was surprised by my face.

"You're the biggest fool I've ever met and if you survive the week it will only be because every scrap of my energy has been devoted to attempting to keep your foolhardy head attached to your body."

My mouth fell open in shock. It was Osprey.

His toothpick bobbed angrily in his mouth as he pulled his hand from my neck and moved his hands to grip mine, pinning me to the bed.

"I thought you were Juste Montpetit," I breathed.

"Obviously," he whispered. "And obviously, you were fool enough to try to kill the crown prince after I've told you in every way possible that it's a bad idea. I told you I would stop you. I told you that your family would suffer. Are you merely a fool, or are you so arrogant that you think you can avoid the consequences and just kill a man and go on living your life?"

"I don't like feeling helpless."

"Murder is not the answer to that." I could feel his chest heaving against me.

"What are you going to do with me?"

"I told you that if you kept trying to bite me, I would bite you back," he warned.

I fought against his grip, freeing one hand and hitting him solidly in the face. Something crunched and he grunted but when my hand drew back it was only the toothpick that had shattered, leaving him with a bloody lip. He caught my hand and this time his grip was too tight to break no matter how hard I fought.

"I'm only trying to protect you from yourself," he whispered. "Why do you have to fight me?"

"You're going to report me to Juste Montpetit and then they're going to take my head. Don't you think I'd fight to prevent that?"

He shook his head. "I'm not going to do anything of the sort. Swear to me you won't seek him out to kill him again. Swear that you will *try* not to be such a violent wild tiger and *try* not to get yourself killed. What if it hadn't been me in this tent? What if it had been someone else? What if it had been one of the Claws – or worse, your intended victim? He's trained in combat, too, House Apidae. He would take you apart."

I was breathing too fast, my cheeks hot. I hadn't thought it through.

"You attacked me without even confirming I was the person you wanted to murder. What if you killed an innocent person? If I'd been a hair slower, you would have killed me."

I felt my eyes growing glassy but I clenched my jaw stubbornly.

"I didn't kill you," I said in a small voice.

He snorted. "I'm beginning to like you, you violent little thing, but you have to promise me that you won't get yourself killed on me before I can get you somewhere safe. Promise me."

I hesitated.

"Promise, or I will turn you in and let them drag you to Karkatua in a cage. We're a week out from that port city. Do you want to spend it like that?"

"I promise," I said reluctantly, my face hot with shame.

"Promise you won't seek out Le Majest again."

"I promise," I said, my voice so faint it was barely a whisper.

He sagged in relief, his forehead dipping down enough that it grazed my own. The scent of his sweat filled my nose. It was oddly nice smelling. Like autumn winds.

"Good," he gasped.

"You ask for a lot," I grumbled as he released my hands, letting me sit up.

I realized, suddenly, that I was on Le Majest's bed. In horror, I scrambled off of it, straightening the covers as Osprey stood, tending his bleeding lip. He slipped off a leather cuff wrapped around his wrist. It was sewn with osprey feathers.

He grabbed for my hand but I pulled back. He scoffed and grabbed for it again, faster and firmer this time. Quickly, but surprisingly gently, he tied the cuff around my arm.

"I've asked for a lot. Here's something I'm giving in return. My cuff. And with it you have my promise that I will do everything I can to try to keep you alive, only please stop tempting fate. Please, stop biting at me at every turn. Fighting together means trusting each other."

I swallowed and nodded, tucking the cuff under the edge of my shirt.

There was a sound at the edge of the tent and he stepped back and to the side so suddenly that I gasped. He shuffled at some papers at the desk as Counsellor Butiez stepped into the tent.

"What's going on in here?" he asked, looking around.

"The Hatchling is going to deliver some pigeon messages to Essana for Le Majest," Osprey said quickly.

"All of the crown prince's correspondence goes through me," Butiez said suspiciously. "He left no word of a message going through you. You should not take liberties just because of your recent promotion."

"This message is private," Osprey said shortly, handing me a scrap of paper. "See that Wing Essana gets this immediately Hatchling."

"I demand to see the message," Counsellor Butiez said, suddenly red in the face.

"You demand?" Osprey asked, lifting an eyebrow. "That's not good. First the crown prince chooses to divert a message from your sight and then you start making demands? I heard it was the same with

Counsellor Swares before he slipped on those stairs outside Kestrel City. Did you attend his funeral?"

Even in the low light of the tent, Butiez seemed to pale. He licked his lips. "If the Hatchling is delivering messages, then I have some of my own to send with her. Some that you know nothing about."

"Really?" Osprey challenged.

I watched him cross his arms, clearly provoking the Counsellor.

"Follow me, Hatchling," the Counsellor said grandly, sweeping out of the tent. I glanced at Osprey, surprised by his wink and then hurried after the counsellor.

I should remember in the future what a smooth manipulator Osprey was. I certainly couldn't have gotten rid of the counsellor and his questions so easily.

We exited the tent and he scurried to the desk, pushing a handful of paper rolls at me.

"Take the whole lot to Wing Essana. Immediately."

He was already back to writing while I was trying to put them in order, still stunned by the quick turn in events. They were addressed to various locations, but one caught my attention. I scrambled to hide behind the crown prince's tent, fumbling at the tight paper roll to open it enough to read what was written.

It was addressed to Far Reach.

It said:

Shrike killed. Find his family. Eliminate them all. C.B.

CHAPTER TWENTY-THREE

My heart was pounding so hard that I couldn't control it. And now my vision narrowed as red filled it.

No.

I couldn't let them send this.

I shoved the roll of paper into my mouth and chewed it up, then spat it out, crushed the paper into the ground with my heel, and kicked dirt over it.

Okay. No message. That meant no killing my family, right?

But that would only last until tonight or tomorrow, when they'd wonder why there was no reply to the message. So that meant one thing.

I needed to act.

I needed to get home and get to my family in time to warn them. I shoved my thumb into my mouth, chewing it slightly.

By chance, I'd stumbled on this in time to do something about it. I could make my family safe.

But I had to be smart.

And I had to stop lying to myself. Osprey was right – as much as I hated admitting that. And Ivo was right, too. If I had acted and tried to killed the crown prince, my family would already be dead just like my father was. I needed a different plan.

First, I needed to make my own note to send in the place of this one. A note telling the Claws to withdraw out of Far Reach. That should buy a little time. Then I could escape when no one was watching and race back there to warn my siblings. But how could I be fast enough? I was not Osprey, who could ride a bird. And these carabaos, while acceptable pack animals, had no speed. I couldn't do it quickly enough.

I looked down at my bee.

If only you were a bird, little bee. Then I could fly on your back to get to my family.

Wait. *I* didn't need to get there. I needed to send a message to them. And a bee could do that, too. Couldn't it? Bees traveled miles and miles. My father had told me that.

I frowned. But could *my* bee travel like that?

There was only one way to find out. I hurried through the camp, looking for Wing Xectare's tent. I knew she had that little desk, and that meant paper and pens. But how would I get in? How would I get access to her desk?

I could pretend I was sent to help her pack.

I pushed down a burst of nerves and approached the entrance.

"Wing Xectare?" I called.

"Enter."

"I'm here to help pack your things," I said meekly, hands thrust behind my back. I'd forgotten to hide the messages.

She nodded with a pleased smile. "At least Ivo is good for something. Start with the linens. They go in that chest."

I hurried to her pallet, carefully gathering and folding blankets and watching her from the corner of my eye. Oh no. She was packing her own desk. I watched as she stoppered the ink bottle and stashed the pens into a tiny drawer on the side. No, no, no! I needed to get her out of here.

My mind raced. What would get her out of the tent? What did she care about?

"I thought I saw Osprey talking with Zayana," I said with a smile. "It must be nice that all Wings can be friends."

Her face froze. "You saw her talking to who?"

"Just Osprey," I said innocently. "I bet he knows so much about how to manage a bird."

She cursed and her grand swan leapt from his perch, shooting out of the tent. "Have this cleared before I get back."

She practically sprinted after the bird. The moment she was gone I hurried to her desk, opened the drawer, and drew the stoppered ink and pen out again. I unrolled the parchment Osprey had given to me.

It had nothing but a scrawl on it that looked like a single wing. I ripped the wing off from the rest and then stretched out the clean scrap of parchment with trembling hands, shaking as I tried to ape Counsellor Butiez's hand.

All Claws return across pass to Astar Harbor. Abandon Far Reach. Leave prisoners behind. C. B.

That should do it, right? I rolled the paper up to look like the others and shoved them all in my pocket.

I could hear voices outside my door. I had to be quick. And I had to write as small as I could. How big of a parchment could a bee carry? It couldn't be large.

I bit the corner of my lip and did my best on the back of the scrap with the single wing scrawled on it.

They want you dead. Run. Aella

Any more and it wouldn't fit. I rolled the message tight and put it in my other pocket, scrambling to return the pen and ink to the desk.

Just in time.

The tent opened and Zayana strode inside. She was bristling.

"You're not even close to done. And Wing Xectare is in a mood. Where were you? I had to do our tent myself and she's only given me five minutes to finish hers."

"Five minutes?" I asked, feigning horror as I collapsed the traveling desk and folded it carefully with the wing nuts made to lock the legs in place. It was a clever invention. Yet another luxury from over the ocean that we would never see here.

Zayana shot me a suspicious look. "Did you say something to her about Osprey?"

"Can I ask you a question?" I needed to head her off. I'd used her as a distraction and now I needed a distraction for her. "What is the significance of the bird that manifests? Like, why do you have a red bird and Xectare has a swan?"

She huffed. "It's not a red bird, it's a cardinal. Cardinals are royal birds, sweet of song, social, dominant and aggressive."

It was like she was describing herself. I hurried to fold the writing chair and swan stand. Half the camp was destroyed from the Forbidding incident but Xectare still had her traveling treasures.

"The swan is stately, violent, and territorial," Zayana said. "There are theories that the bird that Hatches reflects the Wing who it Hatches for. Which makes sense. Other theories say that you call to yourself what you most need. And still others say that you're so imprinted on your house that you always call your house bird."

"Does it matter what bird it is, then?" I asked, rolling up the rug while she tucked the linens and clothing into the large chest.

"Of course," she said, happy now that she was lecturing. Her red cardinal rode on her shoulder, bathing her face in scarlet light. "All birds grant their manifestor better eyesight – though some birds – like Osprey's give added benefits there. Did you know he can see through the water to what lies beneath? That's handy by the ocean. He saw wrecks along our way and kept us from shoals more than once."

I hadn't realized they had traveled over the ocean together. Why did that make me feel like I'd missed out?

The rug had a loose thread almost as long as my hand. I plucked it free, stowing it in my pocket. I could use it to tie the little message.

"Other birds are amazing at long distant travel and can offer their manifestor eyes for miles around. That stamina often instills itself in the manifestor, making them also more enduring. Still others are powerful, mighty in battle. They make their manifestor stronger, or faster. Some confer agility. Others imperviousness to wet or cold. My cardinal is a songbird. Songbirds confer artistic abilities."

"That's pretty amazing," I said as we hurried out of the tent and pulled up the pegs. "What kind of artistic abilities?"

She blushed as I met her eyes. "Dance and song."

I smiled with her and together we hurried to load the tent and interior items into the cart. We were going to make the five minute deadline, which was handy since Xectare was standing there, tapping a foot and watching us.

"At least your conversation has been productive," she said coldly. "You may walk together today and guide this cart. It will be another long day and we hope it will end in a village. Perhaps we will be lucky."

She turned to walk away, but I spoke quickly. "Wing Xectare?"

Her eyes narrowed as she looked back at me.

"I have message rolls to give Wing Essana from Counsellor Butiez."

She frowned. “Hand them to me. I will deliver them to her. Wing Essana has work with the crown prince today and I think it would be best for all of us to keep you far from him. Until you produce a bird manifestation, you are an embarrassment to us.”

“Yes, Wing Xectare,” I said politely, handing her the rolls of messages. My forgery was lost among the rest and with Wing Xectare delivering them, no one would be suspicious. I hid a smile as she took them away.

“Tell me more about these special skills,” I said to Zayana, but my heart was in my throat. Step one was complete. Now I just needed to figure out how to tie a tiny scroll to a spirit bee and convince it to fly to my family.

EARLIER IN THE WINGED EMPIRE

"Promise me that if you hatch, you won't let them hurt Father," her sister whispered, curled up against her like a sleepy puppy. Dala was just six and her shining brass skin was tinted pink in the cheeks.

Zayana blinked back tears. Hatching was an honor. Every family hoped they would have one child to Hatch. Her own father had given her an emerald cloud-silk dress only last night with golden flares where the sleeves met the shoulders.

"I'm proud of you," he said. The first time he'd ever said those words. "If you hatch tomorrow, I will be honored to die for such a great legacy."

She'd had to fight hard to hold back her tears. There had been three roses on the bush behind his head, framed with golden halos as the sun set behind them. An auspicious sign.

"As you request, so I will obey, Father," she'd said instead, and he had smiled.

But if it happened, Dala would miss them both. Being raised at the Winged Court by another lady or lord would not be the same as living with family. Zayana kissed her forehead gently.

"I will do all I can, sweet flame."

CHAPTER TWENTY-FOUR

We stopped for a rest break an hour into the morning journey. At the front of the line, voices were raised with concern. I took that opportunity to slip into the bushes.

I had only a few minutes before Zayana might be suspicious. Just long enough to blow on my palm and summon the little bee.

"Hi little bee," I said gently. "Can you hold still so I can tie this message to you?"

I had it ready, the string wrapped around the tiny tube. I tried to grab the bee, but it darted away. Dust-kissing thing.

Tried again.

Again, it buzzed out of my grasp.

Frustrated, I puffed air out of my bottom lip, blowing stray curls out of my face.

"Please," I begged it. "Please hold still. I need a messenger to warn my family – my swarm, I guess you'd call it. Don't bees send messages? I thought my father said they made messages with some kind of dance."

The bee stilled, landing on my knee. I held my breath as I slowly reached down and oh so gently tied the little message to its thorax with a string.

"Courage," I whispered. "Courage and endurance. Go warn our swarm."

It sat there, still.

"Aella?" I heard Zayana call.

"Please," I whispered. "Can you find my family with that message? Can you go back to Far Reach where you first Hatched? They live near there. I need you to be strong. I need you to be everything we are – devoted, committed, dedicated to our swarm, okay? Be courageous. Be enduring."

My eyes pricked with tears as I tried so hard to use my words to invoke what I desperately needed. I shoved all those emotions into a single word. "Please."

"Aella? Are you lost?" Zayana was so close she was almost on top of me.

"Just relieving myself," I gasped, trying to buy another minute.

"You've been gone a while. Are you ill?"

"Just one more moment," I called and then turned back to the little bee. "Please. Please help me."

A tear of frustration leaked from my eye, splashing over the little fellow. He shook himself, but he hovered upward, circled me once, and then shot off over the rocky slopes like an arrow shot from a bow.

My belly knotted and clenched. I felt like I might be sick. All I could do was hope that he was fast enough. That he could get there in time. He would be well behind the pigeons – but hopefully fast enough that he'd get to my family before the pigeon could return with a second message to the Claws there.

I stood up.

Zayana was right in front of me, her arms crossed over her fancy court dress, her red bird perching on her shoulder. The bird's head tilted from side to side as it watched me, as if it suspected.

"Where's your bee?" she asked, her earth-brown eyes narrowing.

I felt my face growing hot as I lied. "It vanished."

"I guess that might be better. The Wings want you to manifest a bird. Maybe you have to stop manifesting bees first."

I nodded as if I agreed. But I did *not* agree. My bees might not be beautiful or flashy like the birds, but they were loyal and determined. Just like me. I was starting to think they might be the better choice for me.

"Why have we stopped?"

"I don't know." She looked as worried as I was. "Let's see if we can find out."

We pressed through the bushes and back to the pass. We hurried along past the stopped carabaos until we reached a place where the rock narrowed sharply and then widened, sloping downward to show the valley below.

It should have been pine forests in clumps surrounded by tumbled rocks and clay fields. I remembered that from one of the few times I'd been here before. And from here, we should see the small town located at the bottom of the pass where the Forbidding River ran, widening over the plain.

Instead, the Forbidding swelled out over the landscape, tangling it in creeping darkness and twisting wisps. I would never get used to how it made the landscape curl over itself as if the land was made of snakes that could be woven together or spiraled around. Grass grew on shreds of reality that made it seem to hang upside down and flowers were woven through with sky. On the edges of the twisted mass, trees and rocks unfurled at the edges, coming alive as they grasped for more land to Forbid.

I gasped when my eyes reached the point where the town of Far Forest should have been. The town was gone. Lost to the Forbidding. My heart went cold inside me.

All those people.

Gone.

"Did you go through Far Forest on your way to Far Reach?" I asked Zayana quietly.

"Of course," she whispered back.

In front of us, the Wings were arguing with the Crown Prince.

"We don't know that for sure. It would be better to go back and wait until we receive word that the Claw Divisions can come and clear the road," Wing Xectare was saying.

"We don't have enough Claws here to fight, Le Majest," the grizzled leader of the Swan Claws said firmly. His fancy blue jacket had a torn sleeve – probably from the battle two nights ago. "Your royal safety is our top concern and we will not risk you."

"I won't be confined to a backwater village," Juste Montpetit said smoothly. "I'm sure our great Claws and Wings can manage this. Even if we have to push off the road a little into the trees. Or is it too much to ask you to walk through a little mud for the sake of the Winged Empire?"

The road was entirely lost to the Forbidding where it met the town and the river. The dark magic crept up and down the road as if it found it easier to travel where men had been. We would reach the edge of it in hours if we stayed on this road.

"Did you disarm the citizenry on your way through this town?" I whispered to Zayana.

She looked down, refusing to meet my eyes.

"Did you?"

She nodded silently and I cursed. It wasn't hard to guess what had happened here. The people had their arms seized. And when the Forbidding came, they had no way to defend themselves. Just like my family would if I didn't find a way to free them.

"We'll leave the carts here," the crown prince said decisively. "And ride the carabaos down the road, skirting the edge of this indigenous magic. I'm sure we'll come out on the other side and find the road there is clear."

"The other side of what?" Wing Xectare asked frostily. "The river? The only bridge is in that tangled mess. We have no hope of crossing during the spring swell."

"Osprey will ferry us over one by one," the crown prince said, his eyes narrowing. "And perhaps you other Wings can think of how to make your birds strong enough to do likewise. You serve the people. And it's time to show that service."

"We can't," Xectare gasped. "Our birds could not bear the load."

He simply looked at her.

"You serve the people. It's time to show that service."

Did he always repeat meaningless statements when he had no answer? I felt my teeth setting on edge as he spoke.

The Claw leader's jaw clenched but he made the sign of the bird and stepped back in acquiescence.

And where were Ivo and Osprey?

I looked around, finally looking upward instead.

They stood on opposite rocky ledges on the mountain slope to either side of the pass, their eyes shaded as they looked into the distance. With concentration, I picked out their birds far in the distance, surveying the Forbidding ahead.

I frowned. It was all well and good to talk about peace and the defense of the Claws for the Empire, but now they were all seeing how things really were on the fringes of the Empire. Without weapons, the Forbidding took everything from us. And there was no way around what it took. You could only claim it back in battle and sweat.

"Unload the carts. Take only the essentials. We will leave at once," Juste Montpetit ordered.

"Le Majest," the leader of the Claws spoke, his head bent low, "the armaments we seized are in the carts."

Juste Monpetit's lips compressed, but he said nothing.

"Forgive me, Le Majest," the Claw said, kneeling to the ground.

"Do not question the ruling of Le Majest," the crown prince said, and I shivered.

But I couldn't help the spike of hope I felt. We would be leaving weapons behind us. And if I could get word of that to my brothers, they could arm themselves again.

Maybe that little bee of mine would be worth his weight in Imperial gold after all.

CHAPTER TWENTY-FIVE

Zayana and I were tasked with sorting through the items belonging to the Wings. We were just beginning the task as Osprey and Ivo dropped down to our cart.

Osprey paused, worry etched into his expression. He looked both ways before leaning in close.

“Don’t seek him out. Remember your promise to me,” he said, eyes flashing.

I nodded.

“Seriously, House Apidae. I can’t fight this Forbidding and also keep you from being a fool.”

“And I can’t fight it and also teach you how to mind your own business.”

Osprey’s expression set into his usual mix of exasperation and tight self-control. If getting under his skin was a gift, I might be the most gifted person in the Far Stones.

Ivo whistled sharply and Osprey shook his head as if there was more he wanted to say. But he only spun, snatching up his pack and leapt onto the back of his bird. It shrieked at me and launched up into the sky.

Ivo snatched his own pack up with a frown for me. "I've been sent to scout ahead. I'll be back as soon as I can to check on you. Stay with the group. Don't try to be a hero again. Just because you've fought this stuff before doesn't make you a veteran."

He mounted his golden eagle and with a cry of, "Up, Harpy!" he burst up into the sky.

I watched them with fire in my eyes and one hand on my hip, feeling the cuff he'd given me with the other hand. Were they serious? They both said, *Oh Aella, you should join our little revolution*, but then the minute trouble came they were off in the air and I was left down here in a sea of enemies ... and Zayana.

I was starting to really like her.

"You should hide that cuff," she said, rolling her eyes. "He's a fool to give it to you and you're a fool to take it."

"It's only a cuff," I said, slipping the heavy leather onto my wrist and tucking it under my jacket sleeve. "And how do you know who it's from?"

She shook her head, unconvinced, and turned back to packing. What could a cuff mean? And why did it make me feel special to have been given it? I gave a little shiver and got back to work, but the weight of the cuff on my wrist felt oddly comforting as if a piece of that confusing man was here guarding me.

"How exactly are we supposed to strap a writing desk, a Ellovian Bird Perch and a folding chair to the back of a carabao along with her bedding and clothes?" Zayana asked me as we tried to load Wing Xectare's carabao.

The creature snorted at us, rolling its huge eyes and waving its horns threateningly.

"Do you have a sword?" I whispered, looking around to make sure no one was watching. I was much less worried about how to pack than I was about the Forbidding encroachment. I'd heard of the Forbidding swallowing farms, and once it swallowed a town, too. But the people had fled long before the town was taken. This time, I didn't think they'd had the chance.

"Obviously not," she said, but she paused in trying to stuff more clothes into the saddlebags and eyed me with curiosity rather than judgment.

"Did you have to fight the Forbidding on your way here?" I pressed.

"No. I can't believe you live near that awful stuff all the time. It doesn't look right. It gives me a headache just glancing at it. The world is supposed to operate with the ground on the bottom and the sky at the top, but apparently, no one told you people in Far Stones that."

"It's magic," I said, winding twine around the writing desk, folding chair, and perch to bind them all together. It was awkward and ridiculous, but I'd try to tie it so a single knife slice could set them free in case Xectare realized how much a load like this endangered her if she had to gallop. "But that doesn't mean you can't fight it. It doesn't like steel. Steel sets things right. It invokes something true that restores things touched by the tangle of the Forbidding. And it hates fire. Fire cuts it off at the core."

"Interesting," Zayana said. "We don't have Forbidding on the mainland or any of the islands."

"We need to get swords from the cart of weapons the Claws confiscated," I whispered. "That way we can defend ourselves."

"Ridiculous," she said, shaking her head. "They'd take our hands for stealing those. And I don't need a weapon. I have my bird."

"Are Cardinals great at fending off twisting Forbidding magic?" I asked wryly as I finished strapping the desk bundle to one side of the carabao. It stepped sideways as if trying to avoid the rub of the wood and twine against its hindquarter.

Zayana frowned. "Don't get smart with me. Just because he didn't do well in the last attack, it doesn't mean he'll fail next time, right Flame? And just because you grew up on this awful jumble of rocks and dark magic doesn't mean you can tempt me into crimes. If we steal swords, we can't hide them. The Wings will notice immediately and I'll be thrashed. They might even kill you, Aella." She looked over her shoulder before whispering, "The crown prince is not known for his patience."

"Did you see the town?" I hissed back. "Losing a hand is a big risk. Losing your life is worse."

She shivered. "I'm hoping to avoid losing my life, but there is no way that I'll steal a sword. And if you have half a brain, you won't either."

Frustration bubbled up inside me and I fought it back. I liked Zayana. But why was she so quick to submit to these ridiculous rules?

Was it just fear of punishment? Part of me shied away from the idea of losing a hand. She was right that we could easily be caught. But I had a long cloak. If I was careful, I could hide a scabbard. And it could mean the difference between life and death.

We finished with Xectare's carabao and moved to Wing Essana's cart. She was there, opening the doors of all her little wicker cages with a sad expression as her owl watched hungrily. Her pigeons flew out into the sky, heading south to the sea.

"It will be hard to ride without information," she said with a sigh. "These are my eyes and ears in this backward land."

"Backward?" I asked, but it was to try to disguise the smile flickering on the edges of my lips. Without birds, she couldn't find out that I'd sent a forged message. This was good news.

"On the continent," she said, "we have Imperial Towers. Wings with small birds send out their bird to a nearby tower to deliver the message and it follows from tower to tower in a condensed code. I can get a message from one end of the Empire to the other in a matter of hours. It's a magic of its own."

She sighed again and I tried not to look impressed – or afraid. It must be hard to move against the Empire in a world where a message could be delivered so quickly. We should set up something like that here – but we didn't have enough Wings to manage it.

"Finish loading the carabao with the rest," she said, gliding away. "Le Majest is in a hurry."

I joined Zayana beside the stinky carabao. It huffed loudly, rolling an eye at us. I still wasn't used to how easily the others behaved around the horned cattle. They looked like they could split you in half just by nodding their heads the wrong way.

She was stuffing clothing and bedding into the saddlebags and tying the tent behind the saddle. She was leaving behind rugs and porcelain dishes, a mirror clear as a still lake, and a porcelain washbasin like the one the Claws had broken at my home. I looked over her treasures, shaking my head. Imagine being so wealthy that you could just leave all this behind?

"At least she didn't bring anything too valuable with her," Zayana said as she worked. My jaw dropped open and she frowned as she looked at me. "Are you okay?"

Of course I was okay. I was just horrified at the excesses of the people who tread us down under their boots. These things were worth more than all the furnishings in my home. More than ever, I needed that sword. People who didn't understand what wealth was couldn't be trusted to have any sense at all.

"I'll be right back," I said, ignoring her hissed protests and whisper-shouts as I hurried away. I stayed close to the carabaos that were being lined up along the road. Which cart would have the swords?

My frustration grew as I hurried along. They lived a life of luxury and yet they took our means to defend what little we had.

A buzz began in my head.

I paused, feeling it tingle down to my palms.

A golden light blinked into existence, followed by a second.

Two bees sat in my left palm.

"Two of you," I whispered in shock. "Be quiet, be quick."

I followed my own mantra as I slipped between the carabaos.

The cart that had contained my father was covered now. I took a quick peek behind the canvas and recoiled in horror at the smell. There had been no chance to wash it, and the remains of what they'd done were still there. I shuddered and tried not to think about what had been done to my father in that covered cart.

Still gagging, I stumbled to the next one. It was left behind the line of carabaos with a second covered cart, wedged up behind a huge rock.

I slipped toward the nearest one, hiding on the far side of it as I lifted the canvas cover and peaked beneath it. Weapons by the hundreds filled the cart. I snatched up a short sword the length of a man's forearm. It was in a scabbard. Good.

Quickly, I buckled it around my hips, covering the bulge with my cloak. I needed to sneak back the way I came.

But something else caught my eye.

In the bottom of the cart, a small necklace lay. It was strung with a curious type of delicate bead. No, not beads, I realized. Claws. Small bird claws like from a songbird.

Swallowing, I snatched it, throwing it over my neck and hiding it under the neck of my shirt. If they had stolen it, then maybe it was a weapon, too.

I tucked the canvas back in place and hurried around the side of the wagon.

“Aella?” Zayana gasped as I nearly ran into her. “You’re crazy.”

I was about to disagree when the screams started.

Again.

CHAPTER TWENTY-SIX

Zayana's eyes went wide. "What should we do?"

Her little bird leapt from her palm, flying protective circles around her. It dove at me aggressively and I batted it away.

"Hey! Don't hurt him," she said as she grabbed my arm. "Come on."

"Why are you dragging me when you don't even know what to do?" I asked.

I knew what *I* wanted to do. I wanted to slink into the shadows and wait there until the screaming died down and everyone thought I'd been lost to whatever horror was attacking.

But if I did that, I'd lose my chance at this grand plan that Osprey and Ivo had invited me into. I'd lose my chance to protect my family and get my vengeance on Juste Montpetit. I took a deep breath.

"Come on," I said, pulling her along "Stick behind me."

"Why?"

I ignored her question, keeping my cloak close so that she wouldn't see I was hiding the sword. I'd need it if the Forbidding had crawled up this high into the mountains. The carabaos ahead of us had disappeared and I heard an animal scream break out ahead.

"Where did they all go?" Zayana sounded nervous now. "All the carabaos? I only left them for a moment."

I looked around us, watching for the telltale sign of the Forbidding – that way the light bent on the edge of your vision. I didn't see it yet, but dark clouds had swarmed in, seemingly out of nowhere. They blocked the sun, making everything darker.

My stomach dipped. But if the Forbidding was here, then it was as dangerous to stay in one place as it was to go onward. I strode forward, letting the buzz of the bees bolster my courage as I followed the trampled carabao trail out the narrow gap of mountain pass so I could look down on the land below.

Forbidding take it.

This was not good.

Just past the opening through the mountain pass, a carabao struggled in the grip of a piece of ribboned sky. It tangled around the screaming animal like the heads of snakes, if the heads of snakes were perfectly painted to look like a cloudy sky and then fitted to reach down from the actual sky and pluck a carabao from the ground. Other ribbons reached out from where the creature screamed, spiraling outward as they stretched toward us.

I drew the sword, taking a quick look to make sure that nothing was edging in from right beside us.

A stream of curses tumbled through my brain – the only reasonable response to what I was seeing. Zayana gripped my arm in the vice of her hand.

"Look. They're abandoning us."

Past the carabao, the rest of the group were fleeing. The Wings and the Crown Prince and his advisor were all mounted. Some of the Claws rode snorting carabaos. Others ran beside the carabaos, desperately trying to leap up onto their backs as they ran.

I watched in horror as one of the Claws fell under the feet of the carabao he was trying to mount. He was left in a tangled heap behind the carabao. He didn't even twitch.

The tentacles of the Forbidding reached out toward the fleeing Claws, stretching out with such speed that they swallowed up oaks and pines and little glens as fast as I could breathe in and out.

Wing Xectare's swan expanded its full wings, rearing up to snap at a knot of Forbidding at the same moment that it struck toward her. The swan's beak gripped a tangle of reaching grass, ripping it as Wing Xectare rode free.

The Crown Prince ducked beside her and her Swan reared up to knock a second ribbon aside with the power of its magic wings.

My heart was in my throat as Wing Essana looked back at us, her eyes widening with horror as she realized we'd been left behind, but it was too late to turn around. Her carabao plummeted forward, screaming and trumpeting with the rest, and her owl soared above them in loops. Was it searching for a way of escape?

The buzz of my bees was louder as they looped around and around me. There were four now. I didn't know how I knew that, but I did.

"We should go back," I gasped to Zayana as a thick piece of ground erupted ahead of our fleeing party, spattering them with soil and small stones as it surged upward like a giant wave and began to curl up over their heads. The Forbidding was here. We couldn't fight a manifestation this big. We could only flee.

There was no sign of Osprey or Ivo in the sky. Could they have really have gone that far already?

I spun in place and Zayana spun with me, her hands gripping my arm so tightly that I thought she might rip it off. My heart was in my throat. I'd never seen the Forbidding act like this before.

A ribbon of Forbidding reached out of the rocks toward us, spreading between the high walls of rock that formed the narrow gap leading into the pass. It spun, twisting as it lanced toward us between the rocks, filling the carabao trail through the last gap of the pass. There would be no going back the way we'd come.

"Forbidding take it." I cursed.

I shut my jaw with a snap, realizing it already had. I drew my sword, holding the steel out in front of us protectively. Steel could bite it. I had to remember that.

I swiped at the Forbidding ribbon with my short sword, cutting off the edge of it, and then pried Zayana's hand from my arm, moved it to my free hand, and dragged her after me into the valley below, staying close to the edge of the rock face leading out of the pass. The Forbidding was right behind us and fast as I scrambled over the loose shale, I knew we couldn't run fast enough. Suddenly, riding a carabao with the others didn't seem like the worst idea.

CHAPTER TWENTY-SEVEN

We scrambled down the rocky hills.

"It's like the land has come to life and it wants to eat us," Zayana cried.

"That's exactly what it's like," I said, pulling her off the road and along the rocky crags that stuck out at the bottom of the cliff walls. "We'll stay off the road. It seems to be able to travel faster up the roads than on the regular turf."

"It's awful. I can feel that it wants to hurt me. My bird can feel it, too," she said, her voice quavering.

"I bet there's nothing like it in the rest of the Winged Empire," I agreed. "But that's the thing. The settlers here had to carve their way into the land by fighting the Forbidding. And we keep it down with swords and halberds. Fire is best of all. But you can't start a fire in it unless you can get in close and that's why we need our weapons."

"I wouldn't have believed this," she said through chattering teeth. "It was all Wing Xectare could do to keep it off of them back there. And her bird is powerful."

We'd lost sight of the fleeing party and the road as we hurried, following the cliff faces that lined the mountains, weaving between the huge fallen boulders wreathing their base. Faint screams still left us shivering, but I led Zayana deeper into the tumbled rocks toward where the pines stood straight and tall.

A ribbon of Forbidding reached out for us as we stepped down into a gully.

Zayana's scream echoed out through the forest as I drew the short sword and lunged, swiping at it. I cut off the end of the tentacle easily, but three more darted out at us from where the first had been.

I ducked under the waving ribbon, slashing upward to try to keep it off my head and shoulders. The scent of pine filled the air as I cut into the twisting mass.

A tendril of Forbidding slashed out and it was all I could do to turn it aside. Before I had finished the inelegant parry, a second ribbon shot down from above. I dodged to the side, feet quick. Not quick enough. It slid down my arm, slicing through cloak and coat and flesh.

I gasped as hot agony ripped through me, searing my arm and leaving me shaking in the wake of the wound, but I didn't dare pause.

Come on, you tangled mess. Give a little.

A buzz from beside me distracted me for just a moment and then my tiny swarm of shining bees shot out in front of me, distracting the guarding ribbon. It struck toward them, but they hurtled away in a spiral, leading the tentacle away from me. The tentacle tried again, but the targets were small and fast, they spread out, avoiding the strike.

Gratitude surged within me as I darted toward the trunk of the tree. Catch a bird being so useful. Bees were too hard to easily hit, breaking from their swarm and then joining again as they led attention away from me.

I reached the trunk of the tree, skidding across the thick layer of dead needles drifting up in a pile around the trunk. They were bone dry. Perfect. I gasped sharply at the pain that flared through my arm. The spark caught, but the flame was inconstant, burning too quickly through the needles in the harsh wind whipping around us, and spiraling the flames upward in little gusts that made them appear to be tiny fire demons grasping for me.

Cursing as the flames blew out, I tried again.

Something knocked me from behind, sweeping me off my feet. I tumbled through the needles, gasping for breath, and rolled, popping back up to my feet with sword ready. My leg stung but it held my weight as I tried to catch my breath.

An arm of Forbidding swept toward me for a second strike. I danced to the side, parrying.

This tangle of Forbidding was putting up quite the fight. I thought longingly of my brother Alect. If only I had him at my back. We could have taken down this tangle if we were here together.

I swiped again, but a shriek at my shoulder made me duck in response.

Just in time.

A band of Forbidding whistled over my head. Behind it, a little red bird screamed and struck.

Maybe birds weren't so bad after all.

I jabbed the branches with my brand again, and this time something caught fire. Not perfect, but it would do.

I leapt back, spinning, and ran away from the tree. The red bird shot out in front of me, followed by my bees. I brought up the rear.

At least they were all okay.

Two steps and I felt myself begin to slow. Another step and I stumbled.

Blackness danced before me.

Hands grabbed my shoulders, dragging me in between curses to a dancing fire.

"Don't you dare pass out, Aella. I didn't use up all the strength of my bird to save you just so you could faint and leave me to do all the work, do you hear?"

Just like an Imperial lady. Always shirking work.

I heard a creak and I spun again, raising my sword as the dark ribbons rose in a cluster together, splitting in six different directions and shooting toward me.

I attacked in a flurry, but I couldn't catch every tentacle. Behind me I heard a scream and before I could get to her, Zayana crumpled on the ground. I rushed to her, straddling her fallen body, sword ready. Her bird flickered out of existence as she lost consciousness.

Forbidding take it. My heart pounded so hard I thought it might fly from my chest.

This was it.

The end.

I couldn't hope to carry her away and I wasn't fast enough to battle six arms of Forbidding at once. Darkness flickered over my vision as I wavered above her, fighting the pain in my arm, gasping for breath.

I wished I could see my family just one more time. Alect. Raquella. Anfrea. Oska.

A purplish-white flash of light seared my vision.

Osprey?

CHAPTER TWENTY-EIGHT

He was in front of me so suddenly that I gasped. His coat was torn and dirty and there was a trickle of blood running down his hand from a dark stain on his sleeve. He drew his double swords, moving with the grace of a dancer as he wove in and out, around and under the grasping tentacles, slashing and hacking. His bird fought with him, soaring over us like a mighty sentinel. His bright wings cupped the air, talons extended as he dove and dove, ripping at the sudden burst of Forbidding.

"You fool," I heard a voice yell from behind me. Ivo rushed through the tangle of Forbidding, one arm slung over the back of his golden eagle as he half- ran, half was carried by the magic. It might not be strong enough to carry him completely, but he moved as quickly over the ground as someone mounted might.

Osprey spun to meet his challenge, eyes wild and mouth forming a grim line around that ever-present toothpick.

"You have an opinion to offer, Wing Ivo?" he asked formally, one sword snapping out and catching a string of Forbidding as it tried to snake around him. His gaze never left Ivo even as he struck. His chest was heaving, arms flexing in the height of battle rage.

"My decided opinion is that there was a reason you called me here," Ivo said as he joined us. A tentacle of Forbidding reached for him and he hacked it off with more vigor that necessary. "That opinion being that if Le Majest realizes that you are sheltering this Hatchling, you will pay a price your soul cannot bear. Was I wrong about that, Osprey?"

"Forbidding take it!"

My bees buzzed around me as Osprey danced to the side, his double blades twin flurries as he took out his wrath on the nearby threat.

"Wing Ivo?" I interupted as he took a step toward Osprey with narrowed eyes. "Can you help Zayana? She's hurt."

Ivo paused, looking down at my friend.

He clicked his tongue and nodded. "Help me get her on Harpy. He's not that fast under a load, but he's strong enough to carry her to safety. Hurry, now!"

I helped him lift her onto the back of his bird. The bird seemed to almost cup her with his wings so that she wouldn't fall.

"Osprey!" Ivo called. He cursed when the younger man ignored him, striding out to where Osprey fought the crawling Forbidding and grabbing him by the collar. He was almost skewered by one of Osprey's darting blades, but he didn't seem to care as he pulled the other man close to him. "Osprey!"

"We need her, Ivo," Osprey said sharply. "Without her, everything we've worked for will crumble."

"You're risking everything. If he even suspects what she means to us, he'll kill her before I can stop him."

Osprey spun, teeth gritted together as he danced to the side, slicing a waving arm just before it reached me and Zayana. "If she dies here, how is that better?"

"She won't die here. She's been fighting the Forbidding her entire life."

"So had the people in that village. It didn't save them."

"I'm right here." I interrupted. They both ignored me.

"You should take the injured Hatchling back to Le Majest," Osprey said ripping himself from Ivo's grip. "I'll follow you with your apprentice."

Ivo shook his head but he had to fight off a tangle of Forbidding magic, stepping up beside me as I defended Zayana from a creeping vine of darkness.

"We're too vulnerable sitting here. Go!" Osprey said. "You know I'm faster than you. We'll catch up."

Ivo shook his head again. "We need to stick together, Osprey."

"Someone needs to give you a chance to get away, old man," Osprey lunged for the Forbidding again, his osprey screaming as it soared down to join him in the battle.

Ivo made a frustrated sound in the back of his throat and hurried back to me.

"Stay alive," he ordered, pointing at me, and then he was running into a clump of trees. Harpy clung to his side, just barely hovering above the ground with an unconscious Zayana on his back.

I swallowed, worried for my friend. Would Ivo be able o keep her safe? Would he be safe?

I couldn't do anything about that now. I turned back to Osprey, raising my sword and threw myself into the fray. Between his dancing, graceful strikes, I placed my own carefully timed hits.

But the Forbidding was gathering thicker and thicker.

I risked a glance behind my back. We'd kept the way clear for Ivo and Zayana. There were no signs of Forbidding behind us, but what we were fighting was getting thicker, not thinner, despite our best efforts.

"We need fire," I gasped to Osprey as he retreated a step with me.

"We need a place to see. Get the full picture," he argued, stepping backward with me as we gave ground to the Forbidding. "There's nothing to light, anyway. Os!"

And he was right. The tangles of Forbidding writhing toward us were made of earth and green grass – nothing flammable in those ribbons at all.

His osprey dove down and Osprey leapt on his back like I'd seen him do so many times before – and fell through his bird's body, hitting the ground awkwardly.

Our eyes met and I leapt forward, barely slicing the arm off a tentacle before it grabbed him.

"Os," he gasped, reaching for the bird. It shrunk to half the size, landing on his shoulder, but looking more solid. He sheathed one of his swords, reaching up for the bird with one hand as he shoved back the attacking grasp of the Forbidding with the other.

"Is he hurt?" I asked, tension ringing in my voice. The way clear to Zayana and Ivo was starting to creep forward, as dark and tangled as the land on the other side of us. We were nearly surrounded.

"Only tired," Osprey said, his eyes tight. He chewed his toothpick hard as he shifted attention from bird to Forbidding and then back to bird again. "He won't be flying us anywhere, though."

"Then we'll have to fight," I said, firmly.

"Or flee," he agreed, grabbing my free hand and pulling me along the only path free of Forbidding. It was perpendicular to the path that Ivo and Zayana had taken and my throat constricted at the realization that we were running headlong into the wilderness.

I'd heard stories of people lost in Far Stones. Most didn't survive, but those who did told harrowing stories of starvation and sleeplessness as they fought hour upon hour just to survive against the Forbidding. The chances of being rescued by anyone were slim. No one would know where to look for us and with Osprey's bird so diminished, we couldn't fly away.

My bees buzzed around me, but they were little help against the Forbidding.

"We need to find high ground," Osprey said. His hand clasping mine was oddly comforting as we ran side by side, our breath huffing out with every step.

"Fighting the Forbidding takes determination and calm," I said as we ran. "It has a lot to do with trust."

"Have you really been fighting this all your life?" Osprey asked, spitting his toothpick as we sped up.

"Yes."

"Like that?"

"Not that bad, usually," I admitted.

"What kind of trust does it take?" Osprey asked.

I glanced down at the wristband he'd given me. "The kind where you put your future in the hands of someone else."

He paused and I skidded to a stop.

"What?"

"You already have my future in your hands, House Apidae," he said.

The hours bled on as we ran, the Forbidding following, spreading across the land like a stain.

"Is Os getting any stronger?" I asked as the ground began to rise, lined with the tumbled boulders and massive pines of the Far Stones. They were so large that I sometimes thought it made a person feel the size of an insect. A bee, perhaps.

My bees buzzed happily as we climbed, looping around me like tiny fairy lights. I found them oddly comforting.

"Find us somewhere safe," I whispered to them, hardly expecting a response, but they took off in four different directions and I could almost swear I could feel them moving out from me.

"Not yet," he replied. He hadn't let my hand go yet. Perhaps he was worried about being separated. "Do you know where we are?"

"No." I followed a tugging feeling farther up the slope between scattered, towering trees. My bees were leading me. Their faint buzzing echoed through me with every breath.

I felt better between the trees. I could see down the long lanes between their trunks and I could gather wood from the fallen dead. I dropped Osprey's hand and snapped off a nearby branch – weathered and grey – and then scooped up another from the forest floor. Tinder would be harder, but we would do what we could.

The hill was so steep that I was breathless by the time we'd almost reached the crest of the hill.

Two more of my bees darted to my sides and streaked past.

"Why did you come back for me?" I asked him. "You could be with Le Majest. You were already clear that you can't do anything to make him suspicious."

He paused, reaching into his sleeve and pulling out another toothpick. He twirled it over his fingers before jamming it into his mouth.

"Hope is addictive. Once you've had it, it's hard to stop wanting more."

"Wha – " I began, but my words broke off as the tree behind him twisted, reaching forward, branches and trunk ribbons of magic now. "Run."

I dropped the branches and scrambled up the last steps over the crest of the hill, using both hands and feet now that the grade was so steep.

Behind me, I heard a cry from Os, but I didn't dare look back until I reached the top, my heart in my throat. Osprey guarded my back, walking backward, his blades flicking out in front of him as he thrust, slashed and parried, flowing from one movement to the next like a dancer. Something had slit his coat and shirt at the back, revealing flexed muscle and thick scars down his back.

No time to dwell on that now.

Someone had camped here before and left a stack of dried wood next to a ring of stones around a blackened charcoal bare spot where they'd left a tiny wad of tinder and some small sticks.

Thank the skies. I made the sign of the bird.

"We can start a fire," I said, my breath coming quickly, heart racing.

Above the laid fire, my fourth bee buzzed a greeting.

He'd led us to the safest place I could think of. And a place with a fire waiting.

"Thank you," I whispered to him.

I fumbled for my belt pouch and drew out the flint, striking it with my short sword until it sparked.

Come on.

The spark hit the tinder, but the strong wind blew it out. I tried to shelter it with my body as I tried again.

"I can't hold it back for long," Osprey warned. I risked a glance to see him retreating to a spot only a pace away from me, his bird screaming overhead as it dove down toward the tangled trees. It was smaller again – the size of a real osprey.

"I'm hurrying." I struck the flint again. The sparks fell into the tinder pile and I blew gently, still trying to block the worst of the wind.

"Aella!" Osprey warned.

I glanced back, almost struck in the face by a waving tendril of Forbidding. I brought the short sword up, slicing off the tip of it. I burst forward, following my attack with another swipe, flowing into a back hand.

Forbidding take it.

There were too many strands to fight. But what else could we do? If we ran, we'd just be doing this again, only in the dark it would be even harder. And it had to be getting close to dark by now. I spun in another attack.

"Can you nurse the flame? Get it to light?" Osprey called.

I dashed back, blowing gently on the little spark. It was so close to lighting. I blew again and a flame popped into existence.

Something scraped against my back and I twisted, sword up just in time. I hacked at a new ribbon of tree as it reached toward me. Hacked off the tip of a second. Ducked under a lunging arm, scrambling to my feet, and jumped over another one.

The fire shot up into the dried wood, flames licking up the fuel like starving rats set loose on a wheel of cheese.

I looked around, but there was only the Forbidding all around me, tangling so close that it nearly met over my head, leaving only me and the little fire in the center of all that dark, twisted magic.

"Osprey?" I called, an edge of panic to my voice. When had he disappeared? "Osprey?"

I threw more fuel on the fire and it doubled in size, leaping up as high as I was and licking at the Forbidding above us. My breath grew more rapid. I could feel the edges of panic creeping up.

Not enough fire.

Where was Osprey?

Should I go in after him?

Bright orange blazed across the tangled trees and land.

I licked my lips, calling to my bees.

"We'll stick together," I told them, clinging to their buzzing in my mind. I snatched up a branch from the fire and held it in one hand, sword in the other.

Here we go.

I plunged forward in the direction I'd last seen him.

CHAPTER TWENTY-NINE

The shrieks of an angry seabird blasted across my hearing. I hacked through the clawing arms of Forbidding, more like a farmer hacking away weeds than the sleek dancer Osprey had been.

"Osprey?" I called, drawing on the buzz of my bees. I whispered to them. "Find him."

They shot forward and I followed, touching my flame to each branch that swayed toward me. They didn't catch, but their branches scorched, curling away from me. I should have lit a fire sooner. I should have –

And there he was. Just a few steps into the Forbidding, wrapped from head to foot in curls of twisted magic. Os dove toward the mass of Forbidding, small as a goshawk now, but still deadly as he ripped shreds of Forbidding from his manifestor's face. My bees shot forward, buzzing angrily as I hacked my way to him.

Hurry, Aella, hurry. I cut the branches tangling around him, but as fast as I cut, more branches wrapped, squeezing him like snakes.

Gasping with exhaustion, I paused.

I had to trust my instincts. My experience.

I sank to my knees, ducking under the swipe of a tentacle-like branch. It stabbed through my shoulder, right where I'd been injured before.

A cry burst through my lips but I pushed forward. I needed to find the heart of the tree.

My bees glowed bright in front of me, calling me on after them with exuberant buzzing. I could almost feel words in what they were humming, as if they were saying *here, here, here.*

Fighting the Forbidding was all about trust.

I trusted my bees.

I shoved the lit branch into the spot where they'd congregated as they scattered, returning to hover around me. It lit up like a torch, flames shooting upward like arrows.

I scrambled back. Hoping. Desperate.

Was I quick enough? Would it be enough?

The tree was ablaze already as I stumbled out from its grasp, the other trees and tangles shrinking away from the flame – but not quickly enough. Already, flames darted from tree to tree, lighting more and more tangles on fire. There was something so very flammable about the Forbidding. It was like dry tinder. But the arms holding Osprey hadn't relaxed their hold.

Fear seized me, freezing my spine. I couldn't move, couldn't form a proper thought. I'd doomed him to burn to death while I thought I was saving him. This was my fault.

My mind shot back to him standing by while my father was tortured, doing nothing to stop it because he thought it was best. How was this any different? I'd relied on my own judgment – and it was flawed, dooming him, too.

Like a flower blooming suddenly as the sunlight hit it, the tangles of Forbidding opened up and Osprey stumbled forward coughing on the smoke with his face streaked in soot and steam rising from his clothing.

"Osprey," I gasped, rushing forward to drag him out of the reach of the branches. His bird drifted down like a falling leaf, hummingbird sized now, landing on his head like a tiny halo.

I half-dragged him as he stumbled through the smoke, bringing him those few, enormous paces back to the tiny fire.

He fell to his knees as I made the sign of the bird, muttering a prayer. "Skies have mercy. Stars have mercy. Watch us as we struggle and grant us peace."

"I'm not dead yet," he gasped over a raw throat, erupting in coughs again. "Will the fires reach us here?"

"Depends which way the wind is blowing," I said, blinking back confusing tears. The relief I felt was shocking, roaring through me like a fire of its own.

"It is very close," he moaned.

I could feel the heat of it as I fell to my knees beside him. Hot blood poured down my arm and I was suddenly lightheaded at the feeling of the injury.

"Are you hurt?" I asked him.

He looked over himself, eyes wide. "I don't ... I don't .. where's Os?"

"On your head." I sucked in a breath through my teeth, fighting past the sharp throbbing of my arm and then blew over my bees. "Go for help. Find us help."

They swirled upward into the ash-spotted sky, leaving just one bee behind. It sat on my head, buzzing contentedly.

"Where do you think the Forbidding manifestations come from?" Osprey asked, stumbling forward and grasping my sleeve. "There are so many theories but no one ever seems to ask the people who live here."

What? I looked at him, confused and then he tore it off so suddenly that I flinched. He offered me a wry half-smile.

"Sorry. That wound needs binding."

His hands were surprisingly gentle as he inspected my shoulder and then began to wrap the sleeve around it, tightening the cloth as he held my flesh together.

"Who knows. This whole place creeps and slithers. The Forbidding wraps itself around everything and under that, when you clear it away, all you see is the carved snakes left behind by whatever ghosts once inhabited this land," I said, grateful for something to distract me from the pain and the fire hopping from tree to tree around us. It was really bad. A full forest fire beginning. And I could see no way out. "Those carvings are everywhere here but there's no sign of people beyond that. If they ever lived here, they are either long gone or nothing but shadows."

"Shadows?" he asked, raising one of those eyebrows again as he tightened the bandage.

"Yes," I said through gritted teeth.

"Shadows that really love snakes?"

"Yes," I said, my eyes scanning the burning treetops and the tangled Forbidding. No way out. No way out. "Why do you ask?"

"There's a door in the ground under the fallen needles where I fell. And it's carved with snakes," he said, determination filling his face as he released me and jammed a new toothpick between his lips. He still had his swords. He sheathed them as he stood. "And the snakes have shadows."

"What?"

"And I think that if we don't go down into it soon, we're going to be in big trouble because it turns out that pine trees are really, really flammable."

I stood up so fast that the world swam around me.

CHAPTER THIRTY

The flames whooshed from tree to tree, spreading ... well, spreading like wildfire. Which was what it was now.

Osprey brushed inches of fallen needles from the top of a heavily carved stone hatch.

Snakes had been carved so deep into the stone that they appeared to be alive, all tangled up with one another in a huge knot. They were carved in such deep relief that shadows appeared from behind them. It must have been the heat waves, but it almost looked as if they were moving.

There was a crack as a branch fell from a nearby tree and sparks burst up from it in a cloud, sizzling in the needles.

I gasped at the sudden burst of powerful heat. Forbidding take it.

The needles on the ground were alight now. At least the Forbidding had been stopped. I saw no eye-bending magic tentacles anymore. But it was hard to feel too relieved when that meant we were facing the prospect of being burned alive.

Osprey cleared enough of the Hatch to reveal a handle. I stood, hurrying to help him. We both grabbed the handle and at his nod, I helped him lift with all my might. I barely bit back a moan as pain flared in my shoulder and hot blood poured down my arm. Osprey looked exhausted, too, his bird resting on his head.

The Hatch fell open. Beneath it, darkness was thick and deep.

"After you, House Apidae," Osprey said with one of his grim winks.

I held out my hand and my single bee followed it, buzzing around my hand to form a dull golden orb. I lowered it down, but with the bright fires above, all I could see was the first rung.

"Hurry." Osprey's eyes watched the flames around us nervously. The world below was deep inky black. The world above was blazing orange. And there was no way we could know which held more terror.

I swallowed down dread and took a deep breath.

Come on, Aella. It's better than being burned alive.

I sheathed the short sword, and I set a foot on the first rung and slowly began to lower myself into the dark.

It was all I could do not to succumb to a sudden burst of terror. I hated creepy, crawly things and this pit – the one that a hatch with snakes all over it led to – seemed like the ideal place for those. I could already imagine a pit teeming with thousands of snakes below. Maybe that's where they all went. Maybe they were sleeping beneath our feet. That's what snakes did. They slept in pits in the rock – thousands of them, waiting, waiting, waiting.

Come on, Aella. You can do better than this.

I looked up at Osprey chewing impatiently on his toothpick. His eyes were on the trees and his face was bright in the glow of the forest fire.

I lowered myself further. It was our only choice.

My injured arm screamed as I climbed and my bee swarmed round and round me, buzzing irritably, but before I knew it, I was a full body length down the ladder. It felt like it was carved from stone, too. Someone had been worried about grip. They'd carved a ripple pattern in the top of each rung. This ladder was meant to be used.

Above me, Osprey set a firm foot on the rung, lowering himself quickly when a loud *pop* sounded in the trees above.

The bee hummed louder, as if asking a question, and I answered it aloud.

"Sap popping from the fire," I said, climbing faster now, fighting against the exhaustion that had come from using my bees and fighting with the sword. Every muscle was tired, every inch of me screaming that it wanted to sleep.

The Hatch had been too heavy to lower over us. We needed to get clear before flames fell down here, too. I didn't have the option of not going on.

Relentless. Relentless. Relentless.

I swayed a little, blinking against the darkness threatening to swallow my vision.

What other option was there? I'd been working with the best of bad options since Osprey and the other Wings showed up in my village.

I lowered my foot again and jammed it against the ground.

"Nnngh."

That hurt. I lowered the other foot more carefully.

"I'm at the bottom," I whispered.

"Right behind you."

"What do you think, little bee?" I whispered in the darkness as it hummed beside my ear. The light from the flames above was growing more intense, and it bathed the little walkway I stood on in bright orange. Something that looked like glass angled out from me in one direction. It couldn't be glass. No one could make sheets of glass that large. And no one would bring them here.

The walkway continued in the other direction.

Snakes wrapped up along the side of the walkway, large hoods flaring around their heads. Someone had set torch holders in the hoods, but they were unlit. Even with my bee, it was hard to see very far in the darkness, but Osprey's bird was brighter.

I stepped aside so that Osprey could descend. He gripped the wall with trembling hands, clearly exhausted from his use of magic. His osprey had grown back to the size of a real osprey, but it flickered, there one moment and gone the next as if Osprey didn't have the energy to sustain it.

I meant to walk past him, but he reached out, his hand finding my waist in the dark. He leaned his forehead against the rock wall.

"Osprey?" I asked.

"Just one moment. Please."

"We can't rest. Not here. The flames are too close."

"I have to talk to you. About your bees. About your father. About everything."

He looked up and his eyes in the flickering light were tortured.

"Later," I urged. "When we get out of here."

He sucked in a deep breath. "I have so many people to protect. So many lives are resting on me. One mistake and I destroy them all."

"Then why are you here? Why didn't you stay with Le Majest?" The roar of the fire grew louder above and I almost jumped when his hand moved from my waist to find my hand in the dark.

"I want you to trust me, Aella. Fighting the Forbidding might have a lot to do with trust – but so does fighting for our freedom."

I swallowed.

"I want to trust you," I said, reaching to feel the leather cuff he'd given me on my arm. It was sticky with my blood. "But how can I trust you when you have a role to play that will have to come into conflict with me? I won't be Juste Montpetit's property. I won't change my bees to birds – which is sure to enrage him. I won't let him take anything more from my people. And you've already told me how you are bound to him. How your will is not your own. We're going to have to work apart because working together fully is impossible."

"It's not," he argued, his voice soft as down in the warm tunnel. "I'll find a way. You swore you'd work with me."

"And I will," I agreed. "But if it's a choice between you and the freedom of my people, I won't choose you."

He cleared his throat and when he finally spoke, his voice was husky. "I'm not asking you to. Just promise you'll try to trust me, as much as you can."

"Why did you give me the osprey cuff?" I asked, my voice barely above a whisper.

"You don't do that here?" he asked.

"Do what?" The skin on the back of my neck tingled at his words.

"On the continent, we give a personal object – a hair comb, necklace, cuff, or something else to someone to show that our hopes go with them. That they are dearer to us than our personal possessions. I wanted you to be safe. I wanted it so much that I came back for you against Ivo's pleas. Can you understand that?"

I paused. "He's right. You shouldn't have come back for me. You risk too much."

His blue eyes bored into me. "Maybe you're worth the risk."

I swallowed down a bubble of longing. To find someone – anyone – who might offer that kind of devotion after being ripped away from my family was so tempting. It offered to fill a lonely hole in my heart. But that wasn't fair to him. It would be using him for myself. All he'd get from it would be pain.

"We need to get farther down," I said. It was a good excuse. Sweat already clung to my hairline. "Come on."

His bird launched up into the air, spreading his wings protectively over Osprey and lighting the shining angled glass with a lavender glow. Purple light illuminated every shadow.

We scrambled together down the walkway as ash drifted down, following us. The scent of smoke was heavy in the air.

I bit my lip nervously, worried it would be no easier to breathe farther down the tunnel, worried that it would grow too hot and cook us alive in the fire. Worse, there was something about this place that felt secret and terrifying.

I coughed on smoke, not even caring that the air below was dank and still as I hurried faster and faster, trying to suppress my instinctual fear.

We reached another ladder and I checked my sword at my side before I took the lead again, descending into the darkness, my heart in my throat.

Osprey let me lead, his eyes never leaving me, his toothpick migrating from one corner of his mouth to the other as if he was just as full of bleak thoughts as I was.

I took the first step down into the depths.

Don't go much lower. Don't go much lower. Please don't leave us trapped in the earth.

I squeezed my eyes shut for a moment and took a breath. *Breathe, Aella. It will be fine.*

It felt as if the damp darkness was going to swallow me up, and yet – somehow – orange light was still filtering down. My eyes adjusted to it enough that I could make out the rungs of the ladder as I descended. It was narrow and heavily decorated with snake carvings. What was this place? Who would take so much time to carve all these snakes on a ladder underground?

It was long minutes of quiet climbing – quiet sinking into the bowels of the earth – until my feet finally hit the ground again. I stumbled down what seemed to be another passageway toward a glowing doorway ... and stopped.

"What is this place?" I gasped.

The small door was barely large enough to let me through, but it opened into a grand hall carved into the rock. Hanging high above, was the glass I'd seen – panes of it larger than the floor of my home. The dancing firelight of the world burning above lit the pane, making it seem as if the fires of the underworld were gazing down on us. Someone had set the glass into a design – the shape of a bird in flight, talons extended, attacking an S-shaped snake, its fangs exposed and tongue flickering out. Around them, were tiny dots. I stared at them until I realized they were bees.

I shivered.

Who would have made something like that? The shape of the bird and snake cast itself in a pool of light on the floor of the great room and I realized, as I finally tore my eye from the window to the surrounding room, that the floor was made entirely of interwoven carved snakes. At least, I thought they were carved. I hoped they were carved. The floor looked exactly as I had feared a heap of sleeping snakes might look, and they swarmed up the sides of the walls, coating everything in wriggling snakeyness.

My shiver turned into a shudder. This was ... spooky. A sense of something wrong rolled off the floor and was echoed in the strange design in the window. It unnerved me that the artist had chosen bees, almost as if it was declaring the danger of my magic where everyone could see it. Because after all, Ivo and Osprey had chosen me to help with their revolution because of it and it was likely that Juste Montpetit had killed my father because of it. I didn't like seeing that magic pitted against birds in some way. Not because I thought there was something wrong with my magic, but because I was terrified that someone else might think there was.

There were two large doors headed out of the room, their doorways black pits of shadow.

"What do you see?" Osprey whispered from behind me.

Marring the tangle of snakes in the bright patch of light was a dark trail of something wet. Water? But it wasn't running, just a light skim over the floor. What would have left a trail of water down here?

I followed it with my eyes until I found a spot where the shadows of the wall looked thicker and deeper.

I gasped.

The dark shadow wasn't a shadow at all.

It was Juste Montpetit. His face was drawn with surprise. In his hand, he grasped the foot of a dead Claw. The poor man's throat had been slit and the very last of his blood was what had left that wet trail across the floor.

"Le Majest," I gasped.

CHAPTER THIRTY-ONE

I stepped forward, so shocked that I didn't even think of Osprey behind me.

"What's the orange light shining through the stained glass of the window?" Juste Montpetit asked, but he didn't leave the thick shadows. His voice was high and spooky. It made my skin crawl.

"A fire, Le Majest," I answered. "We lit it to keep back the Forbidding, but it consumed the forest and we took shelter down this ladder."

"Fires. I didn't think of fire," he said distantly. His expression bled and morphed in the rippling light of the fire.

"Where are your guards?" I asked boldly. I took another step into the grand room, grateful when the floor didn't slither under my feet. But it might. Who knew what might wake these carved snakes? Nothing seemed quite real anymore. "How did you get here?"

Behind me, Osprey clicked his tongue in irritation. Oh yeah. I was supposed to avoid Le Majest's notice. But I wasn't the one haunting the shadows like a ghost.

It didn't make sense that he was here. He'd been heading south, not west like us. I was almost certain that we had not gotten lost or turned around. But maybe he had.

He took a step toward us, dropping the foot of the dead Claw. He didn't seem to notice that he'd let him go.

"We couldn't ford the river," Juste said, his face tilted upward, eyes riveted on the dazzling window. It must have been made that way so that you could open the Hatch and sunlight would light this underground cathedral. Perhaps it was beautiful then. Or magical. Or holy. Right now, it looked like the depths of hell.

My eyes narrowed in response. What had happened to him? Why was he here alone?

"The land came alive and tried to eat us," he said. "My Claws fought valiantly. My Wings fought with them."

There was a long pause. I stepped farther into the room and the purple light of Osprey's bird followed me, shining on the snakes at my feet and making their shadows long and thick.

I fought down nausea, trying to keep my eyes from lingering on the broken and mangled body behind the crown prince – I recognized the scarred face of the commander of the Swan Claws even though it was drawn in death – or the sculptured snakes staring at me from every corner of the room. All of the sculpted snakes seemed to be looking in the same direction – the spot on the floor where the stained glass window shone the light of the snake onto the floor There was a little platform there, just a step above the ground and only as wide as I was tall. Something was written on it, scrawled in a language I'd never seen and didn't understand.

"It twisted and turned in fragments of itself, like a nest of snakes come alive to eat us all," Juste said, taking another step toward the platform where the light was brightest. "I knew this rocky place would defy me. I broke its teeth. I strangled it. And yet it still had horrors beyond that of man to send against me. But I would not be quelled. I am House Swan. I am crown prince of the Winged Empire. I am Le Majest and all I do and choose is the choice of the sky itself."

Juste Montpetit's voice grew stronger as it echoed through the wide chamber. My bee buzzed oddly out of tune with the cadence of his voice.

"There are ways to quell the Forbidding," he whispered, glancing at me for a heartbeat as if sharing a secret. "Old ways. Ways from when we first arrived at this continent."

"Fire," I said with certainty.

He laughed, long, eerie, and high pitched. "Is that what your father told you? Men do love their little lies. I'll take those too, before I'm done with them. I'll drown them in truth if I must."

I swallowed down a spike of fear. My father didn't like to talk about settling here. Of what it had taken to clear back the Forbidding. When we asked, he had a hollow look in his eyes before he changed the subject.

"Blood," the crown prince said, his words reverberating across the room. He leapt gracefully across the floor and in three delicate hops he was on the little platform, arms spread wide, head tipped up as he let the light of the snake settle over him, turning slightly as if he was bathing in rain instead of sunning himself in the light of the world burning above us.

I didn't like the feel of that word, "blood." I didn't like the ghastly shadows painted in flickering orange over his face.

I worked my way cautiously toward him. Osprey was silent. I risked a glance and realized he was at my shoulder, eyes narrowed and toothpick still as he watched Le Majest. His bird hung above us, lighting the way. His light – though purple – seemed safe and familiar, unlike the flickering orange of the fire above.

I placed my hand on the hilt of my sword.

"You can quell it with blood – if you have enough of it." Juste Montpetit's gaze shot over to one of the deep, black openings leading out of the cathedral.

The doorway that was marked as his path into the cathedral by the dark streak running from that spot to the limp body on the other side of the room. A ribbon of Forbidding twisted along the roof, wrapping out of the darkened door and upward. It did not reach down into the tunnel, as if it was afraid of the blood trail there.

"I am almost out of blood. Other people's blood, at least. And I will not be spilling royal blood today," Juste said, returning his gaze to the window above him.

I shuddered.

"How far did you travel, fleeing the Forbidding?" I asked quietly, taking another step toward him.

"All the way from the river," he said, closing his eyes as if he was bathing in the wicked light. Something moved on his shoulder, twisting around his neck. Just a hint of shadow – wasn't it? It couldn't be more.

"We lost Butiez with the Wings. And it was only me and the Claws left."

Osprey cleared his throat. "They died?"

Le Majest's head whipped toward him. "You're here. You were supposed to be with me. You know you cannot slip that bond."

Osprey looked sick. "I do."

"Perhaps I shall spill royal blood after all." Just's voice climbed higher as if the thought amused him.

"What happened to the Wings?" I asked.

Just Montpetit's smile sent ribbons of cold rippling through my abdomen. "Perhaps they died. Perhaps they abandoned me as Osprey did, in my moment of truest need. And if that is so, then they shall pay in terror and fire."

I swallowed. His threats felt too real – as if he wasn't exaggerating at all what he meant to do.

He continued his story. "We fled to the river, but it was too fast. We couldn't ford it, though we tried. We lost ten Claws to the water before we were certain the crossing was impossible. I watched them get towed under. They did not come back up. The bridge was twisted by the Forbidding."

His eyes shot open and the twisting shadow round his neck glowed a sudden faint green.

With a sigh – long and low – he gasped out words that sounded like a caress. "And there you are. I had wondered if you might come to me here."

That couldn't be...

The thing around his throat moved again and a head darted out over his ear. One eye gleamed brightly as it locked with mine and I gasped.

The crown prince had just Hatched.

Not a bird.

Not a bee.

A snake.

Horror curled in the lowest part of my belly. With it came the sudden urge to flee.

"We killed the carabao on my order," he said, tilting his head to lean into the snake, letting one of his hands drift up to caress it. "But even creatures as large as carabao only have enough blood to cover a small area when you're running for miles looking for escape. We splashed it around too liberally."

"I can only imagine," I said in a small voice. Keep him talking, Aella. Keep him talking while you figure out what to do.

Evil radiated off the snake. I felt my hands twitching in response.

I glanced up at the window. The talons of the bird bit into the snake and the snake was wrapped around the bird's neck. I looked back at the crown prince of the Winged Empire and the snake tangling around his own neck.

He'd called me an abomination for my bees.

What did that mean when it came to his snake?

"Is that a snake?" Osprey asked, his voice guarded.

Juste smiled beatifically. "It turns out I've manifested after all. And it's the best manifestation possible. I don't speak to it – it speaks to me and tells me of the wonders we can manifest. We'll restore peace in the Empire. We'll fill it with justice. Enough bread for every mouth. Enough truth for every heart."

I felt suddenly lightheaded. This couldn't be happening. "What kind of truth?"

"My truth. It's the only kind there is. You will prosper in my world."

"And if I don't?" I'd seen what his kind of "truth" did to my family.

"Then you'll die. We can't have people in the Empire who fight it. We need utter unity. Everyone united under one great Emperor for one great cause. That's what Sephilis says."

"The snake?" I asked.

"It's what he calls himself," Juste said.

I ripped my sword out, but he was leaping from the platform before I moved as if he knew what I was about to do. His hand clamped down on mine, forcing it to stay still while his other hand seized Osprey by the neck.

"By order, Guardian, you will not move," he hissed.

No.

I fought against his hand, pounding on his arm with my other fist, but he was more powerful than I could have guessed. Under all his fancy embroidery, he was hard as a rock.

Osprey's bird went wild, diving into the fray. The purple bird flapped at Juste's face, purple light flashing all around. He loosened his grip on my hand to bat it aside and my sword pulled free.

"Call the bird off, Guardian." He flinched at Osprey's hesitation. "By your vow, you may not harm me."

Under Osprey's tattered coat, something glowed. The feather. It was responding to those words.

Os reared up, swooping upward and out of the fray.

My heart in my throat, I darted forward, trying to take advantage of the distraction.

"No," Osprey shouted, but of course he'd say that. I struck at the crown prince with my short sword and caught something with the tip.

Just his cloak.

It tore, tangling around my sword. It was too hard to see with the bird flapping wildly and the only other light the flickering orange of the fires above.

Nerves made my hands quiver and exhaustion made my movements slow. I fought against them, desperate not to succumb.

"Don't do this, I beg you," Osprey gasped, his hands empty at his sides, not even fighting it as Le Majest squeezed his throat harder.

The crown prince swayed even as he gripped his guardian as if choking Osprey hurt him.

"Don't just stand there. Fight with me," I begged Osprey, even though I knew he wouldn't listen. If only I knew exactly how they had him chained.

I lunged forward again, sword darting into an opening, but Le Majest turned my sword in a quick flick of his wrist. I gasped as I fought to keep my grip on it. This wasn't like any fight I'd ever been in before. I was used to fighting mindless Forbidding, relying on speed and the ability to out-think animal instinct. Fighting a trained opponent was an entirely different thing.

It had been partially successful. Juste let go of Osprey's throat and he sucked in a gasping breath.

I leapt forward as Osprey threw up a hand. His voice was desperate. "For mercy's sake, House Apidae, stop this!"

Juste's snake shot out and uncoiled from his neck to wrap around Osprey's. He grunted, hands reaching up to grip the snake as he gasped for breath. Juste seemed just as breathless, though more in ecstasy than pain.

Juste Montpetit's smile widened. "Silky and deadly you are, my treasure. You light my eyes. Shall we play with our food?"

The snake seemed to swell at his words and Osprey's eyes bulged. Juste swayed from the effort.

I jabbed my sword toward him again, but again he was too fast. I barely slid away from the tip of his blade as it danced toward me.

Where was my magic when I needed it most? Osprey was going to die if I couldn't stop Juste. And I would be moments behind him. But I was so tired. I couldn't feel my bees.

My single remaining bee buzzed angrily around my head as I tried to project my thoughts out to find my others.

To me, bees. To me.

There was no buzz within me. Panic rose up, filling me. Juste was faster and stronger than I was, and his manifestation was much more powerful. What could I do?

"I thought I'd taken all the weapons from you and those fools you call family," Juste said in a low voice. "Their blood will hold back a mile of Forbidding."

Hot fury filled my limbs and I roared, rushing toward him. I feinted low and then slid my blade up and under his guard. He twisted at the last second, and my attack slid off his ribs.

Frustration bubbled up in me as I drew back again. A tiny flicker of golden light flared to life, spiraling down my sword. Yes. Come on. More. I need more.

A very mild buzz welled up in me, stuttering slightly. I shouldn't have pushed my bees so hard.

"How many of those cursed insects do you have, girl? It's like they're flies on a rotting corpse," the crown prince snarled.

"You aren't in your right mind," I said, trying to sound reasonable as I shoved his next blow aside with all my strength. If I couldn't fight, maybe I could talk. Use every arrow in your quiver, Aella. "If you were, you wouldn't be murdering your Claws. Let us help you."

I was giving ground, my muscles burning. He outmatched me without trying. Even with madness in his eyes and his attention split between me, Osprey, and the ribbon of Forbidding snaking out of the tunnel, he was still so much my superior that I could hardly hold my ground. I was already sweat-soaked, my attacks too slow, my defenses too weak.

And Osprey's eyes were bulging as he stood there and let this happen to him, Os's light growing fainter and fainter as the seconds passed.

"I'm not insane, *property,*" Juste sneered, stumbling slightly. Was all the effort too much for him? "I might actually be sane for the first time in my life. I've always known there was something more for me."

"More than being a crown prince?" I leapt to one side, crouching low and jabbing at him sharply, trying to distract him enough that his manifestation might at least release Osprey. My shoulder was on fire, pain flaring through it so sharp and savage that tears flooded my eyes. The wound must have ripped open again. "That seems like a lot of responsibility already."

"More than you know. You think you look upon evil when you look upon me. You think that because I slew your father before your eyes that somehow I am the worst of monsters."

Osprey's eyes met mine at his words, compassion flooding them even as he fought to breathe against the swell of the snake. I looked sharply away. He'd been there. He'd let that happen before. And now he'd let it happen again as he just stood and let the crown prince choke his life out.

He stumbled forward onto one knee. Juste swayed beside him, but kept to his feet.

I had to end this quickly.

"If you're sane, then let's stop fighting," I urged, dodging back from his strike. My hurt arm was on fire. I bit back a gasp of pain. "Let's finish this journey to safety together. Let Osprey go free."

"He'll never be free. My life depends on that. Didn't you look at the Invocation Window? Didn't you see that snakes and birds are locked in battle for all eternity?"

"But you're the crown prince of the Winged Empire," I gasped.

"And now I am also the snake with a crown." There was a hint of elation in his expression with those words.

He struck again, and this time his blade bit into my leg. I moaned in pain, stumbling backward.

To me, bees. To me.

"You aren't making any sense," I gasped.

"The only way to beat a bird is with a snake. They're natural opponents. The bird snatches the snake from the grass and smashes him on the rocks, but the snake creeps into the bird's nest and strangles the bird to death. I will strangle the bird and take his kingdom."

I barely dodged his next strike and he leaned in so close that his free hand grabbed my collar and pulled me to his chest. I could feel his hot breath on my face. It made me sick.

"I thought you were the bird," I objected.

"I've always been the snake," he hissed. "And now my father will know that. Only a snake can bring down a bird. I will bring him down. I will strike when he least expects it. And my poison will have no cure."

The buzzing finally started in my chest, deep and resonant, demanding, certain.

I didn't care about the Winged Empire. I didn't care what bad blood lay between him and his father. But this snake was threatening my family and there was only one way to deal with threats.

A bee could only sting once. Because it died fighting for its swarm and hive.

An image of my father whispering to me, his one eye burning, flashed across my vision.

Be relentless.

I sank to one knee so suddenly that his blade shot across the top of my shoulder, biting through the flesh shallowly. I bit back a scream, focusing instead, on my sting. I leapt back to my feet while he was still recovering his balance, twisted my short sword, and plunged it into his belly.

His scream echoed through the cathedral.

CHAPTER THIRTY-TWO

I watched in horror as he slumped to the ground.

I did that.

I stabbed my father's killer.

A buzzing began inside me. Bees frothed out of my fingers, spinning round and round in a golden cloud. Juste's blood bubbled at his mouth and from the gaping wound in his belly, and his eyes met mine, filled with fury.

My hands shook wildly and my breath came quick.

I didn't mean ...

I shouldn't have ...

"What have you done?" Osprey's words were horrified. I met his wide eyes as his toothpick dropped from his lips. One of his hands gripped his belly and he hunched painfully over it as if he was the one who had been stabbed.

Everything from my hands to my breath felt frozen.

The snake had vanished.

Flakes of ash had drifted down to coat the great window and mar the light it shone, leaving it dappled and shadowy.

“If he dies, you die,” Osprey gasped, agony lining every feature. “And not just you, your family, too. There’s nowhere to go that I can’t find them – and I will be compelled to kill every last one of them.”

I let out a little gasp of terror, choking on it. “I didn’t mean to kill him.”

“It doesn’t matter. Don’t you see that? If only you had been anyone else … anyone but you. I would happily watch you kill him and then slay you quickly.”

He rose from his knees, his shoulders slumping heavily.

Something buzzed in my chest, loud and powerful. Something that seemed to be tugging me to do *something*. Anything.

“I thought you said I was valuable.”

His eyes were haunted and desperate. “And you are. You won’t be the first valuable person whose life I stole. They were all valuable to someone.”

His hand flinched and he made a fist as if trying to prevent himself from drawing his own sword.

I swallowed and looked at Juste Montpetit moaning on the ground.

Please don’t die. Please don’t die. I knelt beside him, hands hovering over his wound. What good was having magic if you could never make it do anything? My eyes were glassy with desperation. Something wet soaked into the knees of my breeches.

Stop the bleeding. I begged in my mind.

"Stop the bleeding," I whispered.

To my surprise, my swarm of bees poured from where they buzzed around my hand and dove into the crown prince's belly, settling there in a seething mass.

My mouth fell open. Were they...

"Can you actually stop the bleeding?" I whispered. But they seemed to be stopping it. Another bee raced in from somewhere else, joining the rest. The blood pool had not expanded. Another bee flew in from the dark doorway, joining the swarm. And another. And another.

My bees were returning. Not *with* help like I'd asked, but *to* help.

"I think it's working," I whispered. "Please, keep it up."

I watched my bees holding the crown prince of the Empire together, thinking about how he said he owned me. But he was wrong. We were owned by no one but the ones we loved and I would do anything necessary to keep them safe and keep them alive, even if that meant holding this man together long enough to deliver him back to his vengeful royal father.

"I think the bees are holding," I said, trying to be calm. "Osprey?"

I heard Osprey muttering something. It sounded like a prayer and pleading at the same time. He didn't seem to hear me.

I swallowed, looking nervously at that door as a loud buzzing pulled my attention. The tentacles of Forbidding were reaching out toward us. They contracted suddenly and then went wild. One of my bees zipped out of the tunnel, narrowly avoiding a snatching tentacle. It streaked toward me, buzzing so hard that the bees holding Juste Montpetit together seemed to buzz louder with it.

"You're back," I said and found myself smiling. It felt weird to smile right now. But I could feel those little bees now. I could feel when they were close and far away. There were still two of them out there somewhere and a part of me reached for them, as if I wouldn't be complete until they had all returned.

The bee zipped to join the others, throbbing with the rest of the swarm. The crown prince moaned, his eyes locking on me for one more furious glare before shutting against the pain. We needed to get him out of here.

I turned to look back at Osprey at the same time his head came up slowly and his fists gripped the handles of his swords until the knuckles went white.

His Osprey had grown again. It circled the room, flapping wildly, leaving little trails and tatters of purplish light falling through the air all around him.

Osprey's blades came out in a pair of perfect arcs and his lips parted in sorrow.

"Skies have mercy," he whispered and then he leapt toward me like an angel of death, his cloak flapping out behind him and his eyes blazing in the bright purplish-white light of his Osprey. He looked like he was stalking me. Like a hunter finding his prey and seizing his moment. "Those are your bees in the belly of my prince."

"They're holding him together," I said, licking my lips.

I pulled my sword tip up again. Adjusting my stance. What was he going to do?

"I'm bound in ways you don't understand. I tried to warn you," Osprey said dangerously. His eyes filled with something that looked like agony. Os shrieked diving forward, but Osprey threw a hand back and the bird stayed hovering behind him.

"What's happening to your chest?" I asked, pointing a trembling finger to where his chest glowed so brightly that I could almost make out the shape of the curled feather under his jacket and shirt.

The great Osprey hovered behind and slightly above him, its wings spread out and towering over us, spilling bright white light over everything. Its eye caught mine and I flinched.

"I am bound, House Apidae. If he dies, I must avenge him," he said. His eyes were desperately sad, but his mouth formed a grim line. One of his hands reached up and clutched his chest where the glowing feather was embedded under the skin. He flinched slightly.

And then his sword struck so fast he made Juste Montpetit look clumsy.

I barely threw myself aside.

I couldn't fight him! I wasn't fast enough or strong enough.

"What are you doing?" I said. "He manifested snakes. He attacked us."

"It doesn't change that you spilled the blood of Le Majest," he said, his voice heavy with pain. Was that the gleam of a tear I saw in his eye?

Help. I needed some kind of help.

The buzzing in my head grew louder and my bees poured from behind me, streaking toward Osprey in an angry swarm. His bird's head struck toward me, but he stayed it with a hand signal and an anguished cry. He could stop the bird, but he couldn't stop himself.

Face twisting with despair, he lunged again, ignoring the bees. I tried to counter his strike, but he was too powerful. The sword bit through my guard, knocking my short sword from my grasp, and sank into my shoulder.

The wailing moan that ripped through my lips didn't even sound like me.

My bees swarmed closer, tightening their ring.

If they could just bind his hands.

He raised his arm for another strike, and they closed in, tangling his hands tightly to each other in a swarming, powerful mass. His sword fell to the ground.

I fell to my knees.

"You're only drawing it out," he said in an anguished voice. "I will have to take your life. Please, let me make it clean. Please don't make me shred you apart with my beloved Os."

My bees clenched tighter and his bird kicked up, drawing back as if preparing to strike.

"Vasyklo," I pled, using his real name. He shut his eyes as if to block out my plea. I thought I might see a tear trailing down his cheek.

"With your death dies my very hope, House Apidae."

My knees trembled and my gaze circled the room, looking for a way out. They settled on Juste Montpetit and the pool of blood growing around him.

"Wait," I yelled, throwing up a hand. "Without the bees, Le Majest is bleeding out. Look."

Sparks danced along the edge of my vision as pain from my wounds flared through me. I gasped, fighting to keep from collapsing on the ground.

"You'll need to make a decision, Vasyklo Petren, sworn in blood to play guardian to the crown prince," I said desperately. "If you let your bird kill me, my bees are gone. If you keep attacking me, they'll remain on your wrists. If you want that prince alive more than you want revenge, then you'll need to make your peace with me and let them return to tending him."

"It's not about what I *want.*" He sounded like he was barely holding back a scream.

"Then what are you bound to do? Is it to revenge him or to save his life?"

His voice was low when he answered. "Return the bees to the prince. I'll not harm you while he needs them to live."

"How comforting." I couldn't help the wryness of my tone as I fell heavily to the ground and everything went mercifully dark.

CHAPTER THIRTY-THREE

I woke to pain through my chest and shoulder.

I moaned.

Everything was too bright. Too bright.

Something buzzed, walking with tiny feet across my face. I closed my eyes and concentrated. Another of my bees. I could still feel that one was away from the swarm, but this one had returned.

"It's okay," I whispered to the bee.

"Aella?"

I grunted, but I didn't have the strength to do anything else as Osprey spoke again.

"You need to lie still. Try to stay conscious. Your bees are stronger when your mind is awake."

Oh yeah. I'd forgotten. He'd spared my life – but only so I could keep his precious royal alive with my bees. I thought I might hate him.

Something moved rhythmically beneath me. Wings, I thought. Was I being carried on Os's back again?

"Almost there," someone cried from a little way off. "Hold him on the back of Harpy. He isn't used to such a heavy load."

"Ivo," I moaned.

"Your bee brought Ivo and Zayana to us," Osprey said quietly. "He has Le Majest on the back of his eagle. We're taking him to the boat."

"Boat?" I murmured.

"Just a skiff, really. Where this tunnel comes out at the river. Ivo had just found it when your bee found him and led him to us. That's a neat trick, by the way. Your bee led me, too."

Was he trying to make up for slicing me apart with all this flow of information?

"Lucky," I gasped. I guess I should have been more specific. I should have told them to go get help that *didn't* want to kill me.

"I'm not going to apologize," Osprey said, leaning down over me. The light in the tunnel was getting brighter. I could see every feature of his proud, unflinching face. "I warned you not to hurt him. I told you what would happen."

"Good for you," I managed between clenched teeth.

He sighed, running a hand over his face and looking off into the distance with gritted teeth.

"I did what I had to do."

"Must be nice."

He made a noise in the back of his throat that sounded like a non-verbal curse. "What do you expect from me?"

I didn't bother answering. Did he really expect me to forgive him for trying to kill me and only stopping because he must to save someone else's life? Did he expect some kind of absolution?

He crumbled, the hard planes of his face softening and his eyes grew glassy as we stepped out of the cavern. Above him, the sky was awash with starlight, spilling out like a spray of water over a dark shadow. The powerful sound of the river filled my ears almost as much as the perpetual buzzing filled my mind.

I could feel my last bee. It was coming closer.

"I'm sorry," he whispered, but he didn't look at me and he didn't stay to see what my response would be.

Ivo's face appeared, streaked in ash and dirt.

"Awake again?" he asked with a wink. "I knew you were too tough to let an injury keep you down. Come on now, you'll have to stand so we can get you in the boat."

He slipped an arm under me and helped to lift me to my feet from the back of Os. Os looked back at me with an angry glint in his eye, as if he held his manifestor's misery against me.

"I was worried I'd lost my first apprentice in years just days after taking her on, but you're too tough for that," Ivo said as he helped me find my feet. I gasped in agony, clinging to him with hands clawing in pain as my head and belly spun with nausea. "I told Osprey that when he feared he'd killed you. She's too tough, I said. She manifests bees, I said. She'll recover, just like the fighter she is. After all, she knows what's worth suffering for, what's worth dying for."

I grunted agreement. But inside my heart was singing. Because he was right. We were both still alive, which meant we could both keep working for revolution. For freedom. For a Far Stones where people could defend themselves in peace.

"He just wanted the prince saved," I said with a moan – because I couldn't let things with Osprey rest even though I knew I should. "He didn't care about killing me."

"You're wrong about that, little bee," Ivo said, but he was helping me shuffle a painful step at a time toward the boat.

My eyes drifted over the boat, finding it hard to focus on any one thing. They'd settled Juste Montpetit into the center of it and Zayana was sitting with his head in her lap and her bird right beside it. She had a kinder heart than I'd ever have. Or maybe she was just more sensible. She looked like the perfect High'un with her Imperial Court dress arranged around her and her straight black hair untangled despite all we'd been through. Her little red bird was perched on her shoulder, worn and tattered.

Osprey refused to look at me as Ivo helped me into the boat. I sank to the floor in the prow, propped against the side of the boat. My eyes flickered closed.

Just for a minute. Only for a minute.

Then I'd get up and fight.

"Flight of stars," Osprey cursed. "We're losing her again. See if you can plug up that hole in her shoulder, Hatchling."

The next time I woke the sun was bright on my face and our boat bobbed along the surface of the water. The water was calm and still, a perfect mirror image of the shoreline and our boat so that I didn't even have to look anywhere but the water to see what was happening.

Everyone else in the boat seemed to be asleep. Ivo was slumped over the tiller. My bees buzzed in Juste Montpetit's wound. I thought I could smell honey. I took in a breath and flinched at the sharp pains shooting through my chest and back.

Flight of wind protect me, mercy of the skies fly over me, give me peace and protection, let me soar from this terror on the wings of eagles.

Without some kind of help, I wouldn't live past the moment that Le Majest healed. Which would likely be weeks but might also be days.

I tried to swallow but my throat was too dry.

Something was walking on my cheek.

The last bee.

I reached up with a shaky hand and let it walk along my finger.

There was a tiny roll of paper tied to its leg with a thread. With trembling fingers, I untied the thread and unrolled the paper.

In a hurried hand that I recognized as Raquella's, a note had been penned:

We flee into the Forbidding. All safe but Father.

I let my eyes fall shut again, the buzz of the bees filling my mind until I was them and they were me and we were one swarm with one sting and one purpose.

My family was safe. For now. I would join them as soon as I was able.

And all because of the bees everyone had feared and disdained. I clung to their song and to the hope in my heart. We were going to find freedom. And we were going to find it together.

***

Find out what happens next in: Hive Magic.

BEHIND THE SCENES:

USA Today bestselling author, Sarah K. L. Wilson loves spinning a yarn and if it paints a magical new world, twists something old into something reborn, or makes your heart pound with excitement ... all the better. Sarah hails from the rocky Canadian Shield in Northern Ontario – learning patience and tenacity from the long months of icy cold – where she lives with her husband and two small boys. You might find her building fires in her woodstove and wishing she had a dragon handy to light them for her

Sarah would like to thank Barbara, Melissa and Eugenia for their incredible work in beta reading and proofreading this book. Without their big hearts and passion for stories, this book would not be the same.

Sarah has the deepest regard for the talent of her phenomenal artist Luciano Fleitas who created the gorgeous cover art that accompanies this book. Without his work, it would be so much harder to show off this story the way it deserves. She also wants to thank her editor, Melissa, who tried her best to make this book better. Any errors remaining are all Sarah's.

Thanks also to the Noble Order of Female Fantasy Authors who keep me sane – sort of. And for my beloved husband, Cale and sons

Neville and Leif who are endlessly patient as I talk to them about bookish passions.

Reviews are always welcome! If you liked this book, please tell someone!

Visit my website for more information:

www.sarahklwilson.com

OTHER SERIES BY SARAH K. L. WILSON

Tangled Fae Series (2020)

Twisted Fae have invaded her world and stolen her sister. Can she save her village and her family by learning to fight and bargain like the fae?

Bridge of Legends Series (2019)

He is possessed by ancient magic. She can smell spiritual residues. Together they seem unstoppable, but is their love doomed?

Dragon Tide Series (2019)

Can Seleska and her baby dragon bring magic back to the world?

Dragon Chameleon Series (2018)

He's a trickster with the most unique dragon out there. Together, they'll have to be heroes.

Dragon School Series (2018)

A disabled teen, a telepathic dragon, a bond that will save the world.

www.ingramcontent.com/pod-product-compliance
Lightning Source LLC
Chambersburg PA
CBHW070537310726
48982CB00010B/1395/J
* 9 7 8 1 7 7 7 2 6 4 5 0 5 *